HEROES & VICTIMS

The Diluvians Series #3

Gerald M. Givens

ISBN: 0-9897985-3-4

ISBN 13: 978-0-9897985-3-2

First Edition

Cover Design by Gerald M. Givens

FOR CAROLE HENRY

Who unconditionally encouraged me to follow my own journey

HEROES & VICTIMS

BOOK IV: The Diluvians

BOOK V: The Contest

BOOK VI: Heroes & Victims

PROLOGUE

Michael Turner opened up the bottle, tossed back three migraine pills, and chased them with a glass of water. He took a deep breath as he stared at the notes he'd taken during the interview. As detailed as he'd been in compiling them, they made little sense. Indeed, the more he reread them the less sense they made.

His partner, Kimberly Reeves, sat across from him at her desk looking just as confused. She'd led most of the interview, but understood just about as much of it as he did. The Embassy paired them together on this assignment six months ago, after three Americans journalists and an English archaeologist went missing in the Egyptian Delta region. The United States Embassy in Egypt had closed this case a few months earlier after no progress was made, but earlier that evening the case had been cracked wide open with the reappearance of the original three missing Americans, along with a fourth who had been reported missing back in Washington, D.C.

"Let's go over their profiles again," said Kimberly. They had gone over the four profiles twice already, but when all sums equal zero, you have to start back at the beginning. He nodded. "Sean Henry…"

"Sean Henry," began Michael, "works for Science Global Magazine as a journalist. His passport shows that he spent a few weeks traveling Europe last Fall and then Egypt before his disappearance six months ago. Last seen before this evening at an archaeological site in Sa el-Hagar, Egypt. Age: 29 years."

"Next, Erin Henry…" continued Kimberly.

"Erin Henry works for Science Global as an editor. She too travelled through Europe last Fall, presumably with Sean, her husband. Also seen last at the dig site in Sa el-Hagar. Age: 29 years."

"Peter Henry…"

"…brother of Sean; practices psychotherapy in D.C. No recent international travels, except for his trip to Egypt six months ago where he was, again, last seen in Sa el-Hagar. Age: 32."

"And last we have Emily Harden…"

"Okay, Kimberly, the stories of the others I'll buy, but Ms. Harden was never in Egypt before tonight. And I'm talking *never*! Not even on a vacation when she was five years old."

"Her story doesn't add up, true," replied Kimberly.

"There's nothing to add up," said Michael. "She claims that she went missing with her friends and had traveled here with them, but then why did she go missing in D.C.? Why are there no flight records, customs forms, or credit card transactions pinning her? There's not even a stamp in her passport. She doesn't even have a passport!"

"We'll have to let the State Department riddle that one out, Michael," she replied.

"I feel like we should detain them a little longer," he said. "Maybe we can find out more information... somehow."

"Michael, this case is confusing, but you have to realize that these people have been through hell trapped in that tunnel. Lord only knows how they survived down there for so long."

"But *how* did they survive? How can they believe they were only down there for three days and more importantly where in the hell is Dr. Julie Vane?"

"I don't know how they survived, but thank God they did. As for the passage of time down there, I can only assume that they're delirious. Maybe they'll remember more at their post interview in D.C. Hopefully then they will be able to tell us more about Dr. Vane and her whereabouts." Michael was silent as Kimberly studied him. There was something he wasn't saying. "What is it?"

"Sean Henry mentioned a name... someone he thought was with them when they disappeared: Matthew Nestor. Remember, he said that Matthew went missing with Dr. Vane."

"I've searched every missing person's database and there's no such person. At this point, we'll have to add this to their delirium. If it seems necessary to bring up again, I trust our team in D.C. will address it."

"I know, but he didn't even answer when you said we've never heard of Nestor."

"Lord, Michael, give them a break! They aren't criminals. They've been through hell, and I'm tired. We'll review this in the morning before we send our reports to D.C. I'm going home."

Without another word, Kimberly collected her purse and left the office. Knowing he couldn't riddle this out in one night,

Michael soon left too.

Michael was unable to crack the investigation the next day and the four survivors were sent back to the States. Two weeks later, he learned that the U.S. State Department had dropped the case altogether and allowed them to resume their lives. It felt like injustice and he couldn't let it rest.

One afternoon, he drove out to Sa el-Hagar to search over the remnants of the closed dig site. He'd been there before at the beginning of the investigation, but perhaps he'd missed something. The site looked the same as it had before. Searching through Dr. Vane's abandoned trailer, he found no clues, just as before. He walked across the site to a spot in front of some old foundations. Early on, he'd been told that this had once been a temple to some god. He wasn't interested in the ruined temple, but rather a rectangular hole in front of it that was covered haphazardly with a tarp. This was the tunnel at the center of his investigation. Several teams had gone down there to search for the three Americans and the archaeologist, but they'd returned each time empty handed.

Removing the tarp, he turned on the flashlight on his phone and entered. The tunnel was damp, cramped, and collapsing in some areas, but he disregarded any immediate danger and continued. His heart sank when he reached a point where the tunnel had caved in completely and he could go no further. Frustrated, he yelled obscenities at the blockage. His pride wounded, he turned and headed back up.

Halfway up, he heard a faint voice calling him. The voice was female. Could it be Dr. Vane? After all this time? Well, if the others had survived, then she may have as well.

"Dr. Vane?" he called out. "Dr. Julie Vane?"

"Michael!" the voice called again. He ran, holding his phone out in front of him. "Michael!" He had to reach her. Nearly sprinting, he tripped over rubble and hit the ground hard, knocking the wind out of him. His phone landed several feet away, the light pointing at him and blinding his vision. Footsteps were coming closer… running now.

"Julie?" he wheezed. Someone picked up his phone and approached him.

"Jesus, Michael," said Kimberly. "What on Earth are you doing down here?" He couldn't speak yet. "Calm down and catch your breath," she said, placing a hand on his back.

After a few moments, he was well enough to speak. "I was just…" he coughed, "checking things out again. You know, research. In case we missed anything."

"I know, Michael, you told the office you were coming," replied Kimberly. "But what are you doing down *here*? You know this tunnel's dangerous."

"I had to see for myself," he pushed himself to his knees and stood, brushing the dirt off of him. "I thought I might find some clue or missing piece to this puzzle."

Kimberly didn't respond immediately, but helped him walk up and out of the tunnel. They climbed into Dr. Vane's trailer to get out of the heat and to finish their conversation.

"I'm worried about you, Michael," said Kimberly. "This investigation is closed and has been for weeks. You have to let this go. Lord knows, we have other work to do."

"I can't shake it, Kimberly," he replied, louder than he'd intended.

"I know," she said, "and so do our bosses. Michael, I hate to be the one to tell you, but you're being transferred back to the States. They have a position for you in New York."

"Transferred?"

"They said you've been over here too long and some time at home would do you good."

He shook his head. "And what do you think?"

"I agreed with them, Michael," she said. He looked betrayed. "You're allowing yourself to become emotionally involved in cases and you can't even tell me why you're so obsessed with this one. I honestly believe that you don't even know." He pushed past her and walked out of the trailer and to his car. "Where are you going?" she called.

"To pack," he replied. "What choice do I have?" He climbed into his car and drove back to Cairo.

Within the week, Michael was in New York City. He made a resolution to put the case that ended his career at the embassy in Egypt out of his mind. Even so, it was hard not to feel spiteful. Instead, he jumped into his new position at the United Nations Headquarters, working with the ambassadors from Egypt.

A year and a half later, Michael was watching the news and a story caught his attention. The anchor was interviewing a couple, Sean and Erin Henry, who had just published a novel titled *Poseidon's Curse*. The story was fiction, a time-travel piece based on the lost continent of Atlantis. That struck a nerve. A spark of anger ignited and his old suspicions and arguments against the couple boiled back to the surface. During the investigation, Michael had become quite familiar with the events surrounding the Henrys' first disappearance nearly three years ago, and he remembered that they had been researching Atlantis before they went missing. Only Sean and Erin had returned from that catastrophe. Dr. Vincent Sanders was an American scientist looking for the lost continent and owned the ship that capsized in early June of that year. He and his crew were never seen again. Dr. Allison Moore, hired by Science Global Magazine, was an oceanographer brought along to verify Sanders' research. She too had gone missing. And lastly there was Dr. Samuel Knight, a geologist and archaeologist hired by Science Global to also verify research. Dr. Knight, too, had not come back.

Michael remembered that Dr. Knight's disappearance had been significant due to the fact that his fiancé, Dr. Julie Vane, had gone missing a little over a year later while the Henrys visted her on their assignment in Egypt. Something was definitely amiss.

Later that day, he attended their book signing and waited patiently in line to meet the authors. They barely glanced up at him as he handed them a book and asked who to make the message out to.

"Michael Turner," repeated Erin as she wrote. When she was finished, Sean having signed it too, she handed the book to him with a smile.

"You don't remember me, do you?" he asked, trying not to sound sardonic.

"Forgive me, I don't," replied Erin. "When did we meet?"

"Oh, it's quite alright," he replied. "The two of you are infamous for forgetting things." He talked louder with every word. "I was a part of the preliminary investigation team when you mysteriously reappeared in Egypt a couple of years ago."

"Yes, now I remember," said Erin. "Please forgive me, that was a very traumatic and confusing time for Sean and me. I'm sure you understand." She smiled.

"I understand, Mrs. Henry. Do you remember, yet, what happened to Dr. Julie Vane? I know her family would be grateful for some closure. Such a pity for them."

"Mr. Turner, do you have a problem?" asked Sean as he handed a signed book to the next person in line. "As I understand it, that investigation is closed."

"Yes, Mr. Henry, I do have a problem," Michael said with a forced smile. "Several persons are missing from your two escapades and it is an injustice to their families and their memories for the two of you to sit back and live your lives drenched in lies about their fates."

"Your accusations are unfounded, Mr. Turner," stated Erin, as a crowd began to form. "We've given ample testimony, confiding all knowledge of those events."

"Lies, Mrs. Henry, you tell lies!" he yelled. Erin waved to the manager of the bookstore, who picked up the phone and dialed. "Is it any coincidence that before your first disappearance three years ago you were researching Atlantis and now, together, you two have written a book on the subject? The two sole survivors."

Standing and lowering his voice to a whisper, Sean said, "Have you any idea how crazy you sound? Read the book, Mr. Turner. If you believe that any of this is true, then you should spend the rest of your life locked away. It's about curses and time travel, Mr. Turner. Don't fool yourself just to try to make sense of this."

"You can't hide the truth forever, Henry," he said as two police officers came up to escort him out. "You can't hide the truth!" he yelled as he was led away.

Michael followed up this incident with several others like it, including dedicating a conspiracy blog to his claims, along with a television interview. Ironically, his accusations only helped to increase the sales of the book. His efforts at justice only abated when the hype of *Poseidon's Curse* subsided nearly a year later.

On his blog, Michael predicted that there would be a sequel to *Poseidon's Curse*, and two years later, nearly five years after the investigation that derailed his career, he was right. He had another chance at the truth.

Book I:
The Sacrifice

CHAPTER I
ZEUS' WRATH

"Good Morning, we're back! I'm Casey Peters and today we're joined by New York Times best-selling authors Sean and Erin Henry, who are promoting their new novel *Zeus' Wrath*. Sean and Erin, welcome to *America Today*."

"Thank you for having us," said Erin. The pair sat on a couch across from Casey with a mob of people outside the window behind them. *America Today* was the first stop on their national book tour.

"So, it has been two years since the wild success of your first novel, *Poseidon's Curse*. What was it like to sit down once again and write as a team?" asked Casey.

"It was complete harmony," said Erin. "When Sean and I write, there is this great creative and collaborative force that becomes apparent."

"Yes, it feels as if we're remembering something, rather than creating it," added Sean, slightly amused that they had indeed based both books off of the events of their adventures in Atlantis and during the deluge.

"Were there any creative differences that had to be overcome?" asked Casey.

"Of course, there were," said Erin. "As cohesive as we may seem, our ideas and opinions on characters and plots do conflict at times."

"And Sean, how do you overcome those differences?"

"We play 'rock-paper-scissors'," he laughed. "No, we simply

weigh the pros and cons of each idea and usually the outcome is a hybrid of the two original thoughts."

"Well, you two have collaborated successfully once again with *Zeus' Wrath*. Can you tell us a little bit about the novel?"

"The story starts one year after the conclusion of *Poseidon's Curse* with our heroes getting married," began Erin, "and shortly after they are summoned to the past to save the world from the great flood. Through some action and suspense, they find themselves facing their darkest fears."

"How does this novel compare to the first?" asked Casey.

"*Poseidon's Curse* focused on creating a new world," said Sean. "The characters were new, the places and settings are fantasy, and there's a lot of adventure. *Zeus' Wrath* takes the story to the next level. The plot is quicker and more multi-dimensional, and the Olympian gods, who were only alluded to in the first book, take a personal role in the new book. I think fans of the first story will be excited with the sequel."

"How exciting! Now, you mentioned in an interview during the release of your last book that some of your story was based on your research and time spent working for Science Global Magazine. Is the same true with the sequel?"

"Our time at Science Global was an important part of our lives," said Sean, "so it's natural that we should pull inspiration from our experiences there. I would say that our childhoods and time spent in college were just as influential."

"And since we left SG about five years ago, we've traveled a great deal, which has in turn added to our pot of inspiration," said Erin. The pair tried not to talk about their time at Science Global publically. Questions about SG always led back to their mysterious disappearances, which they'd rather not address.

"Speaking of Science Global Magazine, you had some adventures of your own during your tenure. There are two reported cases of you going missing during assignments. The second time, you were missing for nearly six months. You've even had two funerals a piece! Surely those experiences must have added something to the creative melting pot."

"Official reports of those incidents have already been made public and this is already a sensitive…" Erin was cut off.

"Indeed, there were reports two years ago from a former U.S. Embassy official claiming that you lied in your original testimony about your second disappearance."

"Michael Turner became obsessed with our story after our interrogation at the U.S. Embassy in Egypt," said Sean. "His allegations are false and his obsession is harassment. If we could, please, finish talking about the book."

"Of course, Sean," said Casey, beaming with pride that she'd struck a nerve. "Since leaving Science Global, you have become full-time writers. How is that going? What is a normal day like for you?"

"It's going very well for us, Casey," replied Erin. "We still contribute articles to various journals and magazines, and we've been writing our novels, but a majority of our time is spent being parents, focusing on our daughter, Allie."

"Naturally," said Casey. "Your daughter was just a toddler when you released *Poseidon's Curse* two years ago. How has she acclimated to your success?"

"She's great," said Sean smiling. "She says she wants to be a writer like us when she grows up. We have her in a good preschool and she starts kindergarten in the Fall."

"That's wonderful to hear," said Casey, turning her attention the camera. "*Zeus' Wrath* is now available wherever books are sold. Get your copy today! Now we turn it over to you, our viewers, or I should say *readers*, who are calling in with questions. Our first caller is Jane from Myrtle Beach. Jane, you're on the air with Sean and Erin Henry."

"Hi, Sean and Erin," said the woman. "I'm a huge fan of *Poseidon's Curse* and I just finished *Zeus' Wrath* last night and I'm blown away!"

"We're glad you enjoy the series, Jane," said Erin.

"Oh, I did very much. The question I'm dying to ask is, will there be a third book in the series?"

Sean took up the mantle to answer. "At this point we have no concrete plans for a third book. We have some notes that could, at some point, become the outline for another novel, but I can't tell you when or if it will happen."

"Well, the folks down here in Myrtle Beach hope you do write another," said Jane.

"Thank you for your question, Jane," said Casey. "Our next caller is Mike from right here in New York City. Mike, you're on the air."

"Hello, Casey," began Mike. "And hello again to Sean and Erin." The man's voice sounded familiar, thought Sean. "Casey, I would like to defend myself, if I may, that my reports against Mr. and Mrs.

Henry's testimonies were not falsified and my 'obsession', as they call it, is only the pursuit of justice." A trickling of rage was building up inside of Sean, and from the look on Erin's face, she too was becoming angry.

"It seems we have former U.S. Embassy official, Michael Turner joining us," said Casey.

"Casey, in my reports I made it clear that the Henrys were only able to give vague answers to questions regarding their disappearances, and I'll also add that these two 'novels', both which I've read, bear dangerously close timelines to both of their disappearances."

"What are you implying, Mr. Turner?" asked Sean. "Are you suggesting that the novels are based off of true events? That we went to Atlantis?" He laughed.

"My point is that something clearly did happen during those disappearances and that those circumstances were extreme in nature. People died!"

"Mr. Turner, could you elaborate?" asked Casey.

"Casey, in both of the Henrys' disappearances, there are four people who are unaccounted for and assumed to be dead. The first time Dr. Samuel Knight, Dr. Vincent Sanders, and Dr. Allison Moore were never heard from again after Sanders' boat capsized, but somehow the Henrys survived?"

"Dr. Sanders' crew was also killed in that shipwreck, Mr. Turner, and you can show some respect for the dead. Lord knows they deserve that much," said Erin.

"What about the second time?" asked Michael. "Dr. Julie Vane was never seen from again after entering the tunnel beneath Sa el-Hagar. It seems to me that if you have a PhD and go on an assignment with these two, you're pretty much marked for death. And there's other evidence that you know what happened. When the pair of you returned from Cyprus, Erin had a crystal necklace, and I believe she wore it to her wedding, but now that is gone. And I won't even go into detail about Emily Harden's magical appearance in Egypt five years ago."

"As I said," said Sean, "your allegations are obsessive and your actions, such as this, are harassing to me and my family. Casey, this interview is over."

Sean stood, Erin following his lead, and walked off the set as they heard Casey Peters ending the segment. His brother, Pete, was waiting a little ways off, but Sean and Erin were intercepted by a producer.

"Mr. and Mrs. Henry, I deeply apologize for that. We didn't..."

Sean cut him off. "Why was he allowed to go on that long...or at all, for that matter?"

"Mr. Henry, I..."

"No, I don't care," said Sean. "We told you before we went on air that Michael Turner and his allegations were not to be brought up, but it seems your host must not have gotten the memo as she backed us into a corner."

The man was left dumbfounded as the pair walked over to Pete. "What the hell was that?!" shouted Sean, loud enough for the whole studio to hear. Pete tried to calm them down as he ushered the couple out of the building.

Sean and Erin's on-air argument with Turner would soon be shown on every news station and all over the internet. Despite their ferocity, the only consolation was that they would probably end up selling more books because of it. They both had guessed that with the publication of their second novel that Michael Turner would come back out of hiding to try and squeeze the truth out of them. They also knew that they hadn't heard the last of him.

"Sean, please calm down," said Erin as the trio stepped into Sean and Erin's apartment. After returning from the deluge and quitting Science Global, the pair had moved into seclusion in upstate New York, where their daughter Allie was born. After the release of *Poseidon's Curse*, they moved back to city life. The convenience of being close to their publisher and editor pushed their decision, not to mention the couple wanted to be closer to Sean's brother, Pete, and his wife, Emily.

"I am calm," he said taking a breath. "I'm calming down at any rate."

"If you let him get to you, then he wins," she said softly, looking into his eyes.

"We don't want a battle, Erin. We don't want to fight him, yet he seems to find a way to pick at us. He makes me wish we'd never written those damn novels."

She raised an eyebrow at him. "He's a bastard, Sean, we know that, but don't let him ruin this for us. Those 'damn novels' are our lives, now. We survived hell. We even beat Hades..."

"Don't say his name," Sean said quietly.

"But we did. We're stronger than a troll like Michael Turner. That's probably why he's so fascinated with us."

"Erin's right, Sean," said Pete.

"It's hard to ignore him, you guys," said Sean. "It's hard because he's right."

"Who's right?" asked Emily, as she walked into the living room. She'd been there all morning babysitting Allie. "You guys are louder than the Macy's Parade. I've just put Allie down for a nap."

"Sorry, Em," said Erin, hugging her friend and sister in-law. "How's she doing?" Sean and Erin hadn't been completely forthcoming with Casey Peters on their daughter's well being. Allie, nearly five years old, had always been a sensitive little girl, yet troubled. Since she was an infant, she'd had problems sleeping and that lack of sleep attributed to behavior problems. The older she got, the more profound those problems became. The fact that the child was napping was a surprise to her parents.

"I took her to the park and ran her ragged," said Emily, "but we do need to talk. All of us," she said. "Allie told me she's been having bad dreams." Emily sighed. "I asked her what she dreamt and, well, she described Hades. I mean, she described him in vivid detail... the pale white eyes, the transparent skin, his long dark robes."

"Hades? When was this?" asked Sean.

"She says she keeps having it," replied Emily. "Almost every night."

"Why didn't she come to us about it?" asked Erin.

"You guys know she's sensitive. You've both been so busy, she might have not wanted to upset you. Don't be mad. Allie and I have been close since the day she was born."

"You're right," said Erin. "Was there anything else about the dream?"

"You're kind of missing the point," said Emily. "She's seen *him*. No child, or anyone for that matter, could make up an identical description of him. That and he spoke to her. She's really scared."

"Does she remember what he said?" asked Pete.

"She didn't want to say, but I got it out of her with a little coaxing. He told her that going to take you from her."

"But we're free of him!" shouted Sean.

"Quiet, you'll wake her," warned Emily. "Sean, never mind us, she's scared to death. She knows nothing about our time in the

Underworld, not that she would understand, and she's afraid that you're in danger... that she's in danger. Part of her thinks that you'll give her up to him to save yourselves."

"Why would she think that?" he asked.

"Sean, she's a child. She's scared."

"Was it real, though?" asked Pete. "Is Hades really trying to communicate with us through her?"

"Pete, this is well within the realm of possibility," said Sean. "That's how Alexia used to communicated with me before. It's completely within Hades' nature to torment a child to get to us. Like Erin said before, we *did* beat him. But I guess his game isn't over yet."

"Daddy?" said a small voice from the hallway. Allie walked into view, groggy from sleep and came to rest in Sean's embrace.

"Great, you woke the baby," said Emily.

"Hi, sweetie," he said lovingly. "Did you have a good nap?"

"No." She began crying. Erin put a hand on her back and soothed her.

"It's okay, baby," she said. "Did you have a bad dream?"

"Yes," she said through sniffling.

"What was it?"

"The bad man came again," she mumbled.

"What bad man?" asked Sean.

"That's what she calls *him*," replied Emily.

"Oh, it's okay, sweetie," said Sean as he propped her on his knee. "He isn't real, okay? There's nothing to be afraid of. He isn't real." He hugged her again.

The silence that took over the room announced that they were not to talk about Hades any further. After a minute or two, Allie was asleep in Sean's arms.

"Did you watch the news?" asked Pete to Emily.

She scoffed. "Yeah, that idiot's back?" she said.

"Yeah, that's who we were talking about when we came in," said Pete.

"Why can he see so clearly through our charade?" asked Emily. "Sure, he's only alleging at the truth, but he's the only one who sees it."

"Many people have questioned us over the years," said Erin, "but in the end the lie is easier to grasp. Remember after Atlantis, Sean? We couldn't even tell our friends and family. God, if Pete and Emily hadn't been dragged into it, we'd still be holding that secret."

"And I wouldn't blame you," said Emily.

"I just wish it didn't have to be a secret," said Sean. "I thought it'd be easier after the books came out, but the reality has been the opposite. I know it's just my pride, but I want to take credit for our actions. If we were still in Saïs, we'd be heroes. Hell, we'd probably be helping to rebuild Athens at this point."

"Sean, it's been five years," said Erin. "Despite the hell we endured, I know you want to go back, but we can't. Clearly," she said pointing to Allie, still sleeping. "We live here now."

"You're right," said Sean. "I do want to go back. If we could somehow take Allie, we wouldn't have to pretend. We could be happy."

Erin sighed. "We can still be happy, love." She placed a hand on his shoulder. "We have a great life here and I love you, even when you're acting the fool. I don't think we're unhappy, it's just that we've done the impossible and it's hard for our now 'mundane' lives to live up to our days of glory."

"I feel it too," said Emily. "Pete and I have talked about it several times. I wish we could go back to Saïs, even just to visit. I miss Aha and Pyrthens."

"Not you too, Em," said Erin.

"Erin, come on," she sighed. "It was lovely there. I got to live in a palace… I felt important."

"Sweetie, you're the most important person to me," said Pete, kissing her cheek.

"You know what I mean, Peter. I was the 'Crystal Bearer'. It was the first time I ever felt like I could make a difference."

"I think we understand each other, Emily," said Sean. "I've never felt as alive as I did then, even when death seemed certain."

"Okay, are you two going through some shared mid-life/post traumatic stress crisis or something?" asked Pete rhetorically.

"I don't know, Pete," said Sean. "You're the shrink."

"Stop it, you two," said Erin.

"Sorry, Erin," said Pete. "It's not my intention to antagonize, but it seems that my brother and my wife are suffering from delusions of grandeur."

"Pete, that's not fair," said Erin.

"Clinically, it's very fair," he stated. "We all have romantic ideas about what it would be like to live in the past, but if you remember the events correctly, none of us would even entertain the idea. Em, I had to stand by while you were snatched away into oblivion right in front of me, and Sean, if you recall, we were possessed by Hades at one point and killed a man." His voice lowered as he said the last few words.

"Don't discuss that in front of our daughter, please," said Erin. "The point is that we can't go back, even if we all wanted to."

"You're exactly right, Erin," said Pete. "Sean, we just have to look at our lives to find the things that make us the most happy and focus our attentions there. I'm happy with my wife and you have a beautiful family who adores you, and let's face it you're not taking my niece anywhere. And if I can't stop you, I'd like to see you try to stop Emily." They laughed.

That evening, Sean and Erin left Allie with a babysitter and they met up with Pete and Emily for dinner. It was a welcome distraction, thought Sean, to double date with the couple. Since their return from Saïs, Sean and his brother had been closer than ever. Having shared in those experiences, it would have been difficult not to feel some deeper connection. In truth, the two couples were quite exclusive in their friendship. About a year after their return, Pete and Emily got married, making Emily an official member of the Henry clan.

"Did you see the news this afternoon, Sean?" asked Pete. "Your spat with Turner ended up being covered by every news station. Apparently the drama between you two outshines your novel."

"Don't remind me," said Sean.

"Hush, Pete, he's only just calmed down," warned Erin. "It's best if we leave it." Sean made a mental note to thank her later. "Besides, the jokes on Turner. I talked to our publisher this afternoon and our sales have spiked. We'll show him who laughs last."

"Sorry, Erin, I didn't want to bring it up, but do you guys have a plan of what to do about him?" asked Pete.

Sean sighed. "What can we do? It will be like last time. He'll only go away when we stop promoting the book, which won't be anytime soon. This book release is supposed to be a happy time, but all I can think about is being underhanded by this wannabe-cop."

"Speaking of your book, when do you two leave for L.A.?" asked Pete. Sean had forgotten about their book tour on the west coast.

"We leave the day after tomorrow," he said. "Are you two still good with watching Allie while we're gone?"

"Of course," said Pete. "We've been looking forward it. Emily just can't get enough of her."

"I can't help but love the child," said Emily. She then frowned. "But let's not forget about Allie's dreams, Sean. She's not around right now, so we can actually talk about it again."

"What's there to talk about?" he asked. "There's nothing that we can do."

"Is there any way to contact Alexia?" asked Emily. "Maybe she can help?"

"I've never tried," said Sean, and he never wanted to. "She always came to me. I doubt it works both ways and I don't want to talk to Alexia. Every time she puts visions in my head, we end up on some whirlwind race for our lives. I know what I said earlier about wanting to go back there, but we'd probably have to save the world again... or watch it be destroyed... again." The table fell silent.

Sean sat up after an hour of tossing and turning. Quietly, he slid out of bed, leaving Erin sleeping sound, and slinked down the hallway to Allie's room. He sat on the edge of her bed and watched her sleep. His daughter was only four and half, and far too young to understand her dreams or the implications of the events that caused them.

Allie was truly something they had brought back from the deluge, he thought. A week after their return to the states, Erin found out she was one month pregnant. It was an intense time in their lives, as they quit their jobs and moved to the country. With a child on the way, they agreed that they couldn't afford to get wrapped up in anymore adventures, but now, despite their efforts, it seemed like something was happening. Something was beginning.

CHAPTER II
TRUE LIES

Michael Turner hunched over his computer typing feverishly. His desk was disheveled with old paper plates and empty beer cans. Not that it stood out from the rest of his townhouse. Only partially furnished, he had lost most of his belongings years ago during a messy divorce. His wife of five years had left him, took half his things, and then he took a job at the U.S. Embassy in Egypt. The move had been good for him, at least in the sense of making him forget about her. He never truly forgot about her, but the distance seemed to make the pain less intense, as if he had been on a very long vacation. But that vacation was long over and the pain came back immediately. He had taken his things out of storage when he returned from Egypt, but most of the boxes were still packed and sitting in various rooms. Boxes full of once-treasures were now used as bedside tables and TV trays. He didn't want to unpack the misery.

Besides, he'd been occupied since the moment he returned four years ago. Between his new position at the United Nations and his newfound hobby of uprooting conspiracy, he'd hardly had a thought for much else. The job at the U.N. paid his bills, yes, but once he was off the clock, his attention was fixed on piecing together the puzzle of Sean and Erin Henry's multiple disappearances. With effort, he knew he could figure them out.

That was Michael's current mission, as he wrote a post on his blog devoted to their story. His prior posts focused mainly on drawing comparisons between their novels and their disappearances. The timelines between the books and the Henrys' disappearances were identical with each. There were threads to their stories that tied them together, but tonight's post focused on how Michael had unhinged the Henrys during their morning show appearance.

"Sean and Erin Henry have once again skirted around questions by giving vague answers or completely ignoring my inquiries," he wrote. *"They still have no solid answer to the appearance of Emily Harden in Egypt and they still claim that they don't know the fate of Dr. Julie Vane."* He continued to ramble on, highlighting any hesitations or ambiguous answers that Sean and Erin might have made. At a certain point, he reached the meat of his post. The truth, as he called it.

"I dare to say that Sean and Erin Henry aren't hiding anything at all, though they continue to evade justice. No, they are clever criminals and they have chosen to mock the world with their truth. Yes, I've alluded to it before, but now I can say conclusively that Poseidon's Curse *and* Zeus' Wrath *are true accounts of the Henrys' disappearances. This includes Atlantis being destroyed and them barely surviving! It also includes their accounts of Hades' Underworld in the second book. I know that this sounds crazy, but hear me out. Their primary characters, Alex and Alice, are both the same ages as the Henrys at the time of their respective disappearances. Also, the list of minor characters clearly mirrors those who were with them at the times of their vanishings. In* Poseidon's Curse, *Alex has a best friend who goes with him and Alice to Atlantis and his friend happens to die at the hands of the Atlantean King. Sean Henry's best friend was Dr. Samuel Knight who went missing the night Vincent Sanders' ship sank. He hasn't been heard from since. Continuing these striking parallels, in* Zeus' Wrath, *Alice has a best friend who goes missing in New York and ends up in Greece, where the 'heroes' come back from the great flood. Well, I have made my case about Ms. Harden before. She is Erin's best friend and she went missing here in the United States and showed up curiously in Egypt.*

"This revelation is fantastic, I know, and I shall continue to highlight the shocking similarities in future posts. But know this... I am very close to revealing the Henrys for who they really are. They will come clean of their transgressions. They won't have a choice in the end."

This was an empty threat, Turner knew, but the effect was made. He truly believed every word written and did not hesitate when he clicked the "post" button. He would root out the truth. He'd stalk them to the ends of the Earth if he had to. He would expose their crimes.

CHAPTER III
GAME OF GODS

Sean woke up sprawled across the foot of Allie's bed. Sitting there in thought, he'd fallen asleep. He sat up slowly and looked at Allie thrashing and whimpering in her sleep. He quickly moved to her side and gently nudged her awake.

"Allie, sweetheart, wake up," he said. She thrashed once more, then opened her eyes and began crying. Pulling her into his arms, he soothed her. "Bad dreams?"

"Yes," she said through the tears. She began to hiccup. "The bad man came back. The ghost man with the black clothes."

"Baby girl, it was just a dream." His heart broke. He wished that it was just a dream, but intuition told him otherwise.

"It's not a dream," she said as if reading his mind. "He's mad at you, Daddy! He's mad at you and Mommy!" She shouted.

"Shh, calm down, Allie." He held her so he could see her face.

"But he's mad at you," she said in a quieter voice. "He told me he was coming to get me and that I belong to him. He said you made him mad and now he's gonna get me." Without thinking, Sean pulled away from her and she resumed crying. He didn't mean to react like that, but for a moment he swore he saw her dark brown eyes turn red. It was just a trick of the light, he thought. Only her night light casting shadows or something like that.

"Nobody's going to get you, sweetie," he said holding her. Standing, he scooped her up and carried her back to his and Erin's bedroom. "You can come sleep with us and we won't let anyone hurt you."

Allie crawled under the covers between Sean and Erin, wrapping her arm around her mom. Within moments, she was asleep again. He felt bad. If her dreams were right, then Hades was still angry with him and Erin. It would also mean that her nightmares were far from over.

Frustrated, Sean decided to try something he never had before. In truth, he wasn't even sure how to do it or if it would even work, but he had to contact Alexia. She would be able to sort this out. Not sure how to start, he closed his eyes and repeated her name over and over again in his head. The repetition turned into a chanting in his brain, "*Alexia-Alexia-Alexia-Alexia...*", and he lost track of time. Feeling as if his efforts were futile, he opened his eyes.

The ceiling ebbed and flowed as if liquid before evaporating into nothingness. Looking around, the bedroom fell away and everything disappeared. Allie, Erin, and even the bed were gone. He then found himself standing. Mountains materialized in the distance, clouds formed overhead, and the sun shone beyond them. He stood on a mountainside high above the earth, but still below the clouds. Although drastic, none of these changes surprised him. He found this odd.

He peered into the distance as the landscape was painted before his eyes, including a lone hawk flying overhead. After a time, the hawk came closer and upon landing it transformed into Alexia.

"It worked," he said aloud.

"Indeed, Sean Henry," said Alexia. She was just how he remembered her, with her long blond hair, blue eyes, and pale skin. Being a God had given her eternal youth in appearance and she embodied the same regal disposition during her mortal life as the Princess of Atlantis. "Have you enjoyed your peace? After two near final deaths, you must have enjoyed these past five years in the mortal world."

"I have," said Sean, "but lately that peace has been disrupted. Erin and I have a daughter now. Her name is Alexia, like you, but we call her Allie for short."

"I am truly honored, Sean Henry," she said smiling. "Having a child can be a heavy burden, but I argue that it does not necessarily break the peace in your heart."

"No, we love her and she's been a joy. A challenging joy, but a joy nonetheless. I need to know if Hades is still angry with Erin and me. Allie's been having these dreams where Hades comes and talks to her saying that he's going to take her to get back at us. I fear for her safety. I learned long ago that nothing is impossible and I'll die before I let anything happen to her."

"Your nobility continues to serve you well, Sean," said Alexia, "but I fear that I have grave news for you and though it will explain your situation, it will not bring you comfort."

"It never was that easy," he said.

"No, Sean, it never was. You remember well that I had to barter your souls to Hades to secure your freedom from Erebus."

"That's not something that I could forget," replied Sean. "I still struggle with the fact that I was possessed and killed a man."

"Indeed, but you also know that it was not your will to do so. You were merely a tool and were used as such. In any case, it is not Hades' possession of your soul that I am referring to, but the soul of your wife. Erin became pregnant whilst he owned her, though just barely, and when Hades reluctantly gave her soul back to her, he kept a small connection to himself within the child. In other words, when you came to your agreement with Hades to free you from his possession, the child was not apart of the bargain. Technically, though I doubt he would care either way, Hades has full rights to the girl."

"I don't understand," said Sean. "She wasn't even alive then."

"The child Alexia was a part of you and Erin when Hades became the master of your souls, and thus had rights to her before she was even conceived. When the deal was broken, she was already alive and her release was not included in that arrangement."

"You knew then and said nothing?" said Sean. "We could have dealt with him five years ago."

"At the time, I am not sure Hades even knew. Since he was present, I felt it unnecessary to bring it to your attention. I was unsure that the child would live. Dying and being reborn, as you were, can be tricky."

"How do we make him stop, then?" said Sean. "I can't let this continue."

"Hades is a God, Sean," said Alexia. "He is stronger, older, and more cunning than many of the Gods. He cannot be stopped, I fear. At least not through mere force."

"Then what?"

"You know the answer to that," replied Alexia. "This will not be the first time you have played the game of gods and faced Hades in order to change his will. The only way to convince him to give up the girl is to bargain with him once again. Hades cares little for the girl, I am sure, but he has a debt to settle with you and Erin. I fear that the only bargain he will accept is yours and Erin's souls in exchange for Alexia's. You must sacrifice yourselves to save her from her fate." At this, Sean remembered the sacrifice Alexia's mother had made for her when she was still a little girl. The Atlantean Queen Azmela had given her life to save Alexia's and now Sean and Erin would have to do the same.

Alexia read the memory in Sean's eyes, as his mind was never far from hers. Sorrow covered her face. Sean felt slightly contented that Alexia truly felt remorse. Sighing, Sean said, "How do we contact Hades?"

"Short of death? You must summon him through the girl."

"Alexia, I can't do that!"

"As grim as it is, she has become a transmitter for him. He's already used her to communicate with you, although rather inefficiently."

"I would rather die than have Hades possess my daughter," said Sean.

"And death would solve nothing, Sean," replied Alexia. "If you die, whether at your hand or another's, you would save no one. The child would still be his. True sacrifice will be required, I assure you of that."

Sean did not reply. Gritting his teeth, he could almost hear Erin shouting at him.

"The choice is always yours, Sean," she said, "but the tormenting will not cease until Hades is satisfied." Before he could reply, Alexia dissolved. The mountains vanished and darkness took over Sean's sight until a bright light blinded him.

Sitting above him, Erin was shouting to him and shaking him. "Sean!" It was morning now and the sun shone through the open curtains.

"There you are," she said. She looked worried. "I've been trying to wake you for five minutes and your alarm was going off for five minutes before that." She had gotten up early to make breakfast for Allie, who woke up at exactly 6 a.m. every morning.

"Sorry, Erin," he replied. "I…I did it. I contacted Alexia. I mean,

18

I tried to reach her and actually succeeded."

"What are you talking about, Sean?" she asked.

"I couldn't sleep last night," he said. He went on to tell her about Allie's dream of Hades. "I brought her back to our bed and that's when I slipped into the dream-state where I contacted Alexia."

"Did she have anything to say about the dreams?" asked Erin.

He told her everything that Alexia said about Erin being pregnant when Hades had possession of her soul, Hades' rights to the girl, and the sacrifice they might have to make in order to save her. By the end, Erin was in tears and crying into Sean's chest.

Erin pulled herself away from him to look him in the eye. "What are we going to do, Sean? I can't lose my baby." She cried. "I just want our daughter to be safe."

"Me too, but this won't end and we have to make a plan," said Sean. "Alexia mentioned summoning Hades through her..."

"No, Sean!" yelled Erin. "There's no way in hell I would do that to my child!"

"*Our* child, Erin," said Sean, "and we're running out of options. Trust me, I know just as well as you what it's like to be possessed by him, but I don't think this will stop otherwise." Erin was in tears again.

"I just wish he would leave us alone," she said almost whimpering.

In the end, they had no choice in the matter. That evening, Sean and Erin were reading in their living room while Allie played with her dolls on the rug. Everything seemed normal and calm until Allie suddenly collapsed on the floor. Within moments, they were by her side trying to rouse her.

"Sean, call an ambulance!" said Erin. "Allie! Allie, sweetie, wake up!" The child lay on her back seemingly lifeless and barely breathing.

Just as Sean began to dial, her eyes opened. No, not *her* eyes. These eyes did not belong to his daughter, but to something vile. They burned blood-red with no whites. Allie's body seized and levitated from her mother's arms, suspended a foot above the floor. Erin screamed and a voice came from the child was not hers either. That is to say, it was her voice mixed with another's. Hades spoke behind the guise of the girl.

"You thought that you had bested me, Sean and Erin Henry. I

have found a hidden piece to our little game."

"You bastard!" screamed Erin. "You knew then and you said nothing! It isn't fair!"

"Sweet Erin, you know better than that. A player does not reveal his secrets at the beginning of the game or else they wouldn't be secrets, and worse off, there would be no game."

"What do you want from us, Hades?" asked Sean. "You have no right to our daughter, but we'll make another bargain with you if we have to. Just leave her alone."

"A bargain? You have spoken with Alexia, Sean Henry," said the lips of their child. "You are resourceful if nothing else. And why should I enter into another bargain with you when I already have the soul of your daughter? She would be the winning piece."

"We'll give you more in return for her, but you must vow to leave her alone," said Sean.

"Name your bargain, Sean Henry."

Sean looked at Erin who, through tears, gave him nod. "Take us instead. You can have our souls back." The words were bitter leaving his mouth. He just wanted a normal happy family, but Hades had deemed that impossible. They would have to leave their daughter with Pete and Emily to raise her as their own. They would, too. Pete and Emily were almost as close to Allie as he and Erin were.

"My, that is enticing. You would give up everything for the soul of your child?" They both nodded. "The sympathy of humans intrigues me. We have a deal. I agree to your bargain, Sean and Erin. Your souls are mine, just as soon as you return to me, and your daughter's soul will be left unviolated."

"And how do we return?" asked Erin. "Should we just kill ourselves here and be done with it?" There was sarcasm in her voice, but Sean shivered at the darkness of her question.

"No, that shall not do," said Hades. "You both are far more valuable and, dare I say, useful to me with your souls attached to the living world."

"Then what?" she asked.

"You must return to the last earthly gate beneath the ancient ruins of Saïs, where I will await you. Do not dither, for I retain possession of your dear Allie until I have you both in my keeping."

"We'll leave in the morning," said Sean.

Without another word, Allie's body dropped lifelessly to the floor. Erin cradled her as she began to wake. Her eyes opened, a dark shade of brown again, and smiled up at them until she saw that they were unhappy.

"What's wrong, Mommy?" she asked. Erin failed to choke back tears and embraced her.

"Nothing, sweetie," she managed to say. "I just love you so much."

"I love you too, Mommy," she said. Erin cried harder.

The next morning, Emily stopped by to pick up Allie and to take Sean and Erin to the airport, where she thought they were going to California, as they had planned up until now. Sean and Erin decided the night before to not tell Pete and Emily what they were going to do. They would only try to stop them and it would only make leaving that much harder.

"She has everything she needs," said Erin, barely holding back another wave of tears. She'd hardly stopped crying. They were just outside the security checkpoint at the airport.

"I know, Erin," said Emily with a smile. "She'll be alright, I promise. You guys have been away without her before. Besides, it's only a couple of days, and I have fun plans for her and me." Emily hugged Allie, who giggled.

"I know," said Erin, who finally succumbed to her tears. "I'm just going to miss her so much."

Emily looked to Sean, who was also very somber. "Is everything alright? I know L.A. isn't for everyone, but you're acting like you're never coming back." She laughed, but she was alone in her joke and Erin cried harder. "Look, sorry I upset you. I know about her dreams, so I'll keep an eye on her and call you if anything happens. She's in good hands."

"Thank you so much, Em," said Erin. "I know she'll be fine with you."

"Of course she will," said Emily. "Now you need to go or you'll miss your flight."

Sean and Erin said goodbye to Emily and their daughter. Taking Erin by an arm, Sean led her away crying still.

Sean suspected that Emily didn't know what to make of their behavior, except that they were obviously worried about Allie's dreams. He turned around to see her taking the child by a hand and leading her out of the airport.

Michael Turner made it a point to know the Henrys' tour schedule in hopes of getting them to publicly declare their injustices. He called one of the news stations in L.A. under the guise of an avid fan to see when they would appear on the morning talk show only to find that their appearance had just been postponed until further notice. A call to their publisher confirmed that the couple had postponed their tour on the west coast due to a family emergency.

He was just about to update his blog about this mysterious tour cancellation, when he got an unexpected call from Kimberly Reeves, his old partner at the U.S. Embassy in Egypt.

"Kimberly," he said, "to what do I owe this pleasure?"

"Michael, I hate to even bring this to you, but I made you a promise and I don't go back on my promises," she said.

"What are you talking about, Kimberly?" he asked. "I'm kind of in the middle of something."

"This will only take a minute. Michael... now don't get excited, but Sean and Erin Henry have just boarded a plane for Cairo."

"They what?" A sense of enthusiasm overcame him.

"You heard me right," she said. "Like I said, don't get excited. I don't know why they're going and I honestly didn't even want to tell you."

"Why did you then?" he asked.

"Because..." she sighed, "I guess on some level, I think it's peculiar. I just don't know why they'd ever want to come back to Egypt after what happened to them last time."

"It's hard to tell why," said Michael, "but I'm certain they're up to something."

"Why do you say that?"

"Because, they've just cancelled their West Coast book tour due to an emergency."

"Hmm. I don't know, Michael," said Kimberly. "That is strange that they'd change their plans so suddenly."

"I think it's worth questioning them about it," he said. Kimberly was quiet on the other line. "You *should* question them, Kimberly. Your duty demands it, given their scandals."

"Michael, I..."

"Think about it this way," he said. "If they arrive in Egypt and go on another one their 'wild mystery tours', you'll wish you'd intervened. You're not arresting them, just questioning. If they're there for a legitimate reason, it will only be a small hiccup in their plans."

Kimberly was silent for a few moments before finally agreeing with him. "I'll intercept them at the airport and question them for you."

"I want to be there, too," said Michael.

"No, Michael, I can't allow that," she said. "You don't work for the embassy anymore and I could lose my…"

"I have a right to be there, Kimberly," he said. When she didn't respond, he said, "Kimberly, I'm getting on the next plane. I have to be there for this."

"Fine, Michael," she said. "I'll see you in the morning."

CHAPTER IV
CAIRO

Their plane touched down in Cairo late into the evening. Somber and determined, Sean and Erin planned to rent a car and drive to Sa el-Hagar immediately to end everything. They had decided that on the plane, seeing as there was no point in wasting time sleeping. They'd soon be dead at any rate.

As they walked out of the gate, Erin noticed that someone was there waiting for them. She recognized the woman as Kimberly Reeves from the U.S. Embassy.

"What is she doing here?" asked Erin under her breath as Kimberly approached them.

"Mr. and Mrs. Henry," said Kimberly, "I'm Kimberly Reeves with the U.S. Embassy here in Cairo."

"We know who you are, Ms. Reeves," said Erin, clearly not amused by her presence.

"Good then. All politeness aside, will you please come with me?"

"And why would we do that?" asked Sean. "We haven't done anything."

"Who said you did anything?" she asked with accusing eyes. "I just have a couple of questions I'd like to ask you. *Did* you do anything, Mr. Henry?"

"We've just had a long flight, Ms. Reeves," said Erin. "Is this something we could discuss in the morning perhaps? All we want right now is a bed."

"It will only take a few minutes, Mrs. Henry," she said. "I insist."

The trio stepped away from the flow of traffic leaving the gate and sat down next to a window overlooking the tarmac. Kimberly looked them over silently for a moment, and got out her notebook.

"What's this about, Ms. Reeves?" asked Sean. "Forgive me if I'm impatient, but as my wife said, we're really tired."

Kimberly was silent for a few more moments, looking from Sean to Erin, and back to Sean again. "What are you doing here?"

"What?" asked Sean. "What business is that of yours?"

"Mr. Henry, given the circumstances of your last visit to Egypt, I'd think you would never dream of coming back here," said Kimberly. "And, given the circumstances of your previous visit, the Embassy is very interested in the reason for this visit."

"I didn't know we had to be interrogated to travel as U.S. citizens," said Sean. "Last time I checked, we had rights."

"You're avoiding my question, Mr. Henry," said Kimberly. "I need to have a full detail of your travel itinerary while here in Egypt or I'll put you right back on that plane."

"We're doing research, Ms. Reeves," said Erin, "for our next book."

"Your next book takes place in Egypt, does it?"

"That's the plan," said Erin.

"Forgive me if I call that bullshit, Mrs. Henry," said Kimberly. "During your tenure at Science Global Magazine, you both were here several times doing 'research'. You can't possibly expect me to believe that with your experiences combined and with your contacts here in Egypt that you actually had to come all the way back here to do *more* 'research'."

"Well, that's our story, Ms. Reeves," said Erin. "I really don't care if you believe it or not."

"Oh, but you do care, Mrs. Henry. If you can't convince me that you have a good reason to be here, I will send you home."

"What do you want from us?" asked Sean. "You ask for our reason for being here and then refuse to believe it when we tell you. Would you believe anything we'd say or does that jackass Michael Turner have you misconstrued to his conspiracy theories?"

"Michael Turner is no longer with the embassy, Mr. Henry," said Kimberly.

"No, because you fired him for being obsessed with us," said Sean. "I looked into it after he started harassing my family. You were his partner, weren't you? Tell me, did you back him in his accusations or did you agree with his discharge?"

"I cannot be held accountable for the beliefs and actions of another, Mr. Henry," said Kimberly, "and you have no right to question me about my loyalties to my job, because I'm pretty damn good at it. As for backing Mr. Turner, I went as far as I could without losing my job. I was there when you returned from Sa el-Hagar naked as jaybirds and speaking a bunch of nonsense. Your story didn't make sense five years ago, Mr. Henry, and nothing you've told us since has made it any clearer. Sure, Mr. Turner became obsessed, but I don't rightfully believe that makes him wrong about you two. You're hiding something and of that I'm convinced." She took a deep breath and silence fell.

"Then what now, Ms. Reeves," asked Sean.

As if reawakening to reality, Kimberly shook her head. Sean could tell that she was beyond frustrated. "I can't deal with this tonight," she said. "You two will be detained until the morning when we can interrogate you properly. Only then may you have leave to travel within Egypt and *only* if I'm convinced."

"You have no right!" yelled Sean.

"Mr. Henry! You're lucky there's no flight leaving for the States until morning, because you'd be on it. Now, you can either come with me back to the embassy or you can spend the night in jail. I honestly don't care which one you choose. Do I have your cooperation?"

After a silent stare, Sean nodded.

Pete and Emily Henry were awakened in the middle of the night by Allie screaming in terror. Moving quickly, Emily made it to the girl's room only moments before Pete. To their surprise, the child was still sleeping, but kicking and shouting.

"Allie," said Emily. Gently moving her, Allie woke and burst into tears. She pulled her niece into an embrace and soothed her. "It's alright, sweetie."

"Did you have a nightmare again?" asked Pete calmly.

Allie cried a few moments longer before mumbling the word 'yes'.

"What happened?" asked Emily. "What was the dream?" Allie refused to answer and continued to cry. Emily and Pete felt at a loss of what to do besides comforting her. After a few minutes, they tried again to get her to talk. As she calmed a little, she began to tell them of her dream. The "bad man" had talked to her again and told her that he would kill "Mommy and Daddy." They were going to kill themselves because of her and it was all her fault. Emily soothed her as she resumed her weeping.

They brought Allie back to their bedroom and eventually the girl fell back to sleep in Emily's arms.

"Hades is truly vile," she said to Pete, "to torment an innocent child like this. It has to end, Pete." He nodded. "I know it's late in L.A., but I'm calling Erin. She and Sean need to know. Not that there's anything they can do about it."

Emily picked her phone up off the nightstand and dialed. After a few rings, the call went to Erin's voicemail.

"Hi hon," she said. "I know it's late, but I just want you to know that Allie had another dream, but she's okay now. It took some coaxing, but essentially Hades told her that you and Sean are going to sacrifice yourselves to save her. He basically blamed her for it and... she was a mess. It doesn't make any sense, but I thought you should know. Call me in the morning and we can talk about it more. I hope you had a good flight. Love you, bye."

Emily hung up and looked to Pete, who was rubbing Allie's back.

"I'm worried about them, Pete," she said.

"Them? Sean and Erin?" he asked.

"Yeah, them and Allie," she said. "Erin was a mess at the airport this morning...like, full on crying. I've never seen her like that."

"She's probably just worried about Allie and these dreams," said Pete.

"Yeah. I guess we'll just talk to them more about it when they get back."

Kimberly Reeves was conflicted. Part of her knew that she should just let the Henrys go on their way without any further hassle, while another part of her begrudgingly agreed with Michael. His suspicions were more of a hunch than anything else. No evidence had proven foul play on the Henrys' part, but then there was the mere fact that they were back in Egypt with seemingly no agenda. It was very curious.

Sitting in a small room with a conference table, she waited for them to arrive. The room was cramped with too many fluorescent lights, but she had chosen it especially to help put pressure on the

Henrys. They might not be up to anything malicious, but she knew for a fact that Erin had lied to her about their reason for being in Egypt. She sighed. This was supposed to be her day off too.

Sean and Erin were escorted into the room and took their seats across from her. There was a voice recorder on the table and she pressed 'record.'

"My apologies, Mr. and Mrs. Henry, if I may have been abrupt with you when we spoke last night," said Kimberly, "and thank you for meeting with me today."

"Did we have a choice?" asked Sean. "Can we just get this over with?"

"Of course, Mr. Henry," she said. "For the record, Mr. and Mrs. Henry, why have you come to Egypt?"

"Like we said last night, we're here to do research for our next novel," said Erin.

"Was this trip previously planned?" asked Kimberly.

"The trip itself has been planned," said Sean, "but our travel arrangements were spontaneous. We didn't know when we'd go, just that we would."

"And what does this research trip consist of?"

"Honestly, we plan to visit museums and monuments," said Sean. "I know that sounds cliché, especially given our knowledge of ancient Egypt, but the research has more to do with the locations and settings. We want our world to be as detailed as possible."

"Is it true, Mrs. Henry that you and your husband canceled your book tour in Los Angeles to make this trip?"

"It is, Ms. Reeves," said Erin.

"Help me to understand why two writers, who are at the beginning stages of releasing a novel, would cancel such a chance to promote their work. I believe that most people would agree that in order to continue to make a living on your work, you should rally at any chance to promote it."

"When inspiration strikes, Ms. Reeves, the artist must respond," said Erin. "I agree that our trip is abrupt, but we believe it necessary."

"And what did your publisher have to say about your trip?"

"I don't believe that concerns you, Ms. Reeves," said Erin.

"Fair enough," said Kimberly. "What about your daughter? Who is watching her during this abrupt escapade?" Erin faltered and barely stopped herself from bursting into tears. "Did I say something wrong, Mrs. Henry? Are you well?"

"I'm fine," said Erin. "I apologize, we don't spend much time away from Allie and I miss her."

"I'm sure that you do, Mrs. Henry," said Kimberly. She genuinely meant it, though Erin's behavior was suspicious.

"She's staying with Sean's brother and his wife," said Erin.

"You're referring to Pete and Emily Henry. I remember them from your investigation."

Just then Erin's cell phone began to ring. Looking down, she saw it was Emily, as if thinking of her triggered her call. She sent the call to voicemail. It was the middle of the night back in New York, she thought. Allie probably had another nightmare. She had to hurry this up. Her baby was suffering.

"To be honest, I am still not convinced," said Kimberly after Erin looked back up from her phone. "By right you shouldn't have come here. I know there are no formal restrictions around you travelling to Egypt, but given your past, this was a terrible idea." Sean and Erin stared at her blankly. She sighed. "I can't allow..."

Kimberly was cut off as the door opened and Michael Turner walked in. At the sight of him, Sean stood and erupted.

"What in the hell are you doing here?" asked Sean.

"I could ask you the same thing, Mr. Henry," he said coolly. "And in fact, I will. Have a seat, please."

"You're behind this, aren't you?" asked Sean. "How many times do I have to tell you to leave me and my family alone?"

"Calm down, Mr. Henry," said Michael. "You aren't helping yourself."

"Fuck you! You don't even work here!"

Michael walked over to the recorder and turned it off. "This conversation will not be on the record. At least not *their* record. I intend to break this story myself."

"Is he even allowed to be here?" asked Erin to Kimberly.

"Yes," she said. "Given his background knowledge and involvement in your investigation, he has been given clearance to be present."

"Now you're the bull-shitter," said Erin. Kimberly didn't reply. "We refuse to talk to this man, Ms. Reeves."

"It's not a choice, Mrs. Henry," said Kimberly. "Mr. Turner has my authority to question you within reason about your presence here today. Under my jurisdiction, you will answer his questions truthfully and in full or we'll know the reason why."

"This is unbelievable," said Sean.

"Believe it, Mr. Henry," said Michael. "Finally, I get a second shot." The two men locked eyes, full of mutual hatred.

"Michael, you'd better get started," said Kimberly.

"Of course," he said, taking a seat next to Kimberly. "Now tell me, Mr. Henry, why are you and your wife here in Egypt today?"

Sean looked at him blankly. "Are we going to have to answer every question a thousand times?"

"Answer him, Mr. Henry," said Kimberly. Sean told him exactly what Erin had just said.

"I believe you're lying," said Michael.

"Shocking," said Sean sarcastically. "You've never believed a word that Erin or I have ever said. Why should this time be different? Here's a question for you, Mr. Turner. Are you capable of believing anything that we say? Because, if not, we're wasting our time. Wouldn't you agree, Ms. Reeves?" Kimberly said nothing.

"I will believe you when you start telling the truth," said Michael.

"The truth is that the U.S. Embassy has no right to detain us," said Sean. "We're not criminals. We've done nothing wrong. The truth is that we're being interrogated because of your obsession with us. Because you had Ms. Reeves put a watch out for us if we ever travelled to Egypt again, am I right? You will jump at any chance to disgrace us and I can't for the life of me understand why. I'm truly sorry you lost your job because we couldn't explain what happened in the tunnel beneath Sa el-Hagar. Not a day goes by when I don't wonder the same. But in the end, we haven't wronged you."

"You can't understand why, Mr. Henry?" Michael said softly. "People are dead. Julie Vane, Vincent Sanders...all of them. There's no justice."

"I won't apologize for surviving, Mr. Turner," said Sean. "I mourn them all, trust me, but we still haven't wronged you."

"Let me tell you a story, Mr. Henry," said Turner. "Five years ago, Ms. Reeves and I were called to Sa el-Hagar to work with the Egyptian authorities to investigate the disappearance of three Americans and an English woman. That's *three* Americans, by the way, not four," he said referring to Emily's appearance. "The dig site was searched over thoroughly, with no trace of you and your companions. We suspected foul play, yet none of our inquiries turned up with any information. That is until we spoke with one of Dr. Vane's graduate students. Her testimony led us to the tunnel near the ruined temple and after searching for weeks, we found nothing. Not a trace of you.

"The case was closed after a month or so. The four missing persons were declared dead and I went on with my life. Of course you know the rest of the story. You and your friends popped up out of the ground and reopened the case. Dr. Vane was not with you and you had an extra person. Emily Harden, as was her name then. You somehow took a case that was pretty much cut and dry: 'four missing persons who probably died when a tunnel caved in' and you turned it upside-down. There are more questions than answers in your testimony, so when I went to find the truth on a closed case, I was sent home. It ruined my life. I was sent to New York and back to a life that was long gone."

"I'm sorry our testimony wasn't sufficient," said Sean, "but your life being ruined is all circumstantial. We couldn't have helped it."

"Yes, Mr. Henry," said Michael, "you could have. I am not an irrational man, though you may think otherwise, and I am a servant of justice. You have done nothing but lie to us and you're hiding something. What happened in the tunnel that you're so ashamed of? What don't you want the world to know? Is it that your novels are true accounts? Or did you kill Dr. Vane?"

"Michael, that's enough," Kimberly said quickly.

"No, it's not enough," he said. "They haven't answered. Look at them. They say they're not criminals, but are they really so innocent?"

"Who are you talking to, Michael?" asked Kimberly. "This isn't a witch hunt. I apologize for my colleague, Mr. and Mrs. Henry."

"I'm not finished!" he yelled.

"Yes, you are," she said. "I'll be lucky if I don't lose my job for your accusations. This is over. Michael, you need to leave. Mr. and Mrs. Henry, you'll be on the next flight out of the country. I can't let you stay."

"You can't send us back!" yelled Sean. Erin started crying.

"I'm not convinced!" Kimberly yelled back. She took a deep breath.

"Sean…" Erin cried. "Sean, our baby."

"What was that, Mrs. Henry?" asked Kimberly.

"Nothing," said Sean in response. "She misses Allie. That's all."

"Well, she'll see her soon," said Kimberly. She was packing up her notes and arguing with Michael as she prepared to leave.

Sean trembled inside. They couldn't afford to be sent back to the States. They were on a mission and if they waited too much longer, who knows what Hades would do to Allie. He had to think quickly. There had to be a way out of this.

Kimberly moved to open the door with Michael Turner looking sour behind her. "Wait!" said Sean. It's sounded as if his voice wasn't his. Here goes another lie, he thought. He was getting tired of them.

"Yes, Mr. Henry," said Kimberly. Erin, too, looked up at him; questioning what he was about to say. She'd just have to trust him.

"Mr. Turner's right," the words were bitter.

"Aha! I knew it. What happened in the tunnel?" he asked.

"Not about that," said Sean. "About a year ago, we started to remember things that happened. We think we know where Julie Vane might be. We thought about just leaving it, but it kept eating away at us. We couldn't handle it anymore. That's why we're here."

"Is she alive?" asked Kimberly.

"Of course she's not," said Michael. "Where is she?"

"She's not alive," said Sean, "but I think I know where her body might be. She's still in the tunnel. I know the way. We were going to rent a car and drive to Sa el-Hagar this morning, but then of course we were made to come here instead."

"Is this true, Mrs. Henry?" asked Kimberly. Erin nodded. "Why didn't you just say so before? We could have saved a lot of time and energy."

"Because we do feel bad about it, okay?" said Sean. "We can't remember what happened to her, but we know where she is. At least we think we do."

Kimberly walked up to Sean and looked him in the eye as if she were measuring something. "I still can't say that I believe you, Mr. Henry, but it would please me to know what happened to Dr. Vane, as I'm sure it would her family. I assume you won't be able to tell me the directions through the tunnel to her exact location, so I will take you and your wife there myself. But mark my words, if this is just a wild goose chase, there will be consequences. For starters, I'll have your passports revoked and that will be the end of your traveling anywhere. Do I make myself clear?" Sean nodded. "Then let's go."

When everyone left the room, Erin stayed behind alone to check her voicemail. Kimberly didn't argue, understanding her need to check on her daughter. After hearing Emily's message, she started to cry all over again. It would be early morning in New York, but she called Emily anyway.

"Erin, she was screaming, but she was still asleep," said Emily. "I've never seen anything like it. Isn't there anything that we can do to help her? He's torturing her." There was no need to say who 'he' was.

"I can't think of anything," said Erin through tears.

"How about getting ahold of Alexia?" asked Emily. "You said that back in Atlantis, she could talk to Sean in his head and through his dreams. Can it work the other way? Can he 'call' her?"

"He's never tried," she lied, "but I'll ask him to. We'd do anything at this point. I'm so worried about her."

"We all are, sweetie," said Emily.

"But I promise you this," said Erin. "Sean and I will take care of it. She's going to be alright."

CHAPTER V
FURTHER IN

Sean and Erin did their best to remain silent during the drive to Sa el-Hagar, despite Michael Turner's insistence on continuing his interrogation. Sean ignored him and stared out the window. Just Michael's presence had set him off again, and he clearly had some influence over Kimberly Reeves. There had been no stopping him from joining them at the old dig site.

"Enough!" shouted Sean after he couldn't take anymore. "Just stop! We aren't answering anymore of your damn questions, Michael. You're fucking ridiculous."

"Ridiculous?" he asked. "Trying to discover the truth behind several deaths is ridiculous?" Sean didn't respond. "I didn't think so."

"Mr. Turner," said Erin. She placed a hand on Sean's knee. "Why didn't you want to return to the States after you were let go from the embassy?"

"What?" he said. "I never said I didn't want to go home."

"You did, actually. You said that you were sent back to a 'life long gone'. What exactly were you running from when you took your job in Cairo? What happened before that was so bad that you would blame us for your ruined life?"

"Now you're the one asking ridiculous questions, Mrs. Henry," said Michael.

"You know what I think," said Erin. "I think that someone long ago hurt you bad, and returning to the States just reminded you of the pain you fled, so now you're mad at us. I think that you're scared and lonely, and harassing us has been your only means of finding sense in the world. I also think that you wish our books were true, because if they were, then there might be some fantastical way for you to permanently escape your pain." Michael looked at her with rage, but said nothing. "And even though you're mad at us and may even hate us, I refuse to hate you. I pity you, Michael." He looked out the window. No one talked the rest of the way.

Several hours after leaving Cairo, they pulled up to the abandoned archaeological site. To Sean, it looked exactly the same as it had five years ago.

"Hasn't anyone worked out here?" asked Sean.

"Not since the dead walked," said Kimberly. "You and your friends created quite a stir with the locals when you reappeared. Some think the site is haunted, though I'm sure the liability of having lost researchers has dissuaded others from resuming Dr. Vane's work." Sean said nothing. "The locals say it's watched over by the angel of death. Some claim to have seen a man in the darkness, ten-feet tall, skin as white as a ghost, and shrouded in darkness." Her description made Sean shiver.

"Better get searching," said Michael as he climbed out of the car. "You two still have a plane to catch."

"Michael, you still have no authority," said Sean. "And with the way you've treated my family these last five years, you're lucky I don't kick your ass right now."

"Sean!" said Erin.

"Cool it, you two," said Kimberly. "Mr. Henry, just because I called off Mr. Turner's questioning, don't think for a second that I believe a word you've said today. Here's your chance to convince me. Now, if you please, lead the way."

Hot-headed, Sean stalked off across the dig site to the ruined foundations of what he knew to be the Temple of Neith. Trepidation filled him as he approached. He hadn't had a private moment with Erin since they left, so they had no plan as how to escape their chaperones. Sean had a thought to just run to the tunnel and try to beat them to the dark pool, but he thought better of it since Michael wasn't going anywhere. He wouldn't let them run. The only other option he saw was to lose them in the tunnel somehow.

Just as it had been left, a tarp haphazardly covered the entrance where a sphinx once stood. Moving it aside, Sean began the descent. Turning on the flashlight on his phone, he led the way.

"So, Mr. Henry," said Kimberly.

"We're past formalities, Kimberly," said Sean.

"Okay then, Sean, what exactly do you remember from being down here?" she asked as they continued further in.

"We got lost almost immediately," he said, making the story up as he went along. "We tried to turn back and only ended up going in circles or running into dead-ends." They moved deeper into the tunnel. "Our flashlights were no help. We didn't know what to do."

"But what *did* you do?" asked Kimberly.

"The only rational thing we could think of," he said. "We split up. In retrospect, it wasn't such a rational idea, but we were growing desperate. Dr. Vane went off in one direction and we all went off in others. In time, Erin, Pete, Emily and I found each other again, but not Dr. Vane."

"Emily Harden wasn't with you, Mr. Henry," said Michael.

"As I was saying, we never saw Dr. Vane again." They continued on. "Time stopped seeming to matter and after what felt like several days, we found the entrance to the tunnel and... well you know the rest of the story."

"Several days turned out to be six months, Sean," said Kimberly. "You said you remember where Dr. Vane is."

"Sort of," he said. "I remember where we split up and which direction she took. I only assume that by following, we'll find her."

"That's hardly encouraging," said Michael.

"Michael, if you keep trying my patience..."

"Sean, stop," whispered Erin. He swallowed his rage.

"How much longer until where you parted ways?" asked Kimberly.

"Further in," he said.

They were silent for a time. Sean began to grow anxious that there weren't any forks in the road to lose Kimberly and Michael. Not that he remembered there being any, but he had been hopeful for something... anything so that they could get rid of them. This anxiety was nothing compared to what he shared with Erin. They would soon sacrifice themselves. What would become of them? What would become of their daughter?

As if the thought shaped reality, the tunnel opened up to reveal a familiar large underground cavern. Stalactites hung ominously from various points, but the true draw-of-the-eye was the large pool of water, glistening in the dim light. The air was damp and cold.

Erin began to weep at the sight and turned to bury her head into Sean's chest.

"Sean, we'll never see her again," she cried. Sean fought to keep his composure.

"Who won't you see again, Erin? Dr. Vane?" asked Kimberly.

"What?" said Erin, looking up at Kimberly and Michael. "Dr. Vane? No. My little girl." She resumed weeping.

"Sean, why is she so worried about Allie all of a sudden?" asked Kimberly. Sean didn't answer, but looked toward the dark pool.

"We're not here to cry about how much you miss your daughter, Mrs. Henry," said Michael. "We're looking for Dr. Vane, or what's left of her. Shouldn't we continue?"

Sean laughed. "There's nowhere else to go, Michael. I'm sorry, but this is the end of the line."

"What?" asked Michael. "You lied again, didn't you? You never knew where to find Dr. Vane. You just let us down here on some goddamned wild-goose chase! WHY?"

Sean was silent for a moment, mentally preparing himself. "Congratulations, Michael. You were right." Michael's eyes opened wider.

"I was right?" asked Michael. "About what?"

"Everything," said Sean. "You were right about everything. Keeping it a secret doesn't matter anymore. Our novels – both of them – are more memories than anything else. Erin and I have brought death upon our friends."

"You lie!" shouted Michael.

Sean laughed at him. "What do you want, Michael? I've finally told you the truth and now you don't believe it. Whatever. I honestly don't care what you believe."

"Sean, what you say is crazy," said Kimberly. "I've read both of your books too and there isn't a drop of realism in either of them. Now, I don't know how deep below ground we are and your switch in story is making me nervous. Why have you brought us here?"

"We haven't brought you anywhere, Kimberly," he said. "We tried to come on our own, but you kept insisting on being present. Yes, I lied when I said that Julie Vane was down here, but only to keep from being deported."

"Again, why are you here?" she asked. She looked at her cell phone, but this far below ground she didn't have any service.

"To finish what we started five years ago, Kimberly. This is our atonement. We're here save our daughter from a fate worse than death." Kimberly stared at Sean in disbelief. Her face turned to awe and fear as she glanced behind him. She dropped her phone.

"Yes," said a voice from behind Sean. "A fate worse than death it is, Sean Henry." Sean knew that hissing voice and he slowly turned around to face Hades. Just as he remembered the Lord of the Underworld, Hades stood taller than any man, semi-transparent skin glowing with dark sinewy robes flowing around him.

"Who the hell is he?" shouted Michael as Kimberly began to scream. With a wave of his hand toward the pair, Michael and Kimberly fell to the ground.

Erin pulled away from Sean to see the collapsed bodies.

"Are they dead?" she asked, choking back tears.

"No," he said. "But their time too shall come." Sean felt a wave of relief. As much as he disliked them, he didn't wish for their death. He wanted no one else killed on his account.

Sean and Erin stood side-by-side facing the Dark Lord. "We have come, Hades," said Sean. "Be done with it and vow to leave Allie alone from now on."

"Indeed, that is our agreement. I will gladly have your lives in exchange for Alexia's namesake. So touching of you to name her so."

"It seemed fitting," said Erin.

"Be done with it, then," said Sean. "We don't need linger any further. Our lives for Allie's. We wouldn't have it any other way."

Sean and Erin took one last look at one another, as if making a final mental resolve to go through with the arrangement. Holding hands, they walked into the water where Hades stood, the familiar cool gassy feeling around their ankles and shins.

"You thought you had bested me when you escaped Cerberus, but I knew all along that Erin was with child. That is why I agreed to the challenge and that is why I allowed you to escape unhindered. Now I will have you absolutely with no bargains to change my way. Forever my servants, you become." Hades placed a ghostly hand over each of their heads, and taking a last breath, the pair fell lifeless into the water.

Book II:
The Land of
Gods & Monsters

GERALD M. GIVENS

CHAPTER I
SURFACING

Kimberly's head felt split open. Taking a deep breath, she opened her eyes to darkness. Fighting vertigo, she sat up and reached for the dim glow of Sean's cell phone, which still had its flashlight turned on. Erin's phone was a few feet away. Where had they gone without their phones in this dark? Behind her, she noticed Michael Turner sprawled on the ground and she quickly began to wake him.

"Michael," she said shaking him. "Michael, wake up!" A few tries later he stirred.

"What the hell happened?" he asked grabbing his head as he sat up. "Where are the Henrys?"

"I don't know," she replied. "They were in front of us in the tunnel and then we found this cavern, then…" her voice caught in her throat. She suddenly remembered.

"And then they must have knocked us out and ran," said Michael. "Well, they can't run forever. I swear to God I'll find them, trust me on that."

"It's dark as sin in here, Michael," she said, "and they left without a flashlight. They didn't knock us out."

"Then what do you think happened, Kimberly?" he asked.

She looked at the dark pool. "There was something over there in the water," she said. "It looked like a man, or maybe… a ghost."

"A ghost?" he mocked her. "Like the one the locals say haunts this place? You must have dreamt it, Kimberly."

"Don't tease, Michael," she said. "I have the wherewithal to know if something was real or if I dreamt it. This was definitely real. It looked like a man, but larger, and all white. Those sightless eyes bore into me and then… I blacked out."

"I don't know what to say to that," said Michael. "Sorry, I'm not trying to be a dick, but you could just as easily be in shock." He sighed. "Let's get the hell out of here. We don't want to end up like Julie Vane."

"That's not funny, Michael," she replied.

"But it's true."

When they finally surfaced, the pair climbed back into Kimberly's car. She asked Michael to drive, since she was still feeling out of it. That and she had an idea.

"Who are you calling?" Michael asked as Kimberly put Sean's phone to her ear.

"Someone who might know what's going on," she said. "Peter Henry, Sean's brother."

"What? Why?"

"Because he might know something," she replied. "Sean insisted that those novels they wrote were truth, and if anyone would know for sure, it'd be his brother." She still hadn't swallowed that pill yet. How could they be true?

"Tell him that if he knows where his brother is, he better hope that I never find him."

"Hush, Michael. It's ringing."

After a few rings, Pete answered. "Hey, Little Brother! How's L.A.?"

"Peter Henry?" said Kimberly.

"Sean? Who is this?" asked Pete.

"Mr. Henry, this is Kimberly Reeves with the United States Embassy in Cairo," she said.

"Kimberly Reeves?" he asked. "What are you doing with Sean's phone? And why are you in Los Angeles?"

"Mr. Henry, I'm not in Los Angeles, I'm in Egypt and so was your brother," she replied. "Up until a few moments ago, that is."

"What? Is he alright? Where's Erin?"

"I don't know the answer to that, Mr. Henry, but I'll explain what has happened as I ask you a few questions."

"Where is my brother?" Pete demanded. "Is this some trick? Did Michael Turner put you up to this?"

"Your brother and sister-in-law showed up in Cairo last night, Mr. Henry," she began, ignoring the comment about Michael. She told Pete about how Sean and Erin had lied to her, telling her a story about trying to find Julie Vane, and then she told him about the cavern and the "ghost" man. "We were knocked out and when we woke up, Sean and Erin were gone. This phone was left behind."

"What? But they boarded a plane for L.A., not Cairo."

"They showed up here, Mr. Henry," she said. "We found out that they canceled their book tour in California at the last minute."

"They never told us," he said.

"Mr. Henry, what were they doing here? Do you have any idea?" Peter was silent. "Mr. Henry?"

"I think I know, Ms. Reeves." He sighed. "My wife and I will be on the next plane to Egypt. I'll explain everything when we arrive."

"What? Okay," she said surprised. "Come to my office at the embassy the moment you get here. I'll have a car waiting for you at the airport."

"Will do, Ms. Reeves."

Pete ended the call and stared at the phone. Anger welled up inside him. "Those selfish bastards!" he yelled and threw his phone across his living room. Emily rushed in at the noise.

"Pete, what's wrong?" she asked. "I just put Allie down for a nap."

Pete looked at her and for some reason he felt a little better. The sight of his wife always lightened his mood, but the pain was still there. Calmly as he could, he told her about the call from Kimberly Reeves.

"Those lying bastards!" Emily yelled.

"Shh… Allie," said Pete.

"Oh to hell with her nap, Peter!" continued Emily. "Her mom and dad just killed themselves! And they couldn't even tell us the damn truth! Ahh!" Pete tried embracing her, but she fought him off. "This… this is why Erin was so fucking upset when she left. Remember, I told you she couldn't stop crying for some reason. Well, we just found the reason."

"I told Ms. Reeves we were heading to Egypt to explain things," said Pete.

"Egypt?" she laughed at him. "And what are we going to do in Egypt? Who's going to watch the baby while we're gone? I assume with Sean and Erin gone, we're now her legal guardians."

"After we explain things to the embassy, I'm going down that damn tunnel and getting them back," he said. "Sean and Erin will be slaves to Hades forever unless I find a way to change things."

"And leave me behind?" she replied. "You need to think this through, Pete."

"Someone has to stay with Allie," he said, "and I won't leave them to their fate."

"Allie?" she began to cry. "I love that child with all my heart, you know that Pete, but I cannot... no, will not let you go down there alone. Do you even have a plan?"

"Somewhat," he said meekly. "When we passed the first time, Hermes met us on the other side and guided us through the Netherworld. I don't know how else to get help other than to meet him there, and what happens after that is anyone's guess. I planned on you coming with me as far as Cairo."

"No, Peter!" she argued. "I can't lose you again. I won't do it. If you go, I have to. They're my family too."

"But Allie..."

"We'll figure it out," she said. "Get our tickets. I'll start packing."

The next day, Pete, Emily, and Allie arrived in Cairo, having explained to Allie that they had to come to help her mom and dad. When she asked what was wrong, they told her not to worry. They climbed into the car Kimberly Reeves sent for them, they sped away to the embassy.

Pete was annoyed to find Michael Turner sitting in Kimberly's office as they walked in, but there was nothing he could do since Michael was now officially entwined.

"Greetings, Mr. and Mrs. Henry," said Ms. Reeves. "Thank you for making it here so quickly."

"Indeed, Ms. Reeves," replied Pete.

"I'll have one of our aides take Allie, so we can talk, if you'd like," she said. "And maybe some coffee?" she added, seeing the fatigue on their faces.

"That would be great." He faked a smile.

After Allie was occupied and the coffee had arrived, Kimberly shut the door and sat behind her desk. "What's going on, Mr. Henry?"

"Before I answer any questions," he replied. "I need to know

46

what Sean and Erin told you… about everything."

She looked at him for a moment. "You Henrys keep secrets well, don't you?" Pete raised an eyebrow. "Okay. To put it plainly, Mr. Henry, they told Michael Turner and I moments before they disappeared that their novels were true stories and they were the main characters. I've read these books and I have a hard time believing them to be true. I mean 'Atlantis' and 'great floods'? And they were the heroes? Forgive me if I don't completely buy it. Michael here is torn between believing them and thinking this is just another one of their lies. In the end, it doesn't matter except what you're going to tell me next. So I'll change my initial question to you. Were Sean and Erin right? Are their novels real?"

"I'll answer this, Pete," said Emily. "Ms. Reeves, I know how all of this must sound. Five years ago, I was on the other side of this story, but then things happened. Crazy things. I was taken by an amulet back in time, rather forcefully. I was thrust into a world that I didn't understand and for a while I questioned my own sanity. I get that it's a lot to take in, but yes, my brother and sister were telling the truth."

"Say that I believe you," said Kimberly, "then what?"

"Then you'll need to believe what we're about to tell you," said Pete. He and Emily explained Allie's nightmares and Hades, and how Sean and Erin must have sacrificed themselves for the sake of their daughter. From Kimberly's description of the white figure beneath Sa-el Hagar, Hades must have taken them.

Kimberly blotted her eyes with a tissue before responding. "I can't say that I believe you, but I'm afraid it's the only explanation we have. Why couldn't you tell me this on the phone yesterday? Why did you have to fly all the way here for this?"

"Because I have to save them," said Pete.

"Save them? How?" asked Kimberly.

"When we passed through the last time… yes, Ms. Reeves, the books are real… the last time we were met by Hermes in Purgatory."

"Hermes? Like the God?" she scoffed. "This is too much for me."

"Kimberly, you have to trust me. Trust me without understanding. That's the only way you'll be able to accept any of this."

"I'll try to do my best," she said. Michael Turner laughed from his seat against the wall. He was being too quiet for comfort.

"Once we meet up with Hermes, we'll ask for his help. From thereon, who knows, but it's the only shot we've got."

"Why do all this?" asked Kimberly. "Sean and Erin sacrificed themselves willingly to save their daughter. Aren't you going against their wishes by saving them?"

"You haven't met Hades, Ms. Reeves," said Emily. "He's ruthless and cruel. They're worse than dead in his service."

Kimberly sighed. "Which of you is staying behind to watch the child? You have thought of her needs, right?"

"Ms. Reeves, last time we went through the passage, we came back out the same one," said Emily. "I was hoping that you could watch her, just for a little while, until we return."

"You mean *if* you return! Mrs. Henry, the child has already lost her mother and father and now you're going to make her lose her aunt and uncle too? What am I supposed to do if you don't come back?"

"I know it's hard to make sense," said Pete. "If we're not back within two weeks, send her to my mother. I'll leave her information with you."

Kimberly was dumbfounded. She had lost control of the situation and didn't know how to fix it.

"We both have to go, Ms. Reeves," said Emily. "I have a power there that might be useful and two heads are better than one. We're more likely to survive with the two of us."

"I... I guess I'll drive you to Sa-el Hagar," said Kimberly, stunned.

Hours later, the four plus Allie stood at the entrance to the tunnel in Sa-el Hagar. On the ride over, Pete and Emily did their best to explain to Allie what was happening and where they were going. To their surprise, she took the news well. Her only concern for them was to get her mommy and daddy back. The sun was close to setting as Pete stared into the hole.

"Pete, are you sure you want to do this?" asked Kimberly.

"I'm sorry, Ms. Reeves, but we don't have a choice," he said. She nodded.

"Mr. Henry, if it's okay with you, I'd like to join you," said Michael. Kimberly reacted first.

"No, Michael!" she said. "You can't."

"Michael, she's right," replied Pete. "This isn't a field trip where you can just tag along. There are dangers larger than you know where we're going."

"With all due respect, Mr. Henry, I've read the books and I'm well aware of what awaits me," he replied.

"Why?" asked Pete. "Why do you want to go?"

"I have my reasons," said Michael.

"That's not good enough," said Pete. "We need a reason."

"Michael, please don't do this," said Kimberly.

"I have to!" Michael said. "I don't have anything left here. I don't want to go back to the States and I can't stay here. Just let me come with you. I'm aware of the dangers."

Pete looked to Emily, who seemed just as torn as he was. Michael would likely get himself killed or worse, but the man was his own keeper. If he wanted to take the risk, it was his to take.

"If we let you come," said Pete, "then you have to do *exactly* as we say. There are rules in the Underworld and I won't have my family's safety jeopardized by your whims."

"As you say," replied Michael.

"Then it's settled," said Pete. Kimberly was on the verge of crying, and Allie was oddly stoic. This bothered Pete, but he didn't know what to do for her. Emily was always better with kids.

As if that was her cue, Emily knelt down in front of the child. "Allie, baby, you be good for Miss Kimberly, okay?"

"I will," she replied. The two embraced one another.

"Well, this is it," said Pete to everyone. They said their final goodbyes and Pete, Emily, and Michael entered the tunnel.

Pete felt a wave of déja vu as they made their way underground. He held Emily's hand the entire way. Her anxiety was felt in her firm grip. The tunnel seemed to go forever until suddenly they stood in the cavern with the dark pool. The air was cold and clammy.

It was then that Pete realized that the other two hadn't done this before. "Don't drink the water, whatever you do," he said, hearing Sean's voice in his head. Not until they were completely submerged could they take in the water and not fully die. "We just walk into the water until it's above our heads. At a certain point we'll… well… cross over." Emily squeezed his hand tighter.

"God, I hope this works," said Emily as they approached the water's edge. Michael followed silently behind them.

Pete closed his eyes and took a step in. Like before, the water felt like cool gas. He took another step, as did Emily. Then another.

Once his head was below the surface he stopped, holding his breath. He knew that soon he'd have to open his mouth and accept death. He clenched Emily's hand tighter and opened his mouth. The water rushed in, filled his mouth and nostrils and spilled into his lungs. He burned for air as panic took him. After several long moments, his body convulsed and he went still. His mind slowly began to relax and fade. Fatigue swept over him and he felt light. Weightless, a current came and swept him deeper into the dark pool.

Kimberly didn't move from the opening to the tunnel for several minutes. Or maybe hours, she couldn't tell. She felt conflicted. She had hardly spoken to Michael in the last few years, and now he had been here. It almost felt like old times, and just as suddenly, he was gone again. What was that she felt? Was it love? She had never thought of him in that way. He'd been like an older brother or cousin to her, but had there been something else? There was an emptiness within her that had not been there moments before. She began to cry.

She took the little girl's hand and began to walk back to the car. The child bothered her as well. Not the fact that she was suddenly a temporary guardian of a little girl she didn't know. Oddly enough, that part didn't really faze her. It was how calm the child was in the midst of all that was happening. Her parents left her to save her, and now her aunt and uncle left to save them, yet the girl had hardly flinched when Pete and Emily told her they were going.

"Don't be sad, Miss Kimberly," she said at her side. Looking down at her, Allie smiled at her.

"Sorry, Allie," she replied. "I'm not good with goodbyes." She gave a weak grin.

"They'll be alright," said Allie. "I know it."

Kimberly stopped walking and knelt down in front of her. "I don't want to upset you, but we can't know that. I pray for their safety, but no one can tell what will happen."

"The pretty lady can," said the girl.

"Pretty lady?" asked Kimberly. "What pretty lady?"

"She was in my dream. After the bad man went away, she visited me and said they are going to be okay."

"Sweetie, that's just a dream," said Kimberly. "Trust me, I want that too, but it was just a dream."

"No," said Allie loudly. "It's not just a dream. She told me that we will help them."

"We?" asked Kimberly. "You and me? How can we help them from here?"

"She'll tell you," said the girl. In a quick motion, Allie place a hand to Kimberly's head and she fell back.

When Kimberly opened her eyes, she was standing. The wind swept around her and she was on a mountainside. Only a thick blanket of clouds lay beneath her and the sun high above. The air was cool and smelled of winter. In the distance, a bird flew toward her. In time, it landed on the mountain beside her and transformed into a woman. She had long golden hair, falling around her in ringlets while her white and gold dress billowed with the wind. She was taller than any woman she'd ever seen before.

"Greetings, Guardian," said the woman. Kimberly was stunned and couldn't find a voice to speak. "You have been brought here to aid those who would require your help."

"Who are you?" her voice squeaked out.

"A friend," she replied. "I am known as Alexia to some, Neith to others."

"Why do you call me 'guardian'?" asked Kimberly.

"I call you what you are. You are to help guide and watch over the daughter of Sean and Erin Henry."

"I'm only watching over Allie until Pete and Emily get back," she said.

"Indeed, but you will do more than that," said Alexia. "With the child's help, you will save her family and save your beloved."

"My beloved?"

"Michael Turner," she replied. "He is in more danger now than he knows. Without your help, he will be lost."

"What? He just left," said Kimberly. "I don't know what this is, but I'm no hero. I wouldn't know what to do."

"No one is a hero until they become one. I will tell you what you shall do. Within Sa-el Hagar is the ancient city of Saïs and beneath my temple, the Temple of Neith, is a chamber with a certain stone. The Crystal of Saïs must be found and with it you will be able to find and save your friend. The child is the key."

Kimberly felt confused, not for the first time that day. Damn Sean and Erin for getting her into this! "Once we get the stone, then what?" she asked.

"Wait," replied Alexia. "The child will let you know when it is time, but you must find it first. Go quickly."

Kimberly had so many questions, but before she could speak, the world dissolved around her and turned to black. Tiny lights appeared above; millions of them strewn through the sky. They were stars she realized.

"You slept forever," laughed the child as Kimberly lay there.

"What was that?" she asked, sitting up. "Was that...?"

"I told you she was pretty," said Allie.

"Yes," she replied. "She was."

"Did she tell you the plan?" asked the girl.

"She mentioned some of it," said Kimberly as she tried to put her thoughts together. "But I'm afraid she may have left some things out."

"What did she say?" asked the child excitedly.

Kimberly looked down at her. What was she doing? This child should be at home with her family, not out here in the middle of nowhere Egypt. She could just take her back to Cairo and wait for Pete and Emily, or better yet, send the girl to her grandmother now, but Allie clearly knew something. It was in her eyes and Kimberly could not ignore that. She sighed.

"We have to find a crystal," she replied.

CHAPTER II
PURGATORYING

Pete was suddenly aware of himself. Not as if he was waking up from a deep sleep, but as if he now realized that he had never been asleep to begin with. It was unsettling at first, until he understood where he was. The sensation was reminiscent of his first trip to Purgatory. Any moment now, Hermes would rouse them with a song. He waited.

"Why have you come here?" said a voice. Pete was confused. Hermes sang to them before, as if calming them to the fact that they were dead. This voice sounded angry. "Do you wish so intently for your souls to be destroyed?"

Pete sat up and looked around. Emily and Michael sat up too. As before, their "bodies" seemed to glow from within. Not really solid and not yet transparent. Pete always thought they looked like white shadows. A figure stood just within reach of their glowing.

"Hermes," said Pete. The figure stepped closer, clad in golden armor around his chest and torso. He looked just as Pete remembered him, skinny and young in appearance. His golden sandals had real bird's wings attached to them, matching the small golden helmet upon his head. Clasped tightly in his right hand was his all-too-familiar caduceus, a silver staff with two snakes coiled around it and two white bird's wings attached at the top. As funny as it looked, Pete knew the power the staff contained.

"Did you become deaf as you passed over, Peter Henry?" asked

Hermes. "And you, Emily, in you I am most disappointed. After your last visit to the Netherworld, I pegged you for never wanting to return. And who is the third? Is he blind for having followed you into the dark pool? Answer me!"

Pete had never seen Hermes so angry. "His name is Michael," said Pete, "and he was determined to come with us."

"A choice that will surely lead to his demise," said Hermes, looking down at Michael in disgust. Speaking to Pete and Emily, he asked, "What demons have possessed you to return here unbidden? Has the sky fallen and I not made aware? Has the Netherworld become your final refuge?"

"We didn't know where else to go," Emily managed to say.

"Were you so won't for a holiday that you chose death?" asked Hermes rhetorically. "Explain yourself or I shall hand you over to Hades now!"

Pete hadn't known what to expect from Hermes, but he never imagined the messenger god would be angry with him. "Sorry, Hermes, Emily is right. We didn't know where else to go. Hades has taken Sean and Erin and we came seeking your help to get them back."

"If that is your quest, then it is vain," replied Hermes. "I am not ignorant that Hades has command of them and I also know that it was of their own accord. His actions were not as before, binding them to him unbidden. Your brethren walked willingly into his grasp."

"How can you say that?" asked Emily. "You know the circumstances that led them there. He's been playing them for fools ever since we escaped Cerberus."

"And who is to blame, my dear, for them being fools? Hades did not bestow them dim wit. *That* they earned of their own merit."

"Hades misled them and possessed their daughter," said Emily. "It was torture for her. Allie had no part in the deal we made with Hades to escape the Underworld, yet now she seems to have paid the price of her parents."

"I say that Sean and Erin have paid the ultimate price, Emily," said Hermes.

"No," she said. "Allie is now without both her mother and her father."

"And now she is also without her aunt and her uncle," he replied. "You have not been so kind to her in your own actions. A better man might say that it would be kinder to the child for you two to stay with her and care for her in your brother's stead. No, instead you're here playing both heroes and victims."

"You're right," said Pete. "We could have stayed with her. Part of me wishes that we had."

"Then why are you here?" Hermes asked again.

"Justice, I guess," said Pete. "You know Hades. You know the kinds of things he'll make them do. I can't even imagine. Nothing good can come of it and since you Gods haven't seen fit to stop him, we're left to figure it out."

"Hades' actions have not gone unnoticed," replied Hermes, "but a deal is a deal. Sean and Erin knew that, and that is why they made the pact in the first place. It was their souls for Allie's. The deal may have been ill-conceived, but they agreed to it."

"There has to be some sort of loophole," said Emily. "Doesn't Hades have a weakness? Can't we outsmart him like we did before?"

"In all fairness, we did not exactly outsmart him," said Hermes, "hence your current problem. As far as loopholes or weaknesses, there is nothing to play. The deal was clean and Sean and Erin consented, however dire their circumstances may have been."

"How can you show no compassion for them?" asked Emily. "We're here because they would have done the same for us. When I was taken to Saïs by the crystal and they thought I'd been taken to the Underworld, they did the same for me. They would have fought me out of the clutches of Hades and I intend to repay them in kind."

"Your quest is futile," said Hermes, exasperated. "It will only lead to death or worse. There is nothing we can do short of imprisoning the dark lord himself, and even then the vow of your kin would still bind them to him."

"Well, we can't just do nothing," said Emily. "Need I remind you, Hermes, of how I helped you and Alexia save mankind from annihilation? Of how I was ripped from my world and forced into service as the Crystal Bearer? Of the hell that I endured at your hands? You talk to us about debts. Well you and Alexia owe me a debt for that, and since I don't know how to contact her, you'll have to pay the bill."

Hermes was silent. Pete could tell that he was taking her words to heart. He looked defeated.

"I was truthful in saying there is nothing that we can do, at least to my knowledge," said Hermes, "but there is one who may know how to sway the dark lord. The one who is closest to him. She is familiar with his deals, still having to live with hers. I cannot make any promises, but I can take you to her."

"Who is 'she'?" asked Pete.

Hermes looked sad. "Persephone. His wife." He turned and walked away. "Follow me," he called, "if you truly wish for this to be your path." Pete, Emily, and Michael hurried after him, lest they be lost in Purgatory.

Time in the Netherworld was uncertain, Pete remembered as Hermes led them along. He couldn't tell how long they trailed after the messenger before they came to the Acheron. It was hardly a river, thought Pete. Wisps of white vapor streamed passed, ebbing and flowing against the shore, reminding him of white smoke. He became tense at what was to come.

"I will not assume that either of you thought to bring an obolus for the crossing?" asked Hermes. They hadn't. Pete fretted for a moment. The ferryman, Charon, would not let them cross without payment and then their quest would truly be in vain. "Fear not. As the Crystal Bearer said, I will pay this bill." From nowhere, he made three golden coins appear and handed one to each of them. "Hold onto them tightly," he said. "You do not want the lost souls to get them."

"Lost souls?" asked Michael, his confidence seemed to have been left with his body.

"Look about you," replied Hermes. Slinking from the shadows, souls just like them wandered and murmured aimlessly. "They are the unfortunate ones, those who have died without being given means for passage. They will never know rest. Pity them, but do not give in to their pleas, for then you shall take their place until such a time when all comes to an end." Pete drew Emily closer to him, and even Michael huddled closer toward the group.

"Hermes," said Pete, "will we... you know... have to go through it again?"

"For someone who has walked blindly to his own death, Peter Henry, you seem very disturbed in facing it," said Hermes, still angry, despite his compliance. "Of course you will have to go through it again. No one crosses Acheron without cleansing."

"Cleansing?" asked Michael.

"Just wait, dear wanderer," said Hermes. "It would not serve you to tell you now."

Chime… Chime… Chime

"Ah, here he comes now," said Hermes. Pete became anxious at the sound.

Chime… Chime… Chime

"I must leave you now," said Hermes. "As a God, I cannot cross as you do. Fear not, I will meet you on the opposite shore." The wings on his sandals and helmet began to flutter, and without another word, he rose and flew away.

"You're being quiet for a change," said Pete to Michael. "Not what you were expecting?"

"What can I possibly say to Hermes, the fabled Messenger God?" replied Michael. "From the sounds of it, this isn't exactly what you were expecting either. What is this cleansing?"

Chime… Chime… Chime

"You'll see," said Pete. "I wouldn't want to spoil it for you."

The chimes became louder, until the sound seemed to press in on them. After a bout of suspense, the ferry finally appeared, chiming one last time before stopping at the shore.

Charon's Ferry looked sadder than Pete had remembered. Barely a raft, it seemed as if it would sink before it'd float. Standing at the back, a tall, thin old man waited. Charon wore white robes that flowed down and melded with the vaporous river. With both hands, he held tightly to a thick wooden staff, just as old and gnarled as he, with a bell attached to the top. Taking a hand from the staff, he gestured for them to board.

Emily and Michael looked at Pete with uncertainty. Apparently he'd become the leader of this outfit without ever knowing. Gathering his courage, he stepped aboard and the others followed. The raft was sturdy, to their relief.

"Peter Henry," said Charon, his clouding-white eyes staring down at the raft. Pete looked at him surprised. "Still have yet to die in truth. I am beginning to believe you like my ferry rides." The old man was making fun of him, Pete realized. After all of the grimness of his first two trips across this river, he never thought that Charon could have a sense of humor. "I do not ever get to see the same face twice, but here you are for a third time. Your reasons are meaningless to me, but here we are. Very well then," he cleared his throat, "thou hast boarded the Ferry of Charon in order to cross this river of woe, the River Acheron. An obolus you must pay or in Purgatory you must stay." He held out his withered palm and they each deposited their gold coin. The raft began to move away from shore, leaving the lost souls and the greater of Purgatory behind them.

"Must I do this again?" asked Pete to Charon.

"It is the only way," he replied. When the shore was gone from sight, Charon began to sing.

"Woe, on the river path... Woe, doth the river hath... Woe, on the river pass... Woe, doth the river mass...

"Upon the Acheron – all souls must become – one with their demons – facing them must begin...

"Remember for the last – wrongs done in past – see them played in day – so they must fade away...

"Woe, on the river path... Woe, doth the river hath... Woe, on the river pass... Woe, doth the river mass... Woe, it has come at last."

Pete was suddenly outside of his body, looking upon himself tied to the walls inside of a ship, being tossed about in a storm. It was the ship the Persephone during the deluge. A crate flew past his face and water gushed in through a hole left from a broken plank of the ship's deck. Emily, Sean, and Erin were tied up beside him and he yelled for them to watch out. As he ran forward to help them, the scene dissolved, the storm was over, and he was standing on the deck of the ship. In front of him, he, Julie Vane, Sean, and Erin wrestled the Athenian Steward, Thebos, to the ground. In the struggle, Thebos took a knife and stabbed Julie in the stomach. She backed away and fell to the floor. In response, he and Erin took their knives and each staked Thebos' hands to the deck. Thebos writhed and cursed in pain.

"Thebos" he heard Sean say, "I have a message for you from the lips of Zeus. In your punishment for your trespasses, death is not the end of suffering." The man screamed as Sean poured oil over his body and set him on fire.

Pete screamed for Sean to stop, but his brother dissolved and he found himself standing in front of a three-headed beast with scales. They were fighting Cerberus at the gates of the Underworld.

"Emily, use the caduceus!" screamed Alexia. Emily stood behind the distracted beast and threw Hermes' staff at its feet. The snakes detached and tied themselves around Cerberus' legs and he fell.

"Run!" yelled Hermes. "They won't hold him for long!" The group then ran off toward the River Acheron, where Pete knew they'd escape.

Cerberus snarled and was replaced by a dark pool. In front of him stood his self and Emily as they prepared to enter the pool.

"God, I hope this works," said Emily. Pete looked away as they walked into the water.

When he looked back, he was on his knees weeping. His tears were white vapor that flowed into the river. Beside him Emily lay curled in the fetal position, sobbing uncontrollably. Michael had also fallen to his knees, white vapor pouring through his fingers as his hands covered his face.

Pete looked up to Charon, questioningly. "We have not reached the shore yet," he said to the withered old man. "Why are they still in pain?"

"Is the answer to your question not an obvious one, Peter Henry?" replied Charon. "You have fewer demons than your companions, as you have passed this way before. Consider yourself fortunate, as you are the first to ever rise from despair before reaching the shore."

Pete watched the others scream and sob. "Is there anything we can do to stop their suffering?" he asked.

"I am afraid not," replied Charon, "and I would not if I had the power to do so. You will remember that this cleansing is meant for those whose time in the world of the living has truly come to pass. Happiness and peace do not come from happiness and peace. They come from pain and suffering. Only after having dealt with and faced their demons will Emily Henry and Michael Turner truly know freedom from them. You know this to be true." Pete nodded in agreement, but he was still torn inside at Emily in pain. His heart lifted when the opposite shore came into view.

Emily and Michael crawled from the raft, much as he had after his first time across the Acheron. Emily climbed to her feet and fell into his arms. Even as just a spirit, he could sense her distress and even feel her heart beating wildly within her.

"You're alright," he said calmly as he kissed the top of her head.

"Peter, I saw..." she cried, "my mother died all over again and then Erin went missing again and Pete... the crystal. I was taken to Saïs and I had lost you all over again." She sobbed. "I saw the deluge and you kill Thebos and then I had to save you all from Hades' sarcophagi. Why?"

"I wish I could take it back," said Pete. "That was preparing you for eternal rest and peace. It was the only way across."

"Indeed it was," said Hermes as he flew down to them. He knelt and helped Michael up to his feet. The once embassy official was stunned. What demons had he faced, Pete wondered. "I am sorry that you had to go through that again, Pete," said Hermes. "You are the first to do so twice."

"Lucky me," said Pete.

The four moved on, Hermes in the lead. The landscape of the Netherworld unnerved Pete as much as it had before. There was no sky, per se, only endless grey-darkness above and an eerie soft glow illuminating the land. The ground was broken at points, with only colorless crags of rock to pervade the bleakness. After a time, they arrived at the top of a steep slope. Far below a massive wall stood that stretched on indefinitely in both directions. Pete could make out the tall gates to the Underworld and a small spot in front, guarding it.

"Worry not, Cerberus sleeps as he always does," said Hermes. He motioned for them to follow him.

"Will he recognize us?" asked Emily as they made their way down the hill. "The last time he saw Pete and I, we tied him up and ran like hell." That scene was still fresh in Pete's mind.

"As ever before, Cerberus pays no heed to those who enter the Underworld," replied Hermes, "but try to leave again and he will not be as calm."

Pete's heart was in his stomach, or would have been if he'd had a body, as they approached the beast. Three giant wolfs' heads, each placed at the end of long snake-like necks, lay curled together with eyes closed. Spikes ran down the back of his house-sized body and he had six legs, each foot with three razor sharp talons. Pete wondered how they had ever escaped such a monster.

Hermes paid no attention to Cerberus and walked right up to the gates. Placing his hand on the stone, he pushed and they opened silently and effortlessly. "Come," he said as they stared at him with uncertainty. Pete could feel the weight of the walls pressing down on him as he passed through the gates. Not for the first time, he questioned their decision to do this, but there was no turning back now.

CHAPTER III
PERSEPHONE

The gates closed silently behind them and Pete looked upon the Underworld. He remembered it vividly. There were hills and valleys in the distance, though no trees or plants to decorate the landscape. Sheer barren rock was all that could be seen. Two roads had been made opposite the gates, one leading to the left and one to the right. Pete felt a stab of uncertainty.

"Hermes, where *is* Persephone?" he asked.

"If you hoped to go to the Elysian Fields, Pete, you will be disappointed," replied Hermes. Hermes had led Pete and the others to the Elysian Fields, the final paradise for the heroes and glorious, on their first visit to the Underworld. Though truly beautiful, that trip had ended in being captured by Hades himself. "Persephone rests in Hades' fortress of Erebus."

"Erebus?" asked Emily. "How on Earth can we see her then? Surely Hades will find us and this will all have been for nothing."

"You asked me to take you to someone who could help," replied Hermes. "Do you think you are the only ones at risk here?"

"There has to be another way," said Pete. There was no way they could sneak into Erebus without being caught. And this time there would be no gods to barter their souls for salvation.

"I am afraid there is not, Pete," said Hermes. "This will not be an easy task, but if you truly want to save your brethren, then I see no other option."

Looking to Emily, Pete resigned himself to their path. The time for turning back ended a long time ago. "Lead us on, then," said Pete.

Hermes did just that, taking the road to the right. The wall and gates to the Underworld vanished behind them as they made their way across the land.

Not far into the Underworld, Pete began to notice his awareness fading. He remembered the sensation from before and summoning his willpower, his mind came back. "We can't fade," he said.

"Indeed," said Hermes. "Though, one should not worry about that at the moment. In a daze, you will not be able to draw attention to yourselves on the road."

Michael looked up as if reawakening from a dream. "Draw attention?" he asked. "Who would be watching us?" He looked around anxiously.

"The Furies," said Hermes. "Pete and Emily will remember them well. They are shadow demons, the guardians of the Underworld and they answer only to Hades."

"I remember," Pete said.

"Just like in the Henrys' novel," said Michael, more to himself than the others. "It's all true. I'd imagined it to be so, but to be here… living it."

"Technically, you're not living," said Pete. Michael didn't reply. "We haven't seen any Furies yet."

"They will appear," replied Hermes. "The closer we get to Erebus, the more we shall see. They will not bother us as they did last time, as I am taking you to where you are meant to go. This path I tread often."

Knowing this made Pete feel a little better. The last time he was taken by the Furies, he woke up in the depths of Erebus as a prisoner of Hades.

As Hermes warned, the further they trekked, the more they saw the Furies. Pete could hardly see the first one, just a dark shadow-cloud hovering above the ground, nearly blending in with the bleakness behind it. Michael had drifted back off into his daze, alongside Emily. Pete forced himself to stay present.

As they approached it, the magnitude of Erebus astounded Pete. At a glance, the fortress appeared to be a dark mountain, it crags and spires shooting high above them. Indeed, lava flowed from it at some points, as if a waterfall. Pete noticed that the spires were actually towers and the fortress had been carved from the mountain.

"The Titans carved her from the core of the Earth," said Hermes when asked about it.

Hermes roused Emily and Michael from their daze as they approached the gate of Erebus. "From here on, you must do your best to stay alert," he told them. "I only have the vaguest of plans and we may have to move suddenly. If you are taken by Hades, I will forsake you. The dark lord trusts me not, from when I aided human causes in the past. I cannot afford another quarrel with Hades."

The doors to the fortress stood twenty-feet tall and wide enough that the four of them could walk through side-by-side with plenty of room to spare. Pods of Furies stood sentinel on either side of the door, but paid no mind to them as Hermes ushered them inside. The interior of the fortress was just as bland as the outside. The air was illuminated by some unseen source and the walls were grey and unadorned. Hermes led them up a large staircase, down a long hall, and finally into a large cave-like room with a vaulted ceiling.

There were hundreds of other souls present, all facing a stone dais with three occupied seats. Pete recognized two of the figures. King Rhadamanthus, ruler of the Elysian Fields, sat to the far left. He had long golden hair that flowed off of his shoulders and a long beard to match. His icy blue eyes dared to pierce the souls of those who looked into them. Seated in the center chair was Hades himself. Garbed in dark-flowing robes, he gazed out over the souls menacingly. In the final chair, to the right of Hades, there sat another large god with dark brown hair that fell in curls around his head. Unlike Rhadamanthus, his beard was short and curly.

"Hermes," whispered Sean, "what is this? What's going on?"

"This is the judgment," he replied. "Here is where souls are sent on to the Elysian Fields, Tartarus, or the Asphodel Meadows. You already know Rhadamanthus and Hades. The last one is Lord Minos. He sees that the final judgments are carried out. If we were to be thrown into Tartarus, he is the one who would do the throwing."

"What are the Asphodel Meadows?" asked Emily.

"It is a plane of indifference," replied Hermes. "There souls do not suffer, but there is no sense of progression or ambition. Once a soul is taken there, it becomes ambivalent to its own existence."

"Why are we here?" asked Pete. "We're supposed to see Persephone."

"Patience humans," replied Hermes. "We had to come here or

the Furies would be suspicious." Hermes looked uncertain about his plan, if he had one at all. Stealing away to Persephone would be difficult at best. "I must leave," said Hermes. "I am not supposed to remain here long. Hades will suspect something. I urge you to stay here and wait for my signal. You will know it when you see it. I will return for you." Before Pete could protest, Hermes was gone.

Pete was panicking inside. With how far they have come, was Hermes just turning them over to Hades? Was that his plan all along? He couldn't express his concerns to Emily or Michael. None of the other souls were talking and doing so would just draw attention. Only one of two things could happen, he thought. Hermes will return, or he won't.

Returning his attention to the room, Pete observed the judgments taking place. Each soul was made to stand before the dais and accept the ruling of the three gods. Rhadamanthus was speaking.

"You have done nothing of valor in your life," he said to the soul of a man. "You are not outright courageous and have known no glory. You have no right to come eternally to the Fields of Elysium where the fallen heroes rest. However you have been kind and virtuous through most of your days and have passed your virtues onto your sons. We have no use for you in Tartarus. You shall reside eternally in the Asphodel Meadows."

"Let it be known," announced Minos. "This man is of the Asphodel Meadows." With that said, the man was led away by a fury. Next, a woman stepped forward. Rhadamanthus' speech was similar, if not the same, to the one before. In the end, the woman was also sent the Asphodel Meadows, as were most of the souls that followed. Once in every dozen or so, someone would be graced with entrance to the Elysian Fields or damned to eternity in Tartarus, but mostly the plane of indifference awaited the masses.

As soul after soul was judged and taken away, Pete, Emily, and Michael were herded closer and closer to the dais. Pete tried to not let his anxiety show, but Emily and Michael were not so composed. Emily looked at him and dared a whisper.

"What are we going to do?" she asked.

He looked straight forward. "We wait," he said. "Hermes said he'd return for us. It's all we can do. No more talking." She nodded.

More souls were judged and they moved closer still. Pete feared that Hades would recognize him or Emily, so he positioned Michael in front of them.

"This man is of the Asphodel Meadows," droned Minos, and another soul was led away. There were only few souls in front of them, though many had filtered in behind them. There was no use in trying to move to the back. Any movement but forward would be noticed.

At last there was no one left before them. Visibly afraid, Michael took his place before the dais. As Hades and the others looked down on him, Hades was called to from the back of the room.

"What is it, messenger? Have you some news from my brothers?" asked Hades to Hermes, who moved through the room and in front of the dais, moving Michael aside.

"It is Ares, my lord," replied Hermes. "He begs that you meet with him immediately."

"Ares? What does my nephew want of me?" asked Hades, unamused at being summoned by a lesser god.

"He did not say," said Hermes. "Do you wish me to reply that you are unavailable?"

"No," replied Hades, "that will not do. I shall go to him now." Hades looked to his fellow gods on either side of him. "We shall resume at a later time." With that, Hades turned to vapor and disappeared, Rhadamanthus and Minos following suit shortly after. The other souls in the room were left in their daze, unconcerned that they would have to wait for their judgment.

"What took you?" asked Pete to Hermes.

"I had to convince Ares to summon Hades," he said. "Do you know how hard it is to convince the God of War to do anything? That is neither here nor there. We must go." Pete shook Michael, who had slipped into the daze and they were off, running at the heels of Hermes' winged sandals.

They climbed higher and higher into Erebus, stair after stair, until finally they came to a door of iron with the image of a setting sun etched on it. Hermes knocked.

"Enter," said a dreamy voice from the other side. Hermes gave a push and the door opened.

Persephone's chamber was unlike anywhere else in Erebus or the Underworld. Pete was taken aback as white and yellow flowers sprung forth from the iron walls, floors, and ceilings, with beds of vibrant green grass growing between them. The air smelled sweet and gave off a brighter, more sun-like light than anywhere else in the fortress. A lone square window at the end of the room looked out upon the bleakness, breaking the spell of the room. Lying on a bench in front of it was Persephone herself. She was nearly as tall as two men, as gods tended to be, with thick red hair that fell well past her hips in flowing waves. She wore a fitting ivory-colored dress with a green cord wrapped around her waist. Her emerald eyes welcomed them in.

"Hermes," she said. "Long it has been since you graced me with your presence." She smiled.

"For such an intoxicating beauty, I would do nothing else but gaze upon you if duty allowed," he replied.

"Indeed, you would," she replied. "I see you have brought me visitors, such a treat. Tell me, Hermes, though I love your visits, why have you come? It is a long way to my tower."

"At great peril to myself, I have brought mortals seeking your council."

"Mortals?!" she said, rising from her bench and rushing over to him. She looked from Hermes to three undead souls. "Here? Does my husband know of this? He will destroy them! Hermes, you know what he is capable of."

"I do, sweet Persephone," he said, "and please know that I took great caution as their escort. Your husband has taken their friends, a trial you are all too familiar with."

"Indeed, I am," she replied. Persephone led them to her bench, where she resumed her seat, the others sitting on the ground around her. "I was only a girl when my father, Zeus, betrayed me to Hades. I was walking through the forest and noticed the loveliest flower growing all alone among a sea of nettles. A single narcissus flower, golden-yellow. As I plucked it from the soil, the ground opened up and swallowed me. I woke up next to the River Styx by Hades, riding his golden chariot. He abducted me and we were wed. My mother, Demeter, was furious, as my father had allowed Hades to do this to me. Her being the God of Harvest, she refused to let anything grow for seven years. To finally appease her, Zeus sent Hermes here to save me and bring me back to Olympus. All would have been fine, but Hades bewitched me. In my captivity, he fed me the seeds of the pomegranate, which bound me to a half-life. When the world is in bloom, I am free to return to Olympus and my mother, but when winter comes, I am forced to remain in the Underworld. And so it has been for time out of mind." She looked up suddenly, breaking her reverie. "But that is my story, how may I counsel thee?" she asked looking to Pete, Emily, and Michael.

"Hades has taken our family," said Pete. "Five years ago, we made a deal with Hades that if we could escape the Underworld, we could have our souls back. We escaped, but our sister Erin was unknowingly pregnant at the time. As the child has grown, Hades has possessed her. In exchange for her soul, Sean and Erin gave up their lives."

"I know of it," said Persephone. "You gave my husband quite a lot of trouble during Zeus' mad deluge. I know Hades is conniving and what he has done is unfair. In the end, your family made a deal with him and he will not go back on it. Even if you were to find them here and take them back to the mortal realm with you, he would still have them. There is no counsel that I can give, as Hermes should have explained."

"I have explained thoroughly," said Hermes. "I thought that you might be able to give them insight that I could not. Though I know Hades greatly, you are closer still."

"Indeed," said Persephone. She closed her eyes for a moment, then opened them. "Little will dissuade my husband from his will. I have spent much time with him these past ages, and there is only one thing that he wants that he does not already possess. Justice."

"Justice?" asked Emily.

"Yes, from his brothers," she replied. "When the Olympians defeated the Titans and imprisoned them within Tartarus, existence was split into three realms for the sons of Kronos to rule. Zeus was given the heavens, Poseidon was given the sea, and Hades was tricked by the two into taking the Netherworld. Hades only desires justice from his brothers, who forsook him, and that I am afraid you small three will be unable to grant him."

"We should never misjudge the power of humans," said Hermes. "They have proven their vigilance before."

"Yes, I suppose they have," she replied. "What are you willing to do to get your family back?"

"Anything," replied Pete. "We've already faced death to come this far."

"Yes, indeed, but you have traveled here before," she said. "Your fear was not in death or coming to the Underworld. You must face greater challenges than that if you are to save your beloved."

"What do you have in mind?" asked Emily.

"Soon, in the world of the living, Poseidon and Athena will have a contest for the patronage of Attica."

"Attica?" asked Pete.

"Formerly Athens," replied Persephone. "After the deluge, the great city of Athens was rebuilt, though not in that name. Because Athena did not protect her city from Zeus' wrath, the rebuilders did not see it fitting to keep the name. Now the city, regrown to match the state of its former glory, is open to choosing a patron.

"The only hope you have in saving your loved ones is to convince Poseidon to beg Hades' forgiveness and welcome him back to Olympus, the condition being that he release your family."

"That's impossible," said Pete. "How are we supposed convince Poseidon of anything?"

"That is your quandary," replied Persephone. "The task is not easy or small, but it is the only hope you now possess. Remember who Poseidon is. Like the sea he governs, he can be terrible and unpredictable. He is also quick to temper. But like the sea, he can also be calm and nurturing."

"What about Zeus?" asked Emily. "We could maybe talk to him?"

"Mortals cannot speak with Zeus directly," said Persephone. "With little or no hope, Poseidon is your path. I now bid you farewell, as it is not wise for you to linger. Hermes will escort you back to the mortal realm. Fortune be with you."

They thanked her and Hermes led them out of the room.

CHAPTER IV
FROM THE DARKNESS INTO THE LIGHT

Hermes took them back the way they came and down so many stairs that Pete was certain they were far beneath Erebus.

"What's the plan now?" asked Pete.

"Just follow me," Hermes replied as he sped on. "We do not have much time before Hades returns."

From the darkness into the light, grey as it was, they emerged from Erebus into a stone courtyard. Faceless statues were crumbling and vines seemed to have grown and then died, covering most surfaces. As if the fortress had provided them some measure of cover, Pete suddenly felt exposed.

Making their way through the yard, a dozen black clouds amassed in front of them. "To where do you take these souls, Psychopomps?" the Furies all said in raspy unison.

"From whence they came," replied Hermes, who was reaching for the caduceus strapped to his belt.

"Not at the bidding of Hades," they replied. "We shall not trust thee to take leave." The Furies moved to entrap them. In one quick movement, Hermes struck the caduceus into the ground and a bright light dissolved the demons, all screeching as they died.

Without wasting a moment, Hermes called for Pete, Emily, and Michael to move on. "That won't hold them back for long," he said. They left the courtyard and crossed the barren land until they came upon a river of flowing magma, Phlegethon, the River of Fire. Hermes stopped in front of it and made a loud cry that Pete remembered well.

"We're taking the fire-serpent, aren't we?" he asked nervously.

"Indeed," replied Hermes. "Ophion will give us passage and you shall take the same tunnel that bore you to Saïs when you were here last."

The lava bubbled a short distance away as the large black serpent surfaced, lashing its head back and forth. His scales looked to be made of iron as he came to slither along the surface and halt in front of them.

"There is no way in hell I'm getting on that thing!" yelled Michael. He was already backing away from the river.

"It is the only way," said Hermes. "He shall not drop you."

"You're joking?" asked Michael. "I think I've done well at holding my peace since we got here, but this is too much."

"Michael, we don't have a choice," said Pete. "We've done this before. You'll be fine, I promise."

"Time flies, Peter Henry," said Hermes, "but you do not. Let us go."

"I thought time didn't exist in the Underworld," said Emily.

"Tell that to Hades when he returns," replied Hermes. "We have to go now!" He struck Michael with his caduceus, not hard, sending him into a daze. "Lead him along, Peter."

Pete did has he was told and guided Michael aboard Ophion; Emily following suit. The scales clinked together, like scratching metal on metal, as the serpent slithered along the top of Phlegethon. He was soon relieved to see the familiar sight of a small shore in front of a rock-wall towering high above. A small entrance to a cave was cut out in its center. Leaving Ophion behind, Hermes led them to it.

"Pete, you will remember the rules of passage?" asked Hermes. Pete nodded, remembering how Hades had explained the rules last time. Once they began to climb the stair beyond the entrance, they were not allowed to look back, lest their souls follow their gaze and trap them in Tartarus for the rest of existence. Pete would have shivered, had he had a body. "Very well, then. You had best lead the way, and I shall follow close behind."

Pete entered the cave, followed by Emily, and then Michael. He placed his foot on the first stair when he heard a commotion behind him. His ascent already started, he dared not look back.

"Run!" he heard Hermes yell.

Pete did not hesitate and climbed quickly, calling back to Emily and Michael to do the same, reminding them time and again not to look back. He was also aware that Hermes was not following, as he said he would. Regardless, he pressed on.

Any small concept of time that he'd had in the Underworld was now completely gone. He had been climbing the stairs for centuries, yet only moments.

"Can we slow down, I'm getting tired," said Michael.

That was good news, thought Pete. "We're nearly there," he replied. "The fatigue means that our souls are passing into the world of the living. We have to keep moving."

A little ways above him, Pete began to see a faint light. Both relief and dread filled him. Being reborn was almost as bad as dying. He approached the source of the light, which was water flowing above them as if supported by a pane of glass.

"We must pass through here and swim to the surface," Pete told them. "No matter what happens... no matter how tired you become, keep swimming. This won't be pleasant."

The water felt cool and refreshing. Finishing the last few steps, Pete climbed into the water and swam. The chill covered his whole body, inside and out. It felt good to feel again, thought Pete as he moved through the water. The next sensation he felt was fatigue. His body was tiring from the exertion, but he dared not stop. Lastly, his chest convulsed and his lungs felt on fire. He needed air; the sweet breath of life. His limbs were beginning to seize, but he willed them to move as he floundered through the water until finally his head broke the surface and life entered him.

As the panic subsided, he floated along the surface, moving toward the shore. He was further relieved as he heard Emily and Michael gasping for breath behind him. The water was full of the familiar bioluminescent plankton that illuminated the sacred lake in Saïs. Reaching the shore, Pete crawled and then collapsed on the rocky surface, Emily and Michael following behind. Sleep then took them all.

Pete took a deep breath and his eyes opened. A blue glow came from the direction of his feet, dimly illuminating the stalactites that hung from the cavern roof. His entire body protested as he sat up and realized he was completely naked. Looking around, he saw that the light was coming from the dark pool several yards away. Next to him, Emily lay on her stomach, and a few feet away was Michael.

Their rebirth washed over him and he was relieved to know they had made it to Saïs.

Stifling the urge to fall back asleep, he began to wake the others. He brushed the hair from Emily's face and nudged her awake, calling her name softly. She opened her eyes and quickly registered where she was.

"Pete, we made it," she breathed. "Thank god." He helped her to sit up.

"Hermes didn't make it," he told her. "I don't know what happened, but he wasn't with us from the start."

"That can't be good," she replied. "Should we wait for him?"

"If he didn't follow us through the cave, I doubt he'd be here anytime soon. Besides, we need to get out of this cavern." She agreed and he moved over to Michael to wake him.

Michael looked confused as he awakened. "Why am I naked?"

Pete laughed. "Because that's the way we're all born. Just be glad you're not screaming like a newborn baby."

"This is incredible," said Michael as he sat up and saw the pool glowing.

"Let's just hope it keeps its novelty," replied Pete. "That water might look pretty, but just wait. Hopefully the Saitians will be as hospitable as they were in the past."

"I thought you knew the king of Saïs," said Michael. "Surely, he'll help you out again."

"Yeah, I've been thinking about that," said Pete. "Persephone said that Athens had been rebuilt and that they are planning a contest for the country's patronage. When we were here last, Athens had just been destroyed. If it's now a thriving country, I'm sure several hundred years must have passed. If Saïs is still the nation it was, it will have a new ruler."

"Then Aha is dead?" asked Emily. She sounded shocked. "It makes sense, but I just didn't realize that everything would have changed. Everyone we know is now dead. Pyrthens…"

"We're not certain of anything yet," said Pete. He looked around warily. "We have to get out of here. Then we'll know more."

"But how?" asked Emily. "We can't go bumbling into the dark. We had flashlights in our time and here we have nothing."

Pete thought for a moment. "During the deluge, the Saitian people lived down here and used orbs filled with water from the lake to provide light."

"But we don't have an orb," said Emily.

"Perhaps," said Pete. "But they lived down here for a while. Maybe they left something behind that we can use to hold the water from this pool. A bowl or a cup or something. I'm sure no one has been down here since."

As best they could, they searched the area surrounding the pool, where the light was brightest, for a vessel. Pete was at a loss when Emily called him over to her. She was digging in the dirt near the water's edge and pulled out a broken clay pot. Half of it was missing, but there was still enough of a curve to it that it could hold a small amount of liquid.

Emily took the pot to the pool and filled it as best she could. "Here goes nothing," she said, and began to lead them out of the cavern and into the tunnel that she knew led to Saïs.

As they climbed, Pete recalled how time seemed to be lost in the passage. Indeed, they'd been walking for hours, or so it seemed, when they were surprised to reach a dead end. The tunnel floor sloped up sharply, ending at the roof of the passage.

"Did we make a wrong turn?" asked Pete.

"There was no wrong turn to make," answered Emily. "The tunnel led us here."

"Are we lost?" asked Michael. "Damn it! I knew I should have stayed at home. We're going to die down here!"

"Michael, calm down," said Emily.

"Calm down?" he replied. "You're lucky I haven't gone bat-shit crazy before this. We went to the Underworld, consulted with Hades' wife, were reborn naked as the day, and now we're stuck in a tunnel with no way out? This is cruel!"

"Just give us a minute," said Pete. "We'll think of something."

Michael took a deep breath, as if to compose himself. "My apologies," he said. "I… I think I've been a good sport about all of this until now. You can begrudge me a little uncertainty."

"Yes, we can," replied Emily. She turned her attention to Pete. "I'm sure there will be plenty more uncertainty before the end. I can't believe that Hermes would've led us here just to hit a dead end. We're missing something."

"Emily," said Michael. "You say that Sean and Erin's books are true?"

"Well, for the most part," she replied. "Some things, like names and some places had to be changed, but other than that, they're dead on."

"Then it's safe to say that the Saitians would still keep a statue of a sphinx guarding the temple of Neith. The same sphinx that covers the passage to this tunnel, if I remember correctly."

"Wow, Michael, you really did read those books," replied Emily. "And you're right." She turned to Pete. "We haven't hit a dead end. The opening is just covered by the statue."

"We aren't strong enough to move that statue," said Pete. "It took a dozen people to move it before. Maybe we could dig around it."

"No, that won't work," said Emily. "We'd starve before we made any progress."

"We could just yell for help," said Michael. "Surely someone will hear us."

"I doubt it," said Emily, as she looked around, holding the water up to the walls. She moved quickly to the opposite wall and some of the water spilled to the floor, losing its glow as it seeped into the earth. "That's it!" she said.

"What's it?" asked Pete and Michael.

"Step back," she replied, "you'll see." Pete and Michael stepped back a ways, giving Emily space.

Pete watched as Emily closed her eyes and placed her fingers in the water. Reacting to her touch, it began to glow brighter. "Look out," she called as she threw the water on the ceiling. The rock absorbed the water quickly, leaving them in complete darkness.

"What good was that?" asked Michael.

"Shh, just wait," she said. Moment later they heard a loud crack and the ceiling caved in and they were covered in a cloud of dust. As the sand settled, light came through an opening. The statue of the sphinx had landed a few feet in front of them. Carefully, they climbed on top of it and out into the light.

The sun was in the middle of the sky and they had to cover their eyes for a time. When they were finally able to see, the great Temple of Neith stood in front of them, just as Pete remembered it. Behind them was the sacred lake itself, with the king's palace built upon an island at its center. The dwellings of the Saitians lined the lake at all sides.

As they stood next to the sunken sphinx, a man in woolen robes ran toward them from the temple.

Book III:
The Oracle of Delphi

CHAPTER I
THE DARK ROOM

News of the Oracle's death stunned all of Attica. So sudden it was that a woman who had barely seen twenty suns had been called to Hades that citizens were in turmoil. Not once since Zeus' deluge had they defied the Gods of Olympus and they often made sacrifices in their honor. Why would they take their voice from this world? Sacrifices were offered more than ever as the Temple of Apollo searched the land for a candidate to become the new Oracle.

Delia was eleven years old when the High Priest of Apollo, Delphinios, came to her village. Duty dictated that each family with a female virgin child was to subject her to testing. The tests, she remembered, were odd at best. When the old man first appeared in her home, he merely looked her over and then asked her questions about the Gods. She answered the questions as she was able, like her father told her to, and the priest seemed quite taken with her. When he was finished, he blessed her in the light of Apollo, said a few quick words to her father, and then left.

At the waning of the following moon, her father, her mother, her elder brother, Doros, and she left their tiny village and walked seven days to the Temple of Apollo at Delphi. At the time, Delia still did not quite understand what was happening. She was merely excited to visit Delphi, a place she had only ever dreamed of. She had heard tales of the Oracle and her visions, and the Temple of Apollo was to be a grand and beautiful place. She wanted to run there for all of her excitement. Her parents did not share in her enthusiasm.

Her father had sold three of their goats to buy enough food for the trip. Her mother could hardly speak to her without crying, and Doros seemed indifferent to everything. If he'd known what was going on, he didn't let on.

"The priest Delphinios has chosen you, daughter, to become a priestess of Apollo," said her father as they approached Delphi. He was leading the donkey, who pulled their small cart of food and supplies. "And in doing so, it will be seen if you are an Oracle."

"An Oracle?" she asked, shocked that anyone would think her special. "But father, I have never been visited by the Gods, nor have I had any visions."

"The priest has seen something within you," he replied. "At the very least, you will honor the Temple and be of service to Apollo, and at most, you will be the new Oracle. May Zeus protect you."

"I shall do as you tell me, Father," she replied, "but will I ever see home again?"

"See it?" he replied. "You may see our village again, yes, but you will not call it home. You will remain here at the Temple and possibly in time you may travel. Delphi is your home now."

Delia became quiet. Had she realized she would be leaving permanently, she would have said goodbye to her friends. She suddenly felt homesick. "Will you be staying too, Father?" she asked after a time.

"Yes, Daughter," he replied. "Your mother and I have chosen to remain in the village and we will visit you as often as we are allowed." The thought of not returning to her village troubled Delia, but having her family close calmed her some.

The Temple of Apollo at Delphi was an enormous complex. Thousands of statues and fountains decorated its many pathways and ornate buildings. At the center of the compound stood a large rectangular building with thick Ionic columns supporting its roof, which was the main temple. Within would be the altar to Apollo. Nearby was a bathhouse, followed by living quarters, and a small theater beyond that. As they were ushered inside the main temple, women in loose tan woolen dresses hurried to and fro. Each had her hair tied back in a braid, held together by golden bands.

"They are the Priestesses of Apollo," whispered her father. Delia was in awe of all she saw. This grand place with its many charms was to be her home.

At the far end, a giant statue of Apollo looked down upon them, a bow in one hand and the sun in the other. One of the priestesses came to greet them.

"May Apollo's grace shine upon you," she said with a bow.

"And upon you, dear priestess," replied her father.

"What child have you brought forth?"

"She is called 'Delia'," he replied. "Might we rest before we continue? We've traveled far and are tired."

"High Priest Delphinios has requested urgency in this matter," said the woman, who could not have been more than fifteen years old. "Please, come with me." Her father made to protest, but the priestess turned before he could say anything. Taking Delia by the hand, he urged her on.

They passed the altar and exited the main temple through a rear door. Behind the structure was a small building, round with a dome roof. Reliefs decorated its exterior, depicting woman interacting with various gods. One that caught her eye was of a screaming woman being drawn toward Olympus by Apollo, all the while being pulled to the Underworld by Hades. She shivered.

The priestess guided them inside. "Welcome to the Oracle's Eye," she said. "Here is where she will speak with Gods, should she prove worthy of their voice." The building was only one room, barely five paces across and two men high, with a round dais in the center. A single torch burned on a sconce next to the door.

"May Zeus protect us," mumbled her father.

"And may Apollo's grace shine upon us all," replied the priestess. "Please wait here. Delphinios will be present soon." She left them standing next to the open door, the single torch burning nearby.

"It stinks in here," Delia said softly to her father. To her delight, he laughed.

"Indeed it does, daughter," he replied. "It is how a mountain smells on the inside."

"It smells like burning wool," she said.

"The scent is sulfur," said a loud voice behind them. "It is the vapor of the Gods. When Apollo slew the serpent Python upon this very hill, the body of the beast fell into the earth and the scent is of his decay. Fear not, the beast has been dead for some time."

"Great priest, may the light of Apollo shine upon you," her father said as he bowed to Delphinios.

"And may his grace befall you," the priest replied. "Forgive me of my haste, but the Gods do not suffer the weary. We must test Delia for the Oracle at once. Please, if you and your family would step outside please. Ah, not you Delia," he said keeping her within the Oracle's Eye. Closing the door, he took her over to the dais. At its center was crack in the earth, the width of a hand, and nearby a chain bolted to the ground with a cuff on the end. "Delia, I believe you know why you are here."

"Yes, High Priest," she said softly. "I am to be tested to see if I am an Oracle."

"Not just *an* Oracle, but *the* Oracle," he replied. He placed her above the crack, where the fumes were strongest. She began to cough. "Sensitivity to the fumes will pass, child." He took the cuff and locked it around her right ankle. "I am afraid this may not be pleasant for you, but it will all be over soon."

Before she could say anything, he walked to the door, removed the torch and stepped outside shutting the door behind him. She was cast into a terrible darkness. Coughing again, she moved as far away from the crack as she could. The iron cuffed chafed at her ankle as she shook it.

"Father!" she yelled. The darkness seemed to weigh down upon her. "Father, I am afraid! Please, let me out!" Her breath began to quicken and her heart began to beat fast within her chest. "I do not want to be the Oracle!" No one answered her calls. She began to scream as terror took her. She did not understand. She had always been a good obedient daughter. The old stories said that only good happened to those who prayed and did as they were told.

She became lightheaded and lay down on the dais. Her head spun and she felt weak. The air was growing hot. "Father..." she whispered. A deeper sense of darkness overtook her as her body became limp. She could feel blood flowing through her veins as bursts of light flashed before her eyes. Red... green... yellow... darkness. They continued in succession. She couldn't move and just stared.

Is this how I die? She heard her mind say. Sweat dripped from her body, as if it were the essence of life leaving her. She felt so weak.

Hours seemed to have passed when the lights suddenly stopped. *It's happened. I have died.* When she looked up, a lone figure stood above her, glowing gold as if from within. She tried to speak, but her voice was silent. The man knelt beside her and helped her to sit up.

"Be calm and be unafraid," he said. He looked odd, she thought.

He wore golden armor and a small helmet with bird wings attached on each side. In his hand, he held a staff with snakes wrapped around it. "I am Hermes, messenger of the Gods." Her eyes widened.

"Hermes?" she managed to say. "Is this the afterlife?"

"No, Delia," he said. "You are still very much alive and have been chosen by the Gods of Olympus to be our collective voice among humans. From this day hence, you are the Oracle of Delphi, Priestess of Apollo." She continued to stare in wonder. "I have a task for you, the first of many. The land of Attica, once known as Athens, has been five hundred years without a patron deity and now two gods vie for her veneration. Attica's patronage to Athena was dissolved when Athens was destroyed. In five years' time, a contest will be held and Athena will contend for her former position and Poseidon shall be her opponent.

"Your task is to make preparations for such a contest, upon the acropolis of the old city. I will return to you in five years to announce their coming, at which time the king of the Atticans will decide the victor. Do you understand all that I am telling you?"

"Yes," she replied. "I think so." He smiled at her.

"This will become easier in time," he told her.

"Why me?" she asked. Her voice found its strength. "I do not question the will of the Gods, Great Hermes, but why am I chosen?"

"You are descended from the old kings of Athens and there is a power in you." He smiled again. "Await my coming on the fifth sun." He stood again and with a flash of light, he vanished.

Delia blinked repeatedly, seeing only spots in front of her eyes. Moments later, she heard a loud click and the door opened. Delphinios walked in with the torch and released the cuff around her ankle.

"What did you see, child?" he asked her.

She looked at him questioningly. What had she seen? It was only then that she realized it was over and she took a deep breath, the sulfuric air ventilating through the open door. Gathering her wits, she told him of Hermes, his task for her, and his proclamation of her being the Oracle.

"May Apollo shine his light upon you always, Great Daughter," he said. "The Gods have bestowed us a blessing. We shall make for the city of Attica at once. King Cecrops must be told of your visions and declare you to the realm as Oracle of Delphi. Rest well tonight, child, as we will leave at first light."

Delia did not rest well that night. So many things were happening at once that she didn't know what to think or what to do. After leaving the Oracle's Eye, she had only moments to say goodbye to her family before she was rushed off to prepare for her journey. Tears welled in her father's eyes as they took her away.

The Oracle's apartments were lavish compared to her small home back in her village. There was a room for her bed, a room for worship and study, a small sitting room, and a balcony looking down upon the Temple complex and the village of Delphi. The priest followed her into her quarters and they sat in her sitting room.

"Delia," Delphinios began, "I will again apologize for my haste, but the Gods do not suffer the weary. Once we have returned from Attica, you will settle into your routine here and begin your training as a Priestess of Apollo, as well as begin your tutelage for the scared position of Oracle." As he spoke, an older woman walked into the room, wearing the tan woolen dress of the priestesses, her grey hair pulled back with a band of gold and a golden sun amulet on a chain around her neck. "Ah, there you are," he said to the woman. "Delia, this is your matron, Helena, Priestess of Apollo. She has looked after Oracles for the last thirty years and will see to your daily needs, as well as your tutoring." He then explained to Helena their travels and need for haste, after which he left.

"*The Gods do not suffer the weary*, he says," said Helena once the door was shut. "If I hear him say that once more, he will see who is weary." She gave Delia a grandmotherly smile, sizing her up in a glance. "You are a pretty thing. Let us get you cleaned up and packed. I know you have not had a moment's rest since you arrived this morning, but I fear there is no time to rest if we are to leave at sunrise." Helena ushered her around the apartment, making sure that Delia's dresses fit, that she had the right size sandals, and spent an agonizing hour detangling her hair.

When dusk came, Helena left her to sleep. As she lay in bed, Delia tried to comprehend the day. As bone tired as she was from the journey to Delphi, she still could not fall asleep. She had slept in ditches and on piles of leaves for the last week, yet this comfortable bed would not give her rest.

An hour after sunset, she heard a faint knock on her door. Covering up with a robe, she answered it to find her brother waiting.

"May I come in, your holy Oracle-ness?" Doros laughed.

"Shut it!" she said as she pulled him inside and shut the door. "I do not know if you can be here, Doros. Helena might chop off your head and give it to the cooks for breakfast." They laughed. She was happy to see him. Two years older than her, Doros was tall and skinny with dark eyes and even darker hair.

"I do not think she will be doing that anytime soon, dear sister," he said. "Once they hauled you off for slaughter, that priest came back to us to ask what our plans were. When Father told him that we were staying in Delphi to start a new life and that Father and I would take up work as masons and Mother would take work at a farm, Gods willing, he was fine with all that except for my lot. He told Father that the Oracle would need protection and that I would start training to be your shadow."

"Protection from what?" she asked, but she didn't give him time to answer. "What's a shadow?"

"It's what they call your protector," he said. "I am to be your bodyguard."

She looked at him, all the jest gone from his face. "You will be protecting me?"

"Do not get all girlish about it," he laughed. "Old Delphinios did not give me a choice in the matter, not that I would have refused. I could be a warrior or I could be some mason's apprentice. I will take the highroad, little sister. I begin my training while you are away in Attica and will be on your guard detail once you return."

"I like that," she said. "I was afraid that being the Oracle would change everything. Somehow it is all not so bad knowing that I will always have you near me."

"I said, do not get all girlish on me," he said. She laughed.

"Come on, I have to show you my chambers," she said and she drug him through all of the rooms, explaining everything as she went along. They sat up talking most of the night, neither really wanting to leave the other, but when a hint of dawn began to show upon the horizon, Doros left to his barracks outside the temple walls.

Delia was able to sleep for an hour before Helena burst into her room, cackling for her to get up, washed, and ready for the road. She was dragged out of bed and a short time later stood in front of a large litter, big enough for at least six people to ride in with thick blue curtains covering all the sides.

"Is this for us?" she asked Helena.

"Well, we are not walking all the way to Attica, now are we?" she replied. Delia had never thought of not walking. She had just spent seven days in trek to the Temple. She felt relieved.

Delphinios joined them a few moments later. "Dear Delia," he said, "I do hope you have rested, though short it may have been. Your father and mother have insisted on seeing you off, so they are coming along now. Once you have said your quick goodbyes, we shall be off. *Quick* goodbyes, mind you. The Gods do not suffer the weary." Delia knew she would begin to hate that phrase.

She smiled big when her parents and Doros walked up. "Father!" she yelled and ran to his arms.

"Sweet child, you behave yourself in the capital and be sweet to the king," he said.

"I will, Father," she replied. "I am to take a litter there! I will get to sit the entire way!" She hugged her mother.

"Yes, but do not forget where you came from," her mother said. "You are made of stronger stuff than that."

"I know," she replied. "Hermes said we come from kings. I will make you proud, I promise." She hugged Doros next.

"Now do not go getting yourself killed before I am able to defend you," he said, squeezing her close.

"And you had better train hard," she replied. "I want you good and soldierly when I get back." She squeezed him harder.

"Delia," called Delphinios, "we must be off, child."

"Yes, High Priest," she said as she finished her goodbyes and walked over to the litter.

"The Gods do not…"

"…suffer the weary," she finished. "I am beginning to understand that." She smiled at Helena.

It took eight men to lift the litter, which also held their supplies for the road. In addition, their caravan had four horses, a guard of twenty Attican soldiers, and an entourage of Priestesses and cooks.

Once they passed the border of the village, waving farewells to the crowds who had come to see them off, sleep began to take Delia.

"She is sagging already, Delphinios," said Helena. "Must be weary from talking to her brother all night." That brought her back.

"How did you know?" Delia asked.

"Sweet child, I have watched after three Oracles before you walked in yesterday. Nothing happens in those chambers that I do not know about." Delia frowned. "Do not look so defeated. It was your first night in a big new place. Your brother brought you comfort, and your wellbeing put aside he is to be your shadow soon. Along with me, he will have complete access to you. I saw no reason to deprive him of that privilege."

"And good of you to do so," said Delphinios, "especially with the girl's parents gone from her so soon. Necessary it is, but a slight cruelty as well."

"Will my father be alright?" she asked them. "I have never seen him so sad."

"Aye, he will be fine in time," replied Delphinios. "There is much that your father and mother will have to learn to accept before they are at ease."

"Like what?"

"Well to start, your father has just lost his bloodline," said Delphinios. "Losing you was hard. I could see it in his face. He pleaded with Apollo while you were in the Oracle's Eye to not choose you, but the Gods' wills be done. But then he lost your brother Doros mere hours later."

"What has that to do with our bloodline?" she asked. "Hermes said we are of kings."

"That you are, my dear, but I fear that with you and your brother that legacy ends," said the priest. "The Oracle can only retain her power so long as she remains virgin. As grand and renowned as you shall become, Delia, you will never know a man's touch and will never have sons of your own.

"As your shadow, your brother must also remain celibate. We find that when warriors of Apollo wed and have children that their loyalties become split between their hearts and their honor."

"But I am Doros' family," she said. "Surely his loyalties would not become split if he were to wed."

"That is not a risk we can take," replied Delphinios. "In your greatness, you will be sought after by many. Your safety must be his singular concern."

"From what must I remain safe?" she asked. "How did the last Oracle come to die?"

"There are many who would see you harmed, my dear," answered Helena. "But that is not a discussion to be had now. Just know that you are an asset to the realm of Attica and that harm to you is harm to us. Rest now. The Gods may not suffer the weary, but seeing as there are none here, you can rest all you like."

Fatigue swept over her and within moments Delia was asleep.

The journey from Delphi to Attica took ten days over mountains, bridges, through villages, forests, and fields. Rains came and went, and they finally arrived on a sunny afternoon.

Delia had never been to the capital before, which had been rebuilt from the ruins of Athens centuries earlier. As they passed the city's northern gates, a royal escort led them through markets, passed houses, and up the hill toward the king's great palace atop the acropolis. The palace was magnificent, she thought. It looked like many buildings, adorned in reliefs and frescos, held together by vaulted walkways and bridges. Towers spired into the sky, seemingly at random, their white stones reflecting the sun's ray.

Giant wooden gates twenty feet tall ushered them within. The litter bearers set them down and palace servants poured out from every door to aid them. The king would receive them in time, but for now they were to retire to their chambers and await his audience.

The palace, named Attella's Crown, was busier than Delia had ever imagined it would be. Everywhere servants and soldiers ran to and fro, all on their individual errands. She was relieved to close the door to her apartments, to just be alone. The feeling was short-lived as Helena burst in after her.

"We will be meeting with his highness just before dinner in the Great Hall," she announced. "At that time he will present you to the realm as the Oracle, making the whole thing official."

"As if Hermes appearing before me was not official," said Delia.

"Indeed," replied Helena, "but do watch your sarcasm in front of the king. Tired you may be from our voyage, but it will do you no favors to get on his grace's bad side."

"Yes, Helena," said Delia.

"What shall we put on you, then?" asked Helena and they set off finding a suitable dress.

Butterflies ravaged her belly as she waited outside the doors to the Great Hall. Delia tried to keep calm, but so many thoughts ran through her head. What if she stumbled walking toward the king? What if she fainted? What if the onlookers called her ugly and made fun of her?

"Stop your fussing," said Helena. "And for the sake of the Gods, take a deep breath. You are as white as a ghost."

Delia tried to distract her mind. She looked at the frescos that lined the hallway leading to the doors. They showed the story of Attella and her rebuilding of the realm. She had been the niece of the last king of Athens. *My ancestor*, she thought. She had survived the deluge, took sanctuary in Saïs across the sea, and returned with the Saitian king's people to rebuild. This palace, Attella's Crown, was built in tribute to her efforts and grace.

Soon Delphinios walked up behind them and announced that they were about to enter. Helena stood to her left and the priest to her right as they heard the palace steward announce them. The doors opened and they walked in.

The arrival of the new Oracle drew considerable attention, thought Delia. The Great Hall was a throne room, vaulted thirty feet high, and was filled with people from every corner of the realm and beyond. Everyone gazed upon her, wearing her modest blue silk dress, her hair tied back in the priestess fashion. Everyone was dressed very well, making her feel common. Their eyes, she noticed, betrayed that thought. They were all looking at her in awe and with deep admiration. The voice of the Gods before them! Halfway into the room, they stopped and waited for the king to call them forward.

King Cecrops sat upon his throne on a dais at the end of the room. From what she could see, he was a fairly handsome man, clean shaven, with red-brown curls that fell to his shoulders. He wore a golden cloak over a white coat and white skirts that fell to the floor.

"High Priest Delphinios of Apollo, may the light and grace of Apollo shine upon you," called the king.

"And may he forever illuminate the realm of Attica," answered Delphinios.

"Whom have you brought before me, dear priest?" asked the king. The formality made Delia more nervous.

"May I present to you, High Priestess Delia of Apollo, the Oracle of Delphi."

"Delia of Apollo, please come forward," the king called.

Her feet moved without her saying so and she glided toward her king. The crowd murmured as she passed. Ages came and went before she stopped before the king and fell to her knees looking at his feet.

Cecrops looked down at her. "What is your age?" he asked to her softly.

"I am eleven, your grace," she replied.

"May Zeus protect us all," he said quietly. "Delia of Apollo," he said more to the crowd than to her, "the High Priest Delphinios of Apollo claims that you have been chosen by Olympus as the Oracle of Delphi. Before the Gods and the realm in which you serve, are you the Oracle of Delphi?"

"I am, your grace," she said.

"How were you granted this gift of voice?" he asked.

"I was taken to the Oracle's Eye at the Temple of Apollo, where the messenger of the Gods, Hermes, appeared to me, your grace. There he named me Oracle, the voice of Olympus, and gave me a task." She was shaking. She wished that her brother were with her. Why couldn't he be her shadow now? The murmuring in the crowd grew louder.

"What task has the messenger given thee?"

"A contest is to be had, your grace," she replied. "In five years' time, the great goddess, Athena, and Lord of Sea, Poseidon, will come to Attica to contend for patronage of the realm. Hermes has charged me with preparing the realm for their coming. That is all, your grace."

"Let it be known," the king said to all present, "that the Gods have seen fit to honor us and bless us with their presence. A feast shall be prepared for their arrival and contest. Games shall take place to honor their glory." The crowd cheered, their voices echoing off the hall's roof. Cecrops looked down at her once again as the room quieted.

"Rise, Delia of Apollo and Oracle of Delphi." The room burst into cheers again as she stood and looked the king in the eyes for the first time. Though he smiled, she sensed pity in his big green eyes.

Five years had passed since Delia was visited by Hermes and named Oracle of Delphi. Five years since she had traveled to the capital and was put on display for the world to see. Five years since she left her family and took up a mantle that she did not then understand.

In that time, she had been visited by many Gods, Aphrodite the Goddess of Love, Poseidon the Lord of the Sea, Ares the God of War, and by Apollo himself. She had become accustomed to being their voice and even come to enjoy the sacred duty. But as the five years crept by, an anxiety grew within her for the contest that was to come. She could not help but feel that something was amiss and that something was wrong in the realms beyond this world.

Delia tried to speak with her brother about her apprehensions, as she spoke to him about everything, but he would only try to pacify her. The pang of anxiety never abated.

As she had done many times in the years since Hermes' first visit, she entered Oracle's Eye and sat. She had never had to wear the chain since her first visit and now she calmly sat before the crack in the dais and let the vapors take her. Sometimes the Gods came to her and sometimes they did not. She honestly did not mind either way. If the Gods did not come to her, she took solace in the quiet peace of being alone.

That peace is what she sought this time, sitting down and taking her customary three deep breaths. Time did not exist within the eye, she found. Once she sat within for two days and her brother had to drag her out for fear of her starving. That same timelessness overtook her and she coasted in a space of thought between this world and the realms beyond.

Her reverie was broken as the ground shook. She could hear shouts from outside, as she stood and made for the door, but it was locked from the outside. She screamed for her brother, for Helena, for anyone to let her out, but no one heard her.

Turning from the door, she screamed and fell to the floor as a tall white figure stood above her.

"Greetings, Delia," he said. "I am Hades."

CHAPTER II
NO LIGHT

Sean drifted... hardly existing... vaguely aware of himself. No body. No breath. No light.

The sensation might have been peaceful, had he possessed the capacity to feel such things. His mind drifted in a sea of indifference. Memories were a distant shadow. He knew only that he could not escape. *"Is this finally death?"* he heard a voice within him ask. No answer came to him. No body. No breath. No light.

Suddenly, as if taking a deep breath, he woke.

The scene before him was painted into his mind in layers. First he saw red-orange light. The light slowly materialized into a lake of fire, which surrounded him. The fire then turned into lava. He was suspended above it, floating in a swirling black cloud that hissed. *"Furies,"* he thought.

Floating beside him in the same state was Erin. She looked at him with a blank stare, but didn't speak. He too felt nothing.

A voice resounded in his head.

"Selfless you are thought to be, to give up two lives in exchange for one. Two souls in exchange for one. My eternal goal is to have you regret your actions. Regret the kiss that cursed you. Regret the friendships that pushed you forth. Regret the peace you felt in the ignorance of your follies. Regret your own daughter."

Hades' voice seemed to come from everywhere and nowhere. Sean could not react. He could not feel.

"Look upon these earthen walls. Look upon this lake of fire. Look upon your prison cell. Look and know that you are damned to this pit. This pit that the heroes… the Titans… and even the Gods fear. This pit of Tartarus. The place of eternal damnation. These earthen walls used to live. They were mortals and immortals alike. Men, Gods, and Titans. They have all become imprisoned here, as will you. Only aware of their captivity and the helplessness in knowing that it will never end. An insanity that you cannot fathom shall become you.

"But you shall not join them yet. No, I have use of you before you suffer your fate. In your chivalry you provide me opportunity. One that I shall not squander, nor from be swayed. You will secure for me dominion over a realm of men. You shall draw a dark center on the face of the world. Seize the land, you shall, and establish patronage to me, Hades, the dark lord of death."

Sean was unable to reply. He became faintly aware of acceptance. Someplace deep within him felt the urge to comply. The feeling was exciting and joyful. He found that he wanted nothing more than to do as Hades commanded.

"Once Zeus denied me the world of men. He and Poseidon both! But through you I have found my way."

In the midst of his reverie, Sean was back to drifting. No body. No breath. No light.

CHAPTER III
TRICK OF THE LIGHT

The door clicked and Delia pushed her way passed Doros and out into the sun. "Dear Apollo, have mercy on us all," she said under her breath. Her brother caught her before she could collapse to the ground. Crying in his arms, she was confused and frightened. Doros did not try to find out what happened as it was not his place to know. Instead, she felt herself lifted into his arms and carried away. In her exhaustion, she fell asleep.

The scene played over and over again in her dreams. Hades appeared before her and threatened her. He told her to remain quiet should anything peculiar happen before or during the competition between Athena and Poseidon.

"If anyone should come seeking advice, aid, or explanation, you will feign ignorance and provide no divinely-given knowledge," he told her. More than death would await her if she failed him.

Delia woke in tears as the sun began to set. Doros, Delphinios, and Helena sat around her bed. Upon seeing her rise, Helena poured her some water from the clay pitcher beside her bed and placed the cups to her lips. She drank it all at once.

"There you go," said Helena as she sat on the bed beside her.

"Is everyone alright?" asked Delia. They all gave her a puzzled look.

"Alright from what, dear?" asked Helena. "Has something happened?"

"There was an earthquake," she replied. "While I was inside the Eye, the entire earth shook. I could hear all of Delphi screaming. I could hear boulders crashing down the mountainside."

"Are you certain this was not a dream or some vision from Apollo?" asked Delphinios from his chair near the window. "Sometimes the visions can be quite vivid."

"No, I am certain it was no vision," said Delia. "I could feel it. Then I screamed for the door to be opened and no one came."

"Doros?" asked the priest.

"High Priest Delphinios, I was stationed outside the door and heard no such commotion, I assure you," said her brother. She looked at him helplessly. "At the agreed time, I opened the door and that is when the Oracle pushed out and fainted. I then brought her here to rest and summoned you."

"Indeed," said Delphinios. "Dear Delia, I do not assume to know the motives of the Gods, and do not know the purpose of these hallucinations, but I fear they have left you in a fragile state. Tell me, what did you see to cause you to push out of the door as your shadow has described?"

"Other than the visions?" asked Delia. "They were not... never mind." She thought for a moment. She could not tell them that it was Hades who appeared. She decided to follow the priest's notions. "As you said, dear priest. The visions were so real that I thought the Temple was collapsing down on itself. I was only trying to escape." The lie hurt. She wanted nothing more than to warn them, but she could not.

"Indeed," replied the priest. "Continue to rest, dear one. Helena and Doros will watch over you, as ever before. The moon wanes. In the coming weeks we shall once again travel to the capital."

"The capital?" she asked.

"Dear child, you really are shaken," said Helena. "You know that you have been summoned to help prepare for the contest. The king has commanded it."

"Oh, right," she replied.

"As Delphinios has said, you rest up," she said. "You will need your strength for the journey."

They left her, all but Doros. He never left her. She was afraid to dream and tried to stave off sleep, but eventually she succumbed to her exhaustion and the scene replayed again and again.

At the advent of the next full moon, Delia and her contingent from the Temple of Apollo journeyed for nearly two weeks across the land to the city of Attica. The trip was much as she remembered from five years earlier. As before, there was rain, sun, mountains, and streams. The closer they came to the capital, the more nervous and uncertain Delia became.

Shortly after her arrival at Attella's Crown, she found herself once more standing before King Cecrops, this time with Doros beside her. The king was much as she remembered him: tall, formidable, and bright green eyes. The crowd in the throne room was much bigger than before, if that were even possible. People had traveled from every corner of the world to be present for the Game of Gods.

"Welcome, Delia of Apollo and Oracle of Delphi," he called to the room. "Your return to Attica brings honor to the realm in this auspicious time."

"Many thanks, your grace," she replied, more confident than before, though still meek. "I have returned to the capital to give the Gods voice in preparation for their contest, and to be of service to you, your grace, as your humble servant."

"The Oracle of Delphi is only a servant to the Gods of Olympus," replied the king. "Please find comfort during your stay and enjoy the feasts and games that precede Athena's and Poseidon's coming. Before you take your leave, I will introduce you to my advisors." Delia was taken aback by two figures that walked up to stand beside the king's throne. She had not noticed them before, but upon looking at the man and woman, she wondered how she could have ever missed them.

"Preparations for the contest have left me stretched thin, so I have appointed advisors to oversee certain matters in my name. The first is Helios." The man stepped forward and gave a slight bow. He was of medium height with long dark hair pulled back and tied with a leather cord. His piercing ice-blue eyes contrasted his tanned skin. "And this vision of Aphrodite is his wife, Hera." Hera stepped forward to join her husband and also gave a slight bow. She was taller than most women she had known and had long golden hair that fell in curls down to her waist. Fair-skinned, she had deep green eyes.

"Should you find yourself in need of anything, please seek them out," said the king.

"Thank you, your grace," she said, looking from Helios to Hera and back again.

"You have my leave to rest," the king said. Delia bowed, eyes still trained the couple.

As Delia turned to leave, Hera smiled and her eyes flashed red. She did a double take, but Hera only smiled more. Uncertain, she turned again and left. Delia walked faster than she should have, her stomach in her throat. *It was nothing,* she thought as she left the throne room, *merely a trick of the light.*

CHAPTER IV
WHISPERS OF HISTORY

The following morning Delia was asked to join Helios and Hera at their villa on the palace grounds, overlooking the city. Delia was hesitant to accept their invitation, but to not accept would seem rude. She had critical thoughts about the couple, but she could not voice them.

She wore a simple ivory dress with light-blue stitching and had her hair pulled back and wrapped with gold ribbon. Helena always said that the Oracle must appear modest without actually being modest. As she walked to the villa, she was both. Doros walked beside her, Helena and Delphinios having stayed at the palace to attend the king.

"A rare moment alone," he said. The sun was nearing its zenith in the sky and a slight cool breeze gave them respite from its heat.

"Indeed, though I do not like the circumstances that make it so," she replied.

"And why is that?" he asked. She did not mind or even notice his informality. Doros was all pomp when surrounded by priests and priestesses, but the moment they left the pair alone, he was her older brother again. Her best friend.

"Call it a feeling," she said. Delia wished she could say more.

"I would have you call it more than that," he replied. She stopped and looked at him. "Delia, you have not been yourself since you had that vision."

"It was not a vision!" she yelled. Tears welled in her eyes. She took a deep breath and held them back.

"Whatever happened, Sister, something is amiss with you," he said. "The priest and Helena may be too blind to see it, but I know you best."

Delia knew he would not let up until he was satisfied. "You are right, as always," she resumed walking. "All that I can say is that I was visited by a certain God whose message for me must remain secret."

"Why visit you only tell you secrets?" he asked. "Do the Gods not want to be heard?"

"I cannot explain, Doros," she replied, "and for the sake of the love you bear me, please leave it be. Know that I do what I must, no matter how much it pains me."

"You bear ill tidings," he said. "I will leave the matter be, for your sake."

"Thank you, brother."

Helios' and Hera's villa was lavish and exotic, making Delia instantly feel out of place. One of their many servants ushered them across the threshold and out to a garden where the couple waited.

Today Hera was wearing a striking green and gold striped dress, accenting both her golden hair and green eyes. Golden bangles clinked on her wrists. Helios was more modest in his attire, donning a simple, yet expensive black and grey tunic with a silver belt. Both rose to greet her.

"Our beautiful young Oracle," said Hera as she pulled Delia into an embrace. "You are most welcome to our humble home." Helios repeated the sentiment.

"Thank you both," she replied, looking around at the many statues, paintings, lavish furniture, and plants that made up their "humble" home. "You are most kind for inviting me."

"We are deeply honored by your presence," said Hera. "You have made quite the voyage from Delphi. One that you have not made since you were first given sight five years ago."

"Indeed," she replied. "Are you both new to the capital? I do not believe that I saw you when last I was here."

"We have lived here for quite some time," replied Helios, offering her fruit from a tray. She shook her head. "We were gone when you last visited, I am afraid. When we are not preparing to host Gods, we assist the king with business throughout the realm. We check in on towns and villages, making certain that they are keeping to the king's laws and maintaining his peace. There is also quite a lot rebuilding happening. Even after five-hundred years, there is still a lot of work to be done to return our realm to her former glory. The good king Cecrops called us back to Attica when you reported your vision of Hermes."

Hera walked over to the garden ledge that overlooked Attica and smiled. "Sweet Delia, do you know our realm's history? I am certain they taught you some of it at the Temple."

"Yes, they did," she replied. "Zeus, in his anger, destroyed the realm with a flood and afterward we rebuilt."

Hera laughed. "That is not a lie, but it is not the complete story. I assure you." Hera returned to her seat next to Delia. "Allow me to tell you. The story of Athens' destruction began with the destruction of Atlantis. You see, many do not remember that the Athenians and Atlanteans were at war during Atlantis' downfall. In fact, most of the Athenian naval force, including the great king Aktaios, was near the shores of Atlantis when it sank beneath the waves. Only one ship made it out, and I fear that the king was not spared. Instead, only his first general, Thebos, and a small party of sailors escaped with their lives to tell the tale.

"Thebos was regarded by the Athenians as a hero and was elected steward of the throne until a rightful heir to Aktaios came forth. That hope was presented in the king's niece, Attella, for whom the royal palace is named. When she bore a son, he would then become king. Athens unfortunately did not last that long. In his new power, Thebos turned the Athenians against Olympus, saying that they had forsaken mankind, having destroyed Atlantis and the Athenian navy. This did not sit well with Zeus. In his anger, he flooded the entire world. All of Athens would have died in that moment had it not been for saviors sent from beyond this world. These saviors we now called the Diluvians.

"Just when all hope was lost, a ship appeared and took both Thebos and Attella away, where she ultimately outlasted the destruction. Thebos was not so fortunate. Attella was younger than you at this point, Delia, but gave birth to Thebos' son shortly after surviving the flood. She lived in Saïs for several years after and upon the child's seventh birthday she moved back to the city with a group of Saitians and reestablished the kingdom as Attica. Years passed by and her son, who had become king of this once-fallen land, had grown old, had sons, died, and his sons' sons died and now Cecrops is king of it all. His grace is of the old blood of Aktaios and of old Athens."

"I have not heard it as such before," said Delia. "Hermes said that I was of the old blood, which makes me a distant cousin to the king."

Hera and Helios laughed. "Yes, it does," he said.

"Delia, might I ask a favor," said Hera. "Would it be alright if your shadow, Doros, left us alone for a moment?"

Delia was more uncertain than ever. "He does not leave my side," she replied. "It is against Temple law."

"I know the rules of the Temple, dear one," said Hera, "but I wish to speak to you of a matter that bears discretion and I would not want to place the burden upon his shoulders."

"I…" Delia began, but was cut off.

"It will only be for a few moments," said Hera, smiling.

Defeated, Delia looked to her brother and nodded. Without a word, he left them.

"Do not be alarmed, Delia," said Hera. "Some things are better left secret. You can keep a secret?"

Delia's stomach was in her throat. She hadn't wanted to believe that these two were involved in Hades' conspiracy. "Yes," she managed to say.

"Good," said Hera. "I tell you this true story about Attica not to entertain you, no, but because there is something more to it that most do not know. That most would not want to believe, despite its truth."

"What truth is that?" asked Delia, managing to keep her composure and not cry. She flinched as Hera put a hand on her shoulder.

"Despite his reputation, Oracle, it was the great lord Hades who saved mankind," she replied.

A wave of nausea swept over Delia. "No," she said. This was Hades playing his game. She knew not to intervene, as he had warned, but her outburst had been unintentional.

"I know a certain God who would frown to hear you say so," said Helios from his chair.

"Yes," said Hera. "The saviors from beyond this world I mentioned? It was Hades who made the Diluvians appear. The ship that ferried them through the storm? It was Hades' own serpent demon, Ophion, taken form as a ship. Without Hades, we would not be. *You* would not be." In spite of herself, Delia began to cry. "Since Hades saved us all from the righteous Zeus, I do not see why Attica should pledge its patronage to any of the Olympians. Athena herself did not even intervene when Zeus' thunderbolt struck down the old kingdom, and Poseidon's trident aided in the destruction. *Hades* is the only one of the High Gods who chose to intervene on our behalf, lest we be destroyed. It is to him that we humans owe our fealty. The Olympians are not worthy."

Delia was shaking and the tears would not abate. "Calm yourself, child," said Helios. "The truth is like a vicious animal. It may tear you apart, but its motives are always justified."

"Have you told the king this history?" she managed to ask.

"No," said Helios. "He is not yet ready to hear it. This truth will be revealed in time, at the right moment."

"Why tell me this?" she asked.

"We may need your help in coercing Cecrops and Attica to declare Hades their sovereign," said Hera. "You cannot deny that they owe him their allegiance. All humans do!"

"Delia," said Helios, "the king puts value in the words spoken from the Oracle. Your words."

Delia was trapped. If she did not comply, then Hades would damn her. If she helped, Hades would rule over Attica and bring darkness into the world.

"Delia, do we have your support?" asked Hera.

Delia looked down at her hands, still shaking. "Yes."

"Good girl," said Helios. "We are delighted." They truly were, Delia noticed. Both Hera and Helios seemed brighter. "Do not be afraid, Delia. We all like to think we are immune and unaffected by the world, like we have some special armor to protect us from the influences of truth. Some would call us weak or vulnerable to be affected so, but it is in the acceptance of the world around us that we are made stronger." Delia only stared. "We know of your prejudices toward Hades, but we cannot sit idly by and let our preferences, personalities, and perceptions keep us locked in our bubble of mis-reality. There are greater plans at work and we must see them and most importantly accept them, else we are to be left behind to rot in the misery of what was or might have been."

"Well said, husband," said Hera smiling.

Delia was afraid to ask her next question, but she had to know

101

for certain. "How do you know of this history?"

"Sweet Delia," said Hera, "though you are Oracle, the Gods can speak with anyone. You are just their *official* voice. Whispers of history have been told and Hades proves righteous."

"We will begin taking action soon to coerce the king to name Hades victor," said Helios, "and you will be on our side."

"But Hades is evil," she blurted out, her temper having gotten the best of her.

"He is NOT!" said Hera, standing to hover over her. Her big green eyes turned red in anger. "Any ill actions he has committed have only been in response to the provocations of his brothers, Zeus and Poseidon. *They* cast him into the shadows! *He* is their victim! But to us humans, *he* can and will be our hero. You let your prejudices cloud reality. You owe Hades your allegiance. Is that clear?"

Frightened, Delia complied. "Yes."

Hera became calm and acted as if nothing had happened. She even said a pleasant goodbye as Delia soon left to return to the palace.

Book IV:
The Diluvians

CHAPTER I
AFTER THE STORM

As Hermes made to follow the mortals into the cave, he found his way blocked by shadows. As before, he raised his caduceus to ward them off, but he froze. The Furies surrounded him, in numbers more than he could count. Panicked, he struck at them as best he could, yelling to the mortals to run, until they overpowered him and his world went black.

When the Furies released him, Hermes was on his back in the stone courtyard outside of Erebus. The grey of the fortress weighed down upon him. He made to stand, but found himself bound by chains.

"Hermes," said a voice he'd been expecting. Of course this was Hades' work. "The great messenger and Psychopomps. You just do not know when to leave well enough alone."

"Where is my caduceus?" asked Hermes, pulling at the chains.

"You will not have further need of that old stick," replied Hermes. "You have been meddling again, Hermes. You and Alexia both. Lucky you are to be here and not in Tartarus."

"And *why* am I not in Tartarus?" asked Hermes. "So that you can make threats?"

"I make no threats, Psychopomps, only promises."

"And what promises would you make to me?" asked Hermes.

"That depends entirely on you, dear messenger," replied Hades. "But first, tell me how three mortal souls wandered all the way from

Purgatory to the cave to be reborn. Ah, that was you, was it not?"

"Why do you ask questions to which you already know the answers?" asked Hermes.

"So that you understand, Hermes, that I see all," he replied. "Tell me, what do the humans intend to do in Saïs?"

"I thought you knew everything," spat Hermes. "Send me to Tartarus and be done with it!"

"Not just yet," replied Hades. "I do not underestimate the influence of humans in divine proceedings. Sean and Erin Henry have proven their capabilities, but since none know of my plans, whatever those three you sent back intend to do shall not interfere. No one and nothing can stop me."

"Plans?" asked Hermes. "What plans?"

"Ah, see there in lies the problem and the solution, as well as my promise to you," said Hades. "I promise to not send you to eternity in Tartarus, but you have to do something for me."

"I will not riddle it out of you," said Hermes. "Make your demands."

Kimberly rolled over and hit the snooze button, but the sound didn't stop. After the fifth try, she sat up and looked at it. The clock read 3:23 a.m. It was then that she noticed it wasn't her alarm, but the sound of screaming coming from her living room. Stumbling out of her bed, she rushed into the next room to find the little girl curled up a ball, screaming her lungs out.

"Allie, wake up, sweetie," she said as she nudged the child awake. It had been one week since Peter and Emily Henry went down into that tunnel with Michael. Things got strange with the little girl immediately after they left. Somehow Allie had knocked her out and she a vision of some goddess named Alexia, telling them to search for a stone. No, not a stone, a crystal.

It had been night when she woke from speaking with Alexia, so Kimberly took Allie to the abandoned trailer at the Sa el-Hagar site and they spent the night huddled together on the small bed. That next morning, they headed off in the direction of the ruined temple. Upon looking at the broken walls and foundation, Kimberly felt lost. "Like trying to find a needle in haystack," she thought to herself, but the little girl seemed to know where she was going.

"It's this way, Miss Kimberly," she called.

"How do you know, Allie?" asked Kimberly. The child ran off

until she came to a corner of the ruins.

"It's down there," she said. "The pretty lady told me so. There's a door underneath this sand." Without a word, the two began to use their hands to uncover the floor, which turned out to be a hatch.

"Well I'll be damned," said Kimberly. She reached for the handle and after several tugs, it came loose. A steep staircase led below the temple into the darkness. Kimberly got out her phone and turned on the flashlight. "Allie, I need you to stay here," she said. "We don't know what's down here and I can't let you get hurt." The girl fussed a little bit, but eventually gave in.

"I must be losing my mind," thought Kimberly, not for the first time that day. She climbed carefully into the darkness, descending about ten feet.

"Do you see anything?" called Allie from up top.

"Not yet," she replied. "Stay there, please."

Shining the light from side to side, she saw she was in a hallway. Hieroglyphics and drawings covered the walls and ceiling and there was a staleness to the air that made her thirsty. She slowly walked forward, careful not to trip over fallen rocks. She turned a corner and the hallway dead-ended into a door. A locked door, she soon found out. There was no handle, and she pushed with all of her strength, but the damn thing wouldn't budge. Giving up, she walked back but as she turned the corner, something ran toward her and she screamed.

"It's okay, Miss Kimberly, it's just me," said Allie laughing.

Kimberly wanted to yell at her, but held back. "Allie, you scared the life out of me," she said. "Didn't I tell you to wait up top? It could be dangerous down here."

"But I'm the key, Miss Kimberly," replied Allie.

Kimberly looked at her suspiciously, but then conceded. "Of course, you are," she said. "Stay with me." Allie held her hand and they returned to the door. Kimberly shined the light, while Allie looked at it. The carving on the door was of a woman, holding light in her hand. Carved lines showed the light radiating and illuminating the world, depicted as trees, humans, water, and animals. As if she'd been told what to do, Allie placed her hand on the light in the woman's hands and the door pushed open.

Allie tried to run in the room, but Kimberly grabbed her first. "I said, stay with me, please." She moved Allie behind her and looked inside. Descending three steps, they entered a room about twenty feet across and ten feet deep. The ceiling was higher here as well. The size of the room was contrasted by the fact that it was completely empty. That was except for a statue at its center.

"That's her," said Allie. "That's the pretty woman."

Kimberly looked closely at the statue and the face was indeed that of Alexia, or Neith as the people who built this temple called her. A contradicting sense of relief and dread filled her when she noticed the gold chain with a crystal pendant hanging from the woman's neck, glowing blue from within. This meant that she and the girl's visions had been real. It also meant that Michael and the others were truly in danger.

After collecting the crystal, they made their way back up and quickly returned to Cairo. Since then, Allie had been sleeping on the couch in her apartment, waiting for a sign of what to do next.

"Allie, wake up, it's only a dream," said Kimberly. Allie opened her eyes and jumped into Kimberly's arms. She was relieved for the screaming to have ended, but wondered what caused it. Soothing her, Kimberly asked what she dreamt.

"It wasn't a dream, Miss Kimberly," the girl said. "It was a weird man. He had bird wings on his shoes and head."

Kimberly didn't like the sound of that. "What did he say, sweetie?"

"It's time to use the crystal," she said.

"Use the crystal?" asked Kimberly. How does one *use* a crystal? Alexia didn't explain anything about that, and she didn't notice an instruction booklet sitting next to that statue back at the temple.

"That's what he said," she replied. Kimberly continued to sooth her until she fell back to sleep.

Kimberly didn't get back to sleep that night, but lay awake wondering what to do with the crystal. "How does one use a crystal?" she asked herself over and over. A little after six, she heard Allie moving around in the living room and went to check on her.

The girl wore the necklace and was holding the crystal in the palm of her hand, staring and it with her face squeezed tight. "It won't work, Miss Kimberly," she said.

"I'm working on it, sweetie," replied Kimberly. She sat down on the couch and Allie sat on her lap, the necklace now around her neck. She began to brush the girl's hair.

"When will I see Uncle Pete again, Miss Kimberly?" asked Allie.

"Soon, I hope," she replied. "Soon."

"Oww!" screamed Allie.

"Sorry, Allie," said Kimberly. "There was a tangle in your hair. I didn't mean to pull hard."

"No, Miss Kimberly, the crystal burned me," said Allie. Kimberly looked at Allie's palms, which were turning red. She felt the crystal, but it was cool to the touch. Suddenly, Allie went rigid and fell against her chest.

"Allie? Allie!" screamed Kimberly, gently shaking her to wake.

Allie opened her eyes in dread. The crystal began to hover in front of them, glowing brightly.

"Oh my lord," said Kimberly. The crystal dimmed and before she could react, it slammed into Allie and then through Kimberly. She had the sense of being pulled forward and backward at the same time, as she clutched Allie close and screamed.

Pete knelt in the center of a courtyard naked with his hands chained to the ground in front of him. His side hurt from being kicked in the ribs and his lip had only just stopped bleeding. Emily and Michael had endured the same and were restrained next to him. On either side of the three stood a guard dressed in bronze armor, each with a pair of daggers on their belts. He knew better than to try to argue with them or try to break free. He felt ashamed that he couldn't keep his wife safe from these men.

When they had emerged from the tunnel, the Grand Priest of Neith had run from the nearby temple and accused them of heresy for destroying the sphinx. They had been arrested before they could explain themselves. Indeed, Pete had tried to explain and for his efforts he was beaten and chained.

Now that same priest stood above him in blue robes and a large golden ankh hanging around his neck on a silver chain. Next to him stood a young woman in a gold, red, and black striped sleeveless dress and a greying man with armor similar to the guards.

"All hail Nefruneith! Queen of the Realm of Saïs and Daughter of the Sacred Lake!" the priest announced. "And Musa, Captain of the Guard and Protector of the Realm." Nefruneith and Musa were stoic at their announcements. Musa turned his head to the priest and nodded.

"It is not usually my business to interrogate criminals within the realm of Saïs," said the priest. "Though in your case, an exception shall be made, for when the sacred home of Neith, may she protect us all, is threatened, I cannot stand aside. I have many questions to ask you and if you answer them truthfully you may just live to see the quarries. If I do not like what I hear, and my dear Queen is also not convinced, I will be forced to question you more severely until we are satisfied."

Pete didn't speak, nor did Emily or Michael. This was not the welcome he had expected from the Saitians, who had once been an understanding and trusting people. The centuries seem to have hardened them.

The priest knelt down in front of Pete. "Who are you?" he asked.

Pete looked at the others and then back at the priest. "My name is Pete and this is Emily and Michael."

"And from where do you come, Pete?" The way he said "Pete" voiced his disbelief.

"We come from another time," he replied. "We passed through the Underworld and were reborn into this world in a secret cavern beneath your sacred lake."

"*Neith's* sacred lake, you mean," spoke the girl-queen Nefruneith. She couldn't have been more than sixteen years old. "And just how would you know about any secrets of this realm?"

"A just question, your grace," said the priest. Pete didn't say anything. "It would be wise of you to answer her grace's question, Pete."

"I know your secrets because I've been here before," said Pete. "Though it was a long time ago."

"You cheat yourself, Pete," said the priest. "You look to have maybe seen thirty suns in your life. I have lived in Saïs all my fifty years and have never laid eyes upon you. When do you claim to have been here?"

"I was here during the reign of the God-king Aha," replied Pete. "During the great flood."

"Aha reigned centuries ago, and the story of the flood is known to every child in this world," said the priest. "You fail in convincing me."

"I am the Crystal Bearer," said Emily. The guard next to her slapped her with the back of his hand, sending her to the ground.

"You will remain silent or I will have these guards cut out your tongue," the priest snapped at her.

"Leave her alone!" said Pete without thinking. He saw a flash of light as the ground rose up to meet him. With effort, he heaved himself back up to his knees. "We have been through fire and hell to get here. We mean no harm to you, your temple, or your realm."

"Then why are you here?" he asked.

"We're passing through," replied Pete. "We're heading to Athens."

"Your words defy you again, Pete," said the priest. "The land you call *Athens* has not been known as such for five centuries. The nation of Attica now stands upon its ruins."

"Five centuries?" asked Pete. "It's been five hundred years since the deluge?"

"It has," said the priest, who seemed to be becoming less certain about them.

"That explains it," said Pete. "We were here in another time. Aha was king, the deluge had just ended, and Emily was the Crystal Bearer that Aha called forth from our time."

"This wench cannot be the Crystal Bearer," said the deep voice of Musa. "She does not bear the crystal!"

"Indeed, Captain," said the priest, "for that I have in my keeping until such a time when the true Crystal Bearer comes forth."

"She has arrived!" said Pete. "Just now, she used the water from the dark pool to break the earth and set us free from beneath the sphinx. That statue doesn't stand guard over the Temple of Neith, but guards something much more sacred and terrible, a gate to the Netherworld. Emily can access the power that Neith has given Saïs."

The priest said nothing.

"The prisoner admits to it!" said Musa. "They willingly destroyed the Sphinx of Neith!"

"His words are heard, Captain," said Nefruneith. "There is more I need to know. Why are you set for Attica, as you say?"

"There will be a contest in Attica between the gods Athena and Poseidon," replied Pete. "We must speak with Poseidon."

"Speak with Gods?" she said. "Your delusions fail you. I have heard enough of your stories and I am not convinced. Guards, take the prisoners to their cells to await their executions."

"Executions!" said Pete before he was struck to the ground again. "But we need to get to Attica soon! We can't wait!"

"Yes, execution," replied Nefruneith. "I do not know you, nor do I approve of your familiarity. You have admitted to your crimes and will pay with your blood. Whatever con you have planned is now at an end. Take them away!"

Pete, Emily, and Michael were unchained from the ground and the guards began to lead them away.

"Wait, leave that one," said Musa pointing to Pete. "I have more questions to ask him. Take away the others." The guards nodded and Pete watched his companions be led from the courtyard.

"I've already told you the truth," said Pete as a guard brought him back to Musa.

"Your version of it, maybe," said the captain of the guard.

"Do what you must to get answers, Captain," said the queen. Musa nodded and she and the priest left. Other than the guard, Pete and Musa were now alone.

"Who has sent you to Saïs?" asked Musa. "Was it that bastard king in Attica?"

"How else can I say it?" asked Pete. "We are only passing through, heading back to Attica. If we were spies, why would we be so bent on returning?"

"I do not pretend to know the motivations of your master," said Musa.

"I don't know the king of Attica," replied Pete. Lights appeared before his eyes and he was on the ground again. Someone lifted his arms and dragged him across the courtyard to a stone column. Attaching a hook to his bound wrists, he was hoisted into the air from the column. He opened his eyes and his face was pressed against the stone. He took a breath and screamed as a searing pain tore through his back. Another lash came and with a crack he screamed again in reply. Then another. And another.

Pete could hardly breathe when Musa turned him around, his bloody back now pressing against the stone.

"Did that loosen your resolve?" asked the captain.

"Why are you doing this?" asked Pete.

"Because you tell lies," replied Musa. "Why are you here?"

"I already told you, to get to Attica to speak with Poseidon," said Pete.

"Wrong answer," said Musa as he turned Pete around again. "Why are you here?"

"I told you!" said Pete. "I already told..." He screamed as his back tore open again.

Emily and Michael were led to a pit on the northern side of the island. The hole was ten feet deep and covered with an iron grate that let in a small amount of light and almost no air. The guard pushed them in haphazardly. Somewhere in the distance they heard screaming and Emily began to weep.

"He shouldn't have yelled at them," she whispered to Michael, her blond hair covered with blood and dirt.

"They're really going to kill us, aren't they?" asked Michael. She could hardly stand him being there. He shouldn't have been there.

"More than likely," she replied.

Michael said nothing.

Day turned to night as the pit slowly darkened and sleep came.

Some time in the hours before dawn, Emily heard arguing from above.

"I told you," a man said to the jailer, "I am told to interrogate the girl. You will let her and her companion come with me." The jailer grunted incomprehensibly and opened the iron grate and threw down a rope ladder.

"You must climb up," said the voice.

"Who are you?" asked Emily.

"Ubaid," replied the voice. "The Grand Priest of Neith."

"Where is my husband?" she asked.

"He is in the custody of Captain Musa," said Ubaid. "Climb up."

Emily did as she was told and climbed up the ladder, Michael following after. The cool night air felt good against her bruised skin.

"I will have them back to you shortly," said the priest to the jailer.

After a short boat ride across the lake, Emily and Michael had been brought to the Temple of Neith. To Emily's relief, he gave them simple robes to wear. "I have consulted the histories," said the priest. They now stood at the his desk. "There is mention of strangers sent from God who delivered our people from annihilation. The crystal bearer was even named Emily. This only proves that you know your history and not that you are who you say. Our task is simple." The priest motioned to a slave boy, who looked to be ten years old, holding a bronze pitcher and a bowl. The boy placed the bowl on the desk in front of Emily and filled it with water. "This is water drawn from the sacred lake. If you have the ability to access the power of Neith, prove it so."

Emily was apprehensive. She looked to the boy, to the priest, and then to Michael. "If I do this, will you let us go? My husband too?"

"That depends entirely on the results of your efforts," replied the priest.

She took a deep breath, closed her eyes and placed a hand in the water. As she opened her eyes, the water was glowing brightly. Suddenly, there was a flash of light and everyone was thrown backwards. Everyone except for her.

When her eyes adjusted, the water puddled on the desk and was dripping onto the floor. The bronze bowl was torn apart.

"Neith protect us all!" said the priest as he climbed to his feet. "Not since the time of the flood has anyone accessed the power."

Michael was also getting to his feet, but the slave boy did not stir.

"I told you, I am the Crystal Bearer," she said as she moved toward the child. "Is the boy hurt?"

"He matters not," said the priest. "He is just a slave."

"He is a human," she said kneeling down at the boy's side. "Does he have a name?"

"We call him 'Xho'."

Emily felt for a pulse and barely found it. "He must have hit his head," she said. "Is there any water left in that pitcher?"

The priest picked it up off the floor and handed it to her. There was a little water left inside. She carefully put it up to the boy's mouth to drink.

"You must not," said the priest. "Slaves do not drink of the lake."

"I don't honor that custom," said Emily, now cradling the boy's head in her lap. Once the water was within his mouth, she closed her eyes, her hand on the boy's chest. The boy's skin began to glow and he opened his eyes. He was in shock, but upon looking at Emily he calmed down.

"You have saved me," said Xho.

"Slaves do not speak, boy!" said the priest.

"Leave him alone," said Emily. "Now do you believe me?"

"It appears that I must," he replied.

"Then will you help me get to Attica?" she asked.

"I shall," he replied, "but before I take you any further, you must know that the queen and her captain do not know of this test. They would be most displeased, but I had to find out for myself. Even having proven yourself, they will not help you."

"Why is that?" she asked.

"In truth, Saïs is not fond of Attica," he said. "We do not trust them."

"But why?"

"Because they are unworthy of our trust," he replied. "You say that you come from the time of the flood. We call the time that follows 'After the Storm' in our histories. After the storm, Attella of the old blood reestablished Attica with her son and the help of God-king Aha, may he protect us all. The building of such a nation was tedious and laborious. If the histories are correct, Attica has yet to return to its former glory.

"In the beginning relations between our two nations were amiable and strong. In truth, we were hardly separate. It was with our people that Attica rebuilt, but time passed and Attella and her son died. Their descendants, after many years of trials, drew away their support until the realms were barely civil toward one another. Attica grew fast in strength, a gift from the Gods, and at a point threatened to claim Saïs as a part of their realm. War would have ensued, had it not been for the queen who fought politically as much as she could to stop the onslaught from happening.

"Attica's current king, Cecrops, has improved our relations, but minimally. We are not at war and nothing more. Betrayal is a deep fracture to heal, but in recent years we have been able to resume trade and commerce.

"You see, the world was broken by the deluge and we Saitians are still trying to put it back together." The priest was somber, the weight of the world seemingly on his shoulders.

"Be that as it may, we need your help getting there," said Emily. "And soon."

"Soon will be necessary," said Ubaid. "Musa will find you missing soon, and the contest betwixt the Gods is coming. We will have to be stealth in your escape."

"What do you suggest?" she asked.

"I will disguise you and take you down to the docks, where we will find you passage on a trade ship bound for Attica. That is your only hope."

"We must free my husband before we go anywhere," said Emily. "I'm not leaving him here."

"Herald of Neith," said the priest, "we will not be able to free him in time for you to leave."

"I won't leave without him!" she exclaimed. "I'll use the water from the lake and tear down the damn palace if I have to." Emily stalked toward the door.

"Then your quest is already at an end," called the priest. Emily stopped and turned to look at him. "As powerful as you may be, you are just one person. There are dozens of guards surrounding your beloved. They have scythes, swords, and arrows. Even with the water, you'd be struck down before you even entered the palace."

"But they'll kill him," she said. "They've already passed sentence on him! I'll raise the fires of hell if I have to."

"And then you will die and your entire quest will be for naught," he replied.

"I've died before!" she said.

"You know in your heart that this death will not be as before," said Ubaid. "There will be no rising from the Underworld, and then you both will be dead. I do not presume to know why you have returned to us, Crystal Bearer, but I would bet on my life that it was not to die mere moments after your arrival."

Emily stared at him, cold. "So we just leave him? Is that your plan?"

"I will do all within my power to secure his release and send him on his way as soon as I am able, but if you remain in Saïs a moment longer, you will be found out and you will die. I do not know what business you have with Poseidon, but you will not be able to fulfill your duty if you remain here."

Emily was silent. She looked to Michael, who hadn't said a word. Part of her resented him. Pete should be standing where he is.

"I'm sorry, Emily," was all he said as a tear escaped his eye. She began to sob.

"Emily," said the priest. "I am sorry, but we must go now." Ubaid took her by the hand to lead her away, as she tried to regain her composure.

"You're right," she said through red puffy eyes. "Damn it, I hate it, but you are. You must promise to save him. Promise me you'll save him!"

"I will do all within my power, be assured," said Ubaid.

"Then let's get this over with," she said.

The priest led them to the door of his office and before leaving, turned to the boy, still resting on the floor. "Clean this mess up and have some tea ready for my return."

"No," said Emily. "He is no longer your slave. I gave him back his life and now he is free. Xho, you will come with me." She held her hand out to the boy. He looked from the priest to Emily with uncertainty. "By the power of Neith, I free you." He looked to the priest once more.

"As you wish," said Ubaid.

"I did not come here to change your customs," said Emily, "just to gain passage to Attica. Nothing more, though I will keep Xho with me to ensure his freedom."

"As you wish," said the priest.

"Then let's go."

Emily was angered by her treatment in Saïs. The nation had once been peaceful and hospitable. When she had been called forth by the God-king Aha, she was given every comfort available and more. The old woman, Pyrthens, had been her caretaker and the king checked in on her from time to time. It would seem that Nefruneith and her captain were not as hospitable as their ancestors.

It was an hour before dawn when the priest led them out of the Temple and down to the sacred lake.

"I thought we were going to the docks," said Emily.

"Apologies, herald," said the priest, "but there is something I must do first. I cannot answer for the queen, but I can give you one small token of my esteem." He reached within his robes and pulled out a small horn that was corked at one end. He removed the stopper, knelt down to the water, filled it, and then handed it to her. "It is not much, but you may have need of Neith's power before your journey is at an end."

"I'm sure you're right," replied Emily, placing the horn in the small pouch at her waist.

Leaving the lake behind them, Ubaid led them through the streets of Saïs. Before, the Saitians had mainly lived in low-built mud-brick houses, but now most buildings were made of stone and mortar. The road was not crowded, due to the early hour. Blue orbs illuminated the path all the way down to the harbor, where people were already up and moving.

Dozens of ships lined the shore. Sailors yelled back and forth, and cargo was being loaded and unloaded.

"How do we find a ship?" asked Michael.

"I know of a trader," said the priest. "Just follow me and stay close." They did as he said and walked down the docks until they came upon a ship that appeared deserted. "Here she is, Kronos. Her captain, Daxteros, will give you passage in exchange for work. With no coin, that will be your only way there."

"Can't you pay for our passage?" asked Emily. "It's the least you can do."

"The Temple has no coin," replied the priest. "Anything we require is provided by her grace, Nefruneith."

Emily turned back to the Kronos. Every other ship at the docks was bustling and busy except for this one. If it hadn't been for the candlelight coming through the yellow-stained glass windows of the captain's quarters, she would have believed it to be empty.

Against her better judgment, they followed Ubaid and boarded the ship. Kronos had a single mast with yellow sails rolled up. They saw no one on board.

"Should we keep going?" asked Michael. "Maybe you were mistaken, priest."

"I am not mistaken," he replied. There was uncertainty in his voice.

They took a few more steps and suddenly Emily felt cold steel at her throat.

"What do you lot think you are doing here?" asked a voice by her ear. In the dim light from the docks, Emily saw Ubaid, Michael, and Xho standing opposite her, jaws dropped. "Any of you so much as flinches, I will spill her blood into the sea. Were you thinking you would take our wares? Steal a pig or two for your starving mommy? You think the ship would be unattended for your pleasure?"

"No, you have us wrong," said Ubaid.

"Well then speak quickly," said the man. The knife was beginning to cut into her skin.

"I am Ubaid, Grand Priest of Neith. We only wish to speak with your captain. We are not trespassers."

"Is that so?" said the knifeman. "Well, we will see what old Dax has to say about it then."

The knifeman kept the blade to her throat as he ushered them toward the captain's quarters. He rapped on the door quickly and they heard movement within.

"Captain!" he called. "We have some trespassers here claiming to be holy men."

The door opened to reveal a tall rugged man with white hairs poking through his well-kept beard. He wore a simple black coat with matching pants. Dark brown eyes peered down at them. A large scar ran down the left side of his face.

"Tam, you idiot!" he yelled. "Let the girl go! Ubaid, forgive my insolent crewman."

"Yes, Captain," replied Tam as he let her go. She rubbed her throat to find a small bit of blood from a shallow cut. "But I found them sneaking around the ship."

"Tam, you are a simple fool," replied the captain. "Bring them in and leave us be."

Once they were all inside, Tam left them, much to his chagrin.

"Forgive his impudence, Ubaid," said the captain. "He takes to his post with a self-imposed sense of authority. There is no lasting damage, I hope." He looked to Emily, who shook her head.

"No crime has been committed," replied Ubaid. "I do, however, apologize for not sending word of my visit, as we have urgent matters."

"Urgent matters?" said the captain. "Do not sound so ominous, dear priest."

"My friends here need passage to Attica and are willing to work for it, but they will need to leave within the morning."

"That is a tall order. I was not planning to leave your beautiful realm for another moon's turn."

"As I said, urgent matters," said Ubaid.

"Who are these friends?" he asked looking to Emily and Michael.

"Forgive my rudeness, Captain," said Ubaid. "This is Emily, Herald of Neith, and her companion Michael, along with the boy, Xho."

"Herald of Neith?" said the captain. "This is important business, Ubaid." He looked to Emily and Michael. "Welcome to Kronos. I am Daxteros, her captain, originally from Attica, but everyone just calls me Captain or Dax. You say you need to leave this morning?" They nodded. Emily noticed that faint light was beginning to peer through the stained windows. They were losing time. "Ubaid, I trust you. You have never steered me wrong, but I must know the reasons why you are in such haste."

"The games," said Emily. "We need to get to Attica before the game of gods."

"The whole world is making its way to Attica," said Dax. "It will be a mess, I assure you. Best you keep away."

"We don't have a choice," said Emily. "With all due respect Captain, we are losing time. Will you take us on?" The captain studied them for a moment, glancing back at the priest several times.

"Yes, indeed," said Dax. "I will take you on, but know that I am

Lord of this ship, despite any loyalties you hold toward Neith, and my word is law. Any defiance and you will take a long walk off a short plank, understood?" They nodded. "Fine. The girl will serve me personally, cleaning and cooking my meals. You," he pointed to Michael, "will help with cleaning out the stalls. I trade livestock, you see. Cattle, boar, goats. They shit everywhere. The smell is something awful, but you get accustomed to it. They boy will help out wherever he is needed. Work until we reach port and consider the debt of passage paid."

"We agree to your terms," said Emily.

"Good," said Dax. "Priest, know that I am doing this as a favor to you."

"One that I appreciate and will repay in kind," said Ubaid. "May Neith bless you and protect you always. I must leave now before my absence is noticed. Herald of Neith, may fortune bless you on your journey."

"You promised to free my husband, priest," said Emily. "If he dies, I will come back for vengeance with all of the power of Neith behind me."

"I pray you will have no need to," replied the priest. "Fare journey."

The sun was above the horizon when the priest rushed back to the Temple. Both Emily and Michael had to lend a hand, but as promised, before noon the Kronos left Saïs and before the day's end, they left the river heading north and out into the open sea.

CHAPTER II
THE GOVERNESS OF CARMOUR

Kronos sailed beyond the sight of land. As Emily watched the last line of earth become engulfed by the sea, she felt a familiar sinking feeling. Their flight from Saïs happened so quickly that it was only now that she began to feel guilty for leaving Pete behind. Who knows what the girl-queen had done to him. Ubaid promised to save him, but that promise now seemed hollow at best. *If they kill him,* she thought, *I swear I'll destroy them all.* She turned her thoughts to the matter at hand: saving Sean and Erin. She had no idea what to do once she got to Attica, or how to gain an audience with Poseidon.

Deep in thought, she didn't notice Captain Daxteros coming up beside her. "Have you been at sea before, Herald?"

The question took her off guard. "What?"

"You seem to long for land a bit too soon," he replied.

"Oh, yes," said Emily. "I have sailed before. Once."

"Not a fond memory, I take it," he read the pained look on her face. "Neith is not lord of the sea as she is of Saïs. If safe passage is what you require, I can only provide the vessel. Pray to Poseidon for your assured deliverance."

"I plan to do that and more, Captain," she replied and then scolded herself.

"What do you mean?" asked Dax.

"What?"

"Do not play coy," he said. "I have brought you on my ship in good faith with only a vague understanding why. I am loyal to Ubaid or you would not be here. Tell me why you need to go to Attica."

"I already told you, to see the game of gods."

"Ah, that I do not doubt, but it is not the whole truth." Dax stared at her.

Emily looked out over the sea as the sun raced toward the horizon. "I'm having a hard time trusting new people," she said. "You seem like an honorable man, Captain, and I ask that you accept that I can't tell you my reasons for this journey. Call it distrust, if you want, but know that I'm grateful for your help and will work as needed to pay my passage."

"As you say then. I will not badger you with questions now," said Dax. "You have work to do anyway and can start by fixing me supper. You will find food stores down below."

"Yes, Captain." Emily turned from the rail and walked away.

The next week passed without incident. Emily did her best to keep her head down and avoid questions from both the captain and crew. She hardly saw Michael, as he tended to the animals, and only had time to quickly ask how he was doing before each running off to their next task. She did keep a close eye on the boy, Xho. He mostly cleaned and ran messages for the captain, but sometimes he helped her prepare meals. Upon her request, he slept beside her on a pallet of bound straw and blankets. It was her fault he was with them, and she often wondered if he would have been better off just serving Ubaid. It was now her duty to keep him safe.

One night, a week into their journey, Emily lay awake staring at the pale light of the moon shining through a crack in the wood. Xho breathed softly beside her. Soon they would arrive in Attica and then what? Hermes was supposed to lead them there, but he left before they had even made it back to dark pool. She wondered where he was now and if he had any design to help her.

Hermes was a trickster, she remembered. When she first met him, he was disguised as a sailor named Sandis. Before then, he pretended to be an intern named Matthew Nestor who carefully manipulated Sean and Erin into going to the Underworld. For all she knew, he could very well be on the Kronos at that moment. Maybe he was Dax? Or Tam? Or even Xho? The boy rolled over and huddle closer to her. She put an arm around him.

"Hermes, where are you?" she whispered to the moon light, closing her eyes.

"Sons of Hades!" she heard a voice shout from above deck. The sudden sound of boots running across the deck made her sit up. More shouting filled as panic overcame the crew.

Carefully, she rose from her pallet and tucked Xho back in, hoping he'd sleep through whatever was happening. She reached for the door of her small cabin, but it tore open in front of her revealing Michael Turner.

"Emily, you'd better come see this," he said pulling her by the arm.

"What's happening?" she asked as they made their way on deck. He didn't answer and ran ahead.

When she arrived, the crew was running everywhere as Daxteros manically screamed out orders. It was only after a few moments that Emily realized what was happening. Running to the railing, the Kronos was surrounded by a ring of fire.

"Keep us in one place!" Daxteros shouted. "We will burn to death if that fire even comes close. Lower anchor!"

"What happened?" she asked Michael.

"I don't know," he replied. "All was dark and then we were just surrounded."

"Hades," she said fearfully. "He must have found us out. There's no way we can win this."

"Hades? What are we going to do?" asked Michael.

"I… I don't know, but lowering anchor won't help and water can't put this fire out."

"Isn't there anything that *you* can do?" he asked. "You're supposed to be supernatural. Wield power. Something!"

"I'm only human, Michael!" she yelled. She thought about the horn of water from the sacred lake, but surely that small amount wouldn't do much.

"HERALD!" she heard a shout. Turning around, Daxteros was calling to her. "Pray to your goddess now, for Poseidon may have forsaken us!"

"Come with me," she whispered to Michael, and they made their way over to the captain.

"Ubaid said you can wield divine power," said Dax, "save us from this and I will forgive your debt and deliver you to the games myself."

"This isn't normal fire," she told him.

"Of course it is not, simple girl," he yelled over the clamor. "What fire burns on water?"

"The fire of Hades," she replied.

A column of flame burst into the sky in front of them. Writhing back and forth, it transformed into a giant serpent.

"Ophion," said Emily. Daxteros looked at her. "The fire demon of Hades." As the serpent's head touched the water it transformed again into a large ship, dark as night itself.

Emily clutched Michael's arm in fear. Everything they had gone through to get this far was all in vain. Leaving Allie, crossing the Underworld, leaving Pete. It was all for nothing.

"Poseidon, deliver us," mumbled Daxteros.

The ring of fire remained as the Persephone, the ship that saved mankind from the deluge, came to a halt side-face next to Kronos. Her sail gleamed red, menacingly in light of the fire. Pale figures stood on her deck, their eyes sightless.

The crew of the Kronos gathered their weapons and waited for the demons to make their move. "Tell your crew to stand down," said Emily. "They can't fight this."

"My men do not fear death, Herald," he replied.

"It's not death they should fear, but what comes after," she said. "Tell them to stand down!"

"If we make it through this, you will tell me who you really are," he told her waving an angry finger in front of her face.

"I promise," she replied. Daxteros gave the order and his men lowered but did not discard their weapons. It was the most that Emily could hope for.

Leaving Daxteros and Michael, Emily walked to the railing and waited. Her heart was in her throat, beating so loudly that it threatened to drown out the sound of the fire crackling. Long minutes later, a tall figure appeared on deck, dressed in all white. Hades kept his head down as he walked to the rail of his ship.

When he did not speak, she broke the ice. "Hades!" she called. "You have come for me! I have deceived you and have no right to ask favors! But if you will grant mercy to Daxteros and the Kronos, I will come to you without a fight and give up my quest."

"I do not come to take you," said the figure in a high ethereal voice, "but to offer you counsel, dear pilgrim."

Confused, Emily called back to him. "And what counsel would Hades offer me?"

"I do not know what counsel my husband would give you."

Emily looked closer as the figure raised its head. Bright green eyes met hers. "But I do know what I would say."

"Persephone!" said Emily.

"Indeed, I have come," she replied. Wind seemed catch in her gown, billowing she rose into the air and flew to land on the deck of Kronos. "Forgive the theatrics, but Ophion was my only means to warn you. Though I am not Hades, his darkness has taken flight. You may be mankind's only hope."

"Persephone," said Emily, still in shock. "Why? What would you have me do?"

"Change your quest," she replied, her green eyes seeming to peer into Emily's soul. "Saving your family must be set aside."

"But I can't. They're all I have left."

"You left your husband to save them," said Persephone. "That was a brave choice and I commend you for your courage, but know that your family will not continue to exist if you do not do as I say."

"What do you mean?"

"Hades intends to intervene at the game of gods and take Attica for his own," she replied. "He has already set his plan into motion to convince King Cecrops to name him patron God."

"Why would Cecrops do that?" asked Emily.

"Hades has a convincing case and the king's mind can be heavily swayed by the Oracle of Delphi," replied Persephone. "My husband has full control over the Oracle, but she remains in her own mind. If you can convince her to disobey Hades, we may have a chance of stopping him."

"How can I do that?" she asked.

"The Oracle is already in the capital, but getting to her may prove difficult as a commoner. You must adopt a disguise. Thousands of people are arriving in Attica everyday for the games, including the governing bodies from lands all over the world. You will become a governess, and will therefore be housed at the palace. There you may contrive a way to meet with the Oracle, as many will be wont to do."

"I don't know if I can convince her," said Emily. "And what do I govern? I can't keep that story straight."

"Emily Henry, you are Lady Elise, the Governess of Carmour, a small island off the eastern coast of Attica. The king will have scarcely heard of it, but will provide you accommodations nonetheless. The island does truly exist, but consists of mostly sheepherders and farmers with no true governing body. The men of this ship will act as your entourage, solidifying your disguise." Persephone turned and summoned Daxteros and Michael over. "The two of you are to be her sword and shield. Any allegiances you have held true in the past are now dissolved. Her life is your own and if she fails in her task, you are just as much at fault. This appointment is not fair, I understand, but necessary. You cannot fail."

"I live to serve the Governess of Carmour," said Daxteros with a bow. "And, of course, the Goddess Persephone. I will see to her safety and deliverance."

"I am assured that you will, sailor. And you, Michael Turner?"

"I… don't know how I can serve her," he said timidly. "I'm not a fighter. I'm just a paper-pusher. I can't fight."

"You do not need to fight, but only appear as if you can. Captain Daxteros will outfit you." Michael hesitated, then nodded and stepped away. "Emily, you must do this or darkness worse than death will blanket this world. You shall arrive in Attica within the moon."

"As you say," said Emily. "Before you go, do you know what happened to Hermes? He didn't make it out of the Underworld with us."

"I cannot say," said Persephone, "but if you do see him again, do not trust him. Hermes is a trickster first and a friend second. He very well may be under my husband's thumb." Kneeling down slightly, Persephone kissed Emily lightly on the forehead. "I must go now. Good fortune, dear one."

Persephone floated back to her ship and disappeared within its darkness. Slowly, the ship moved back toward the ring of fire, transforming once again into the serpent Ophion. As if turning off a light switch, the serpent was gone and ring fire was extinguished. The sudden darkness was shocking and it took several minutes for Emily's eyes to adjust.

She felt a hand on her shoulder and when she looked up, Daxteros stared back at her. "Who are you?" he asked.

"I am the Governess of Carmour."

Three days later, the Kronos made port in Piraeus, a bustling port town a half-day's journey from the capital. After Persephone left, Emily tried her best to explain who she was and her quest to Daxteros.

"So that was your last time sailing?" he asked her after explaining her part in the deluge. "Small wonder you longed for land as you did." Though he seemed to understand, she was not certain that he was convinced. Part of her couldn't blame him. The flood had happened five hundred years ago and was mostly a legend at this point.

Upon reaching port, Daxteros sent one of his men to the capital to announce the Governess' arrival, while he and Emily set out on their own to find her suitable attire. There would be no time to have an appropriate dress made, so they would have to look through shops and stalls for anything that might work. Piraeus was bursting to capacity and they fought their way through the streets and alleys.

"I know of a shop not far from here," said Daxteros, holding her close as to not lose her. They continued to weave through the thrall and soon they arrived at a shop next to a butcher's stand. Emily hesitated. "The lass who runs this shop is an old friend of mine," he told her. "She will help us."

"Daxteros!" she heard someone scream from inside. "What in the name of Hades has dragged the Kronos back to port?" A young woman barely twenty years old ran out and threw herself at the captain. Emily stumbled back as she planted a kiss on his lips.

"Hello, Daria," he said softly and she kissed him again. Daria looked at Emily suspiciously.

"Who have you brought with you?" she asked with a hint of jealousy. "You better not be sneaking around on me." To Emily's surprise, Daxteros turned red. Her brave captain was actually blushing!

"I would never dream of it," he replied. "This is a friend of mine looking for a dress. A real pretty one. Got any that will do?"

"A real pretty one?" she asked. "I may have something that will suit her. Who is she?"

"This is Lady Elise," he replied, the name they agreed to give the Governess. "I gave her passage from Carmour. She wants to impress the king."

"The king?" she asked. "Not a small order then, is it? That may a little bit harder to find. Come inside, we will see what we can do."

Emily followed the pair inside the shop. An older woman sat at a table sewing, bolts of cloth strewn everywhere.

"You may be in luck," called Daria from a back room. "We just finished a nice gown for one of the noble ladies, but she will not send for it for another week at least." She walked out carrying an olive green dress. Sleeveless, it had golden beads and emeralds sewn into swirling patterns around the collar. "We can remake it with enough time to spare. It will only take a few minutes to alter it to fit Lady Elise. Here, try it on."

Within minutes, Emily was wearing the dress, completely in love with it. Other than being a bit too long for her, it was a perfect fit. Daria was at her feet, hemming the bottom into place.

"What will you give me for it, Dax?" asked Daria.

"What will you have for it?" he replied.

"Take me with you," she said. "Take me away from this shop and you can keep the damn thing."

"Aye, and what would I do with you?" he asked laughing.

"I can cook and clean," she replied. "I can mend sails and keep your bed warm at night. I have not stepped a toe outside of Piraeus in over a year."

"I am not setting sail again for a moon's turn," he replied.

"I could come live on the ship in the meantime," she said smiling. By now she had abandoned Emily's dress and had her arms around the captain's neck. "You always promised me a tour of the Kronos."

"I will not be staying with my ship while I'm here," he said. "I am escorting Lady Elise to the capital."

"I will not take no for an answer, my captain," she giggled.

Watching this young girl throwing herself at Daxteros gave Emily a thought; one that would add weight to her disguise.

"Daria," she began. "How would you like to come to the capital with us?" Daxteros' eyes opened wide in fear. Daria's opened wide in wonder.

"Really?" she asked.

"Yes," she said. "I left Carmour in such a hurry that I had to leave my handmaids there. You'll find that I treat my servants well and I can pay you handsomely for your time."

"Em... Elise, I do not think that would be a wise choice," said Daxteros.

"Oh, it is a wonderful idea, Captain," Emily assured him. "I was going to beg the king for one, but if Daria is indeed ambitious to leave her shop, we can both gain something from her presence."

"Oh, Dax, please say yes," Daria begged. "And when you leave, you can take me with you."

"Yes, Dax, let her." Emily had backed the captain into a corner, she thought. Though it worked to her advantage, she feared his wrath later on. Men like Daxteros didn't like tight corners.

Within an hour Emily was wearing the newly altered dress and was making her way back through the crowd, Daxteros and Daria at her side. She would have to keep up her disguise at all times from now on, lest the girl find her for a fraud. Until she trusted Daria, Emily had no plans of revealing her identity.

As ordered, the crew of the Kronos wore their best clothing when they returned and was ready to escort the "Lady Elise" to the capital. Michael had also borrowed clothing from the crew, wearing a brown vest on top of a linen shirt. Xho wore his slave attire from Saïs, though now freshly laundered. He was to be her cup bearer, a roll he was already accustomed to from serving at the Temple of Neith.

It was nearly midday when the caravan set out. The captain had secured her a litter, carried by the crew. Xho rode with her, while Michael, Daxteros, and Daria walked alongside.

"If you do not mind me asking, why would you leave all of your belongings in Carmour, Lady Elise?" asked Daria.

"I am a private woman," replied Emily. "But to rest your mind, know that my trip was not planned and I wished to arrive before the games began. That left little time for packing and even less time to gather my servants. I was only able to bring my bodyguard and my cupbearer."

Daria's curiosity seemed sated for the moment, but Emily knew that she would continue to pry. Emily left the matter alone for the time being.

The sun was near the horizon as they crested a hill that overlooked the capital of Attica. Palaces and temples lined the hill that made up the acropolis and lesser buildings filled in the area between the hill and the city wall. The city was over capacity, noticed Emily, as the land outside was littered with rough-made huts and tents.

"Will they let us enter?" she asked Daxteros from her litter.

"For a Governess and Lady of Carmour, yes," he replied.

Soon they arrived at the city gate. Daxteros announced her as planned and the guards let them pass without incident, only asking that they head to the palace quickly and not tarry as night was coming fast. The streets were darkening and it was full night by the time they reached the gates of Attella's Crown.

The litter was left near the gatehouse and guards ushered them into the palace. The king, they were told, was indisposed for the evening and that she would be received by his advisors. After being settled in her rooms on the second floor of a western tower, Emily made her way to one of the many courtyards, with Michael and Daxteros at her side.

"Presenting the Lady Elise, Governess of Carmour," announced the guard. Her nerves were a mess as she walked in. The king's advisors stood to welcome her.

"Greetings, Governess," said the man, bowing to kiss her hand. "I am Helios, an honored trustee of King Cecrops, and this is my wife, Hera." Hera smiled and welcomed her.

"Thank you for your kindness," replied Emily, "and for receiving me."

"We are honored to have Carmour represented at the games," said Hera. "We have most of the realm, and better yet, the entire world represented here. Tell me, Elise, how fares your isle?"

"Things go as they usually do," she replied. "My people raise sheep and goats or farm, mostly. We are quite simple, I fear."

"Your lives are ones without scruples," said Helios. "A life we all can envy. And of course we know of your occupations. It has been years since we last visited the outer islands, but enjoyed it greatly."

"You have been to Carmour?" she asked, her inflection showing surprise.

"Of course, dear," said Hera, "when your father ruled. You were still a little girl back then, but my how you have grown into your father's seat."

Emily balked. They knew her for a fake, she sensed. If they had been to Carmour, then surely they would know that the "Lady Elise" did not exist.

"Is everything alright, dear?" asked Hera.

Emily snapped out of her trance. "Yes," she replied. "Thank you. I fear that I am travel worn."

"Ah, do not let us keep you from your rest," replied Helios with a knowing smile.

"Thank you for your understanding," said Emily. "Before I retire, I have heard that the Oracle of Delphi is within the palace."

"The rumors are true," said Hera with a smile. "I shall set you up a meeting with her tomorrow, if you wish."

"That would be wonderful," replied Emily, her stomach in knots.

"Then it shall be," said Hera. "Perhaps afterward we shall go for a walk. I would love to hear news from the isles."

"Oh, I wouldn't want to take you away from your many duties," replied Emily.

"You will not be an inconvenience at all, my dear," said Hera.

"As you say," said Emily. "I will look forward to it, then."

Leaving the courtyard, Emily, along with Michael and Daxteros, walked down a long corridor and back upstairs to her rooms. She wanted to run. She wanted to scream. She wanted to scream at Persephone for making her adopt this disguise, which seemed to have already failed. She wanted to scream at Pete for not being there. But most of all she wanted to scream at Sean and Erin for setting her on this damned quest. *After I save them, I just might kill them,* she thought.

Entering her rooms, Daxteros shut the door behind them.

"That seemed to go well," he said to everyone. Daria and Xho were seated at the window looking out over the city. Emily wanted to explode, but couldn't with Daria there. The girl had yet to gain her trust.

"Daria," she said with all the composure she could muster, "would you be a dear and help Xho into bed?" Daria smiled and led the boy away. At least she was obedient. "It went well?" she asked when the girl was out of earshot. "Did you not hear Hera? They've been to Carmour and know that 'Lady Elise' doesn't exist!"

"Emily, please calm down," said Michael.

"Calm down?" she replied. "Michael, you of all people should understand the gravity of this. If we are discovered then we will have no chance of seeing the Oracle or Poseidon. Our entire mission relies on the success of my disguise."

"Well if they know you for a fake, why did they let you stay?" he asked. "Why aren't you rotting in a cell somewhere right now?"

"Good questions," she replied. "There was something off about those two. I can't put a finger on it, but mark my words."

That night Emily dreamed she was back in Washington, D.C. with Pete early on in their relationship and before the flood. Inside Sean's apartment, Pete sat on the couch with Emily on top of him. Passion flowed between them as they kissed. Taking off her top, the Saitian crystal suddenly hung from her neck. Emily stopped and looked at it. Pete, seemingly oblivious to its sudden appearance, pulled her in for another kiss when she heard glass shatter behind them.

She turned to look at the cause, but Pete held her still. "Don't worry," he said. "It's just Allie."

"Allie?" she asked. "Who's Allie?"

"Our niece?" replied Pete as he continued to kiss her neck. In her dream state she knew that Allie wasn't even born then, but something about Pete made her forget that.

"But what about the broken glass?" she asked. A shriek sounded behind her and she pulled away from Pete and stood. Turning around, a sobbing young girl with long dark hair stood next to broken glass, her fingers bloody.

"Oh Allie," she said as she scooped the girl up. "Are you okay?" The girl ceased her screaming. Though there was blood on her hands, Emily saw no cuts. "Where's your cut?"

"I didn't cut myself," replied the girl.

"Then whose blood is this?" she asked.

"Yours, Aunt Emily," replied Allie.

Emily felt a stab in her side, and blood poured from her wound. Before she could react, the crystal glowed bright and she had a familiar sensation of being tugged forward and backward at the same time. Still holding onto Allie, they both were moving quickly through space and time. The pressure was too much to bear and Emily screamed.

Tears trickled down her face as she opened her eyes. Sitting up in bed, she was back in Attica and it was morning. She heard running and then two men busted through the door.

"Emily!" one screamed. It had only been a dream, she reassured herself, breathing heavily.

"I am alright," she said to Michael and Daxteros. "Did I scream?"

"Loud enough to wake the whole damn palace," said Daxteros, holding a short sword. "You sounded like someone was murdering you and doing a good job of it."

"I'm sorry, Captain," she said, feeling at her side where the wound had been. "It was just a bad dream. I... I'm sorry."

Daxteros sheathed his sword. "With all the drama that follows you people," he said, "It is difficult not to be alarmed. Shall I send Daria in with some warm milk?"

"No," she replied. "Thank you, Captain, but I think I'll just get up. I don't want to go back to sleep."

"Perhaps a bath, then?" he asked.

"That would be great," she smiled to reassure him that she was fine. Having a man so concerned about her made Emily miss Pete all the more.

GERALD M. GIVENS

CHAPTER III
DEMANDS & COMPLIANCE

One week had passed since Delia's meeting with Hera and Helios and during that time she had done her best to avoid them. She still knew that Hades would include her in his plot and there was nothing she could do to stop him. What made it worse was that she had to keep it all a secret. After leaving the villa, Doros had questioned her on their way back to the palace, but she would not answer and quickly changed the topic of discussion. She was aware that he knew she was hiding something, but he honored her by not pressing the issue.

Early one morning, walking down the corridor toward her rooms, flanked by Doros and two handmaidens, the moment she had been dreading arrived. As they turned a corner, Hera and Helios seemed to appear out of thin air. She gasped and took a step back. Realizing her behavior, she regained her composure.

"Apologies, Hera and Helios," she said. "I was not expecting you."

"I believe we are the ones who will be apologizing, dear Oracle," replied Hera. "We should have sent word of our coming, but here we are."

"You wish to speak with me?" asked Delia. "I am a bit busy at the moment, but we could meet…"

"Oh, do not be silly," Helios interrupted. "We will only take a moment of your time."

Delia frowned, and then conceded. She knew that she couldn't keep them away. "I am just on my way back to my chambers. Will that be suitable for your counsel?" she asked. Hera nodded with a grin.

Moments later they arrived in the Oracle's apartment and Delia sent away her maids and Doros. "Please do not argue, Brother," said Delia quietly when Doros insisted on remaining in the room. "I will be fine."

"You will be fine just like the last time I left you alone with these two?" he asked.

"Please, Doros… just go."

"I will be right outside," he said then shut the door.

When she turned around, Hera was already sitting down and Helios was pouring tea. The sight of them disgusted her.

"What is it?" she asked them.

"Dear Oracle, we have missed you," said Hera accepting a cup from her husband as he sat down beside her. "If I did not know better, I would think you have been avoiding us."

"What would you have me do?" she asked, taking a seat opposite the couple.

"Be pleasant, to start," said Helios. "You may not have been happy with our last encounter, but that is no cause to be rude. A smile every now and again would suffice."

"Please would be you telling me what you are doing in my rooms," she said. She was walking on thin ice, she knew, but she could not help but show her contempt for the pair. "Clearly Hades has some need of me. Let us not waste time and energy on pleasantries."

Hera gave her a big smile. "Fine," she said. "We shall get to our point quickly and not waste anymore of the Oracle's precious time. Husband?"

"Oracle, the time has come for you to bring our case to King Cecrops," said Helios. "Tomorrow morning, you will announce that Hermes has come to you to state that Hades will be the third competitor in the games."

"If I do that, they will not believe me," said Delia. "They will laugh at me or worse, call me a fake and cast me out."

"Not if you do so carefully," said Helios. "Do you remember our true history of Zeus' deluge? How Hades saved us all? That is the thread you must use to weave your web."

Delia was afraid, but more so angry. "I cannot do it." She stood as if to make herself more menacing. "I will not do it! I will not deliver us into the hands of a monster."

In one quick motion, Hera stood and grabbed her by the throat, slamming her against the wall. Delia tried to fight, but Hera's grip only tightened and her eyes glowed red. "You will cooperate as you have vowed, child, or you will suffer the wrath of Hades himself. He will not be as tolerant of your insolence as we have been and know that there will be no death to escape your suffering." Hera let go and Delia collapsed to the floor, clutching her throat and coughing.

As if to console her, Helios knelt down before her. "Your compliance, child, is not a request. Hades does not make requests, is that clear? This is his demand of you." Through tears, she nodded. Without another word, the pair left.

Doros came in after they were gone, but Delia had quickly composed herself and washed her face. Her throat was still red from Hera's bony hands, but she covered it with a shawl. Her fate was sealed, it seemed.

"I am alright, Doros," she said looking out the window. She could sense his concern. "Us mortals cannot change the course of fate, it seems. Tell me, what is next on our agenda for today?"

"Delphinios sends word that a leader from one of the outlying islands has requested an audience," he replied. "The Governess of Carmour. Shall I send her away?"

"No, that will not be necessary," she replied. "Bring her in."

With Daxteros and Michael as her entourage, the Lady Elise of Carmour made her way across the palace to the Oracle's chambers. Somehow she would convince this woman to forsake the hold that Hades has on her and spare mankind his reign. She took a deep breath and rounded the final corner.

A tall young man stood outside the door, barring entry.

"The Lady Elise, Governess of Carmour, seeks the Oracle's counsel," announced Daxteros.

"The Oracle will see her ladyship shortly," said the guard. "She is presently occupied."

The door opened just then and Helios and Hera emerged. "Not anymore," said Hera with a smile. "Thank you, Doros, for watching over our precious flower."

"It is my duty," he replied.

Hera looked to the Governess and back to the guard again, "These days are perilous. Be sure to not let her out of your sight."

"As you say," said the guard. He looked to Daxteros, "I will tell the Oracle of your arrival," said the guard as he rushed inside and closed the door behind him.

"A pleasure to see you this morning, Governess," said Helios with a smile.

"Yes, it is wonderful to see you as well, sir," replied Emily. "And thank you for arranging this meeting for me. I am very grateful."

"It was nothing," Hera assured her. "We must be going, Governess, but do enjoy your visit with the Oracle. She really is a very special girl."

"I will," said Emily, as they walked away.

Before they turned the corner, Hera looked back. "Governess, do remember you promised me a walk this afternoon." Hera smiled and turned the corner.

"I'd rather die," said Emily under her breath.

A few minutes passed and the door opened. "The Oracle will see you now," said the guard.

They were ushered inside and the door shut behind them, the guard remaining inside the room. Seated on a couch in the center, a young girl in a simple white dress and woolen shawl sat with a cup of hot tea. She smiled as Emily took a seat across from her. Daxteros and Michael remained standing.

"Thank you, Oracle, for meeting with me on such short notice," said Emily. "Hera and Helios assured me that you would not mind."

"It is my honor to serve the realm," said the girl, though she seemed distant and lost in thought. "I do not mind. Many have done the same since I first arrived at the capital. Tell me, child, how may I counsel thee?"

Emily was taken aback by the question. First, for being called 'child' by someone who was little more than half her age and then second because she realized that she did not know how to proceed.

"Is something the matter?" asked the Oracle after the silence became awkward.

"I... uh... wanted to know who you think should win patronage of Attica in the coming contests," said Emily. She gritted her teeth.

"Patronage?" asked the girl, clearly not amused. "Well, the contest itself will tell who the victor shall be. The Gods either do not know or they will not share with me such wisdom. I am simply their humble vassal."

The girl was suddenly on the verge of tears. Trying to seem oblivious, Emily continued. "But surely the Oracle has an opinion on the matter."

"Alas, she does not," said the girl. "Please forgive my rudeness, Governess, but I have suddenly become quite tired and must rest. My bodyguard, Doros, will see you out." With that she rose and began to walk away. Doros came forward, urging them to leave.

"Wait," said Emily. The girl turned around. "We know about your deal with Hades." Emily hadn't meant to blurt it out, but she'd become desperate. The tears that the Oracle had been holding back finally came forth.

"I know nothing of what you say," she said pointing to the door. "You will leave now."

Doros tried to take Emily by the arm, but Daxteros stepped forward. "No, Dax," said Emily. "Oracle, I know what Hades has asked of you and I am here to help."

"Well you can tell Hades that I passed his test," said the girl. "If I fail him..." she continued to cry. Emily was surprised when Doros went to comfort her.

"Hades did not send us," she said. "Persephone did. We cannot allow Hades to take control of Attica. I assure you he won't stop with just this realm. Soon his darkness will cover the whole world."

"Persephone?" she said. "I cannot betray him. I made a vow."

"For the saving of all mankind, you must," said Emily. She walked over to the girl to look in her eyes. "I know what it's like to be a pawn in the game of gods. I have survived Purgatory, Erebus, death, and rebirth, and here I am again, being moved into place. We pawns have to stick together."

"I still cannot break the vow," she said. "I shall be eternally damned."

"I am not asking you to break your vow," said Emily. "I will do the work. I just need you to tell me who Hades has sent to Attica. Who is helping him?"

"Aside from me?" the girl cried.

"I do not blame you, Oracle," said Emily.

"I am Oracle no longer," she said. "Zeus will see to that. I am called Delia."

"Delia," said Emily, "who is helping Hades?"

"It is Hera and Helios," she replied. Though many thoughts

overwhelmed her, Emily found that she was not surprised. This explained why Hera had not called her out. Hera knew she was a fraud before she even arrived. "You do not want to cross them, I assure you, Governess. They wield the power of Hades."

"I too can wield divine power," said Emily as she fingered the horn of water hanging from a chain around her neck. "What is their plan?"

"Tomorrow morning I am to announce Hades' bid for patronage to the king and the realm," said Daria. "Hera and Helios say that Hades aided mankind against Zeus' genocide."

"Hades aided mankind?" asked Emily. "How so?"

"Hera says he sent heroes from another time to save us," replied Delia.

"Heroes?" said Emily. "Hades did not send them, Alexia did, and he was well compensated for his so-called aid. Trust me on that."

"What?" asked Delia. "How do you know these things? Who are you?"

"I was one of those heroes," replied Emily, "and it seems I've returned once again to help save the world."

"You are one of the Diluvians?" asked Delia, her eyes widening.

"Diluvians?"

"The people of the flood," said Delia. "The strangers from the deluge. That is what we call you in our legends."

"Then yes, I am one of them, I suppose," said Emily. "I am Emily, but that doesn't matter now. I have to stop Hades or die trying."

"Emily? What are you going to do?" asked Delia.

"Leave that to me," said Emily. "Just continue as if we haven't spoken. Tomorrow you will tell the king what Hera and Helios have instructed you to, but know that the opportunity may not come for you to reveal this information. I will contact you as I am able." Emily stepped back from the girl to leave.

"May Apollo shine his light upon you always," said Delia.

"And upon you," replied Emily and with that she left.

Emily returned to her rooms to find Hera and Helios sitting on a chaise near the windows drinking tea. She had mistrusted the pair to begin with and now that she knew that they were Hades' minions she wanted to keep her distance more than ever. Before she could say anything, Daria ran up to her.

"I am sorry, mistress," she said. "They insisted on being let in. The woman said that you were expecting her. I did not feel right to refuse them."

"Don't worry, Daria," said Emily. "You've done nothing wrong."

Helios and Hera turned and smiled as she entered. She didn't know whether to run or to choke them. Instead, she returned their smile.

"Lovely to see you again," she said as she approached. "To what do I owe this pleasure?"

"We wished to know how your audience with the Oracle went," replied Hera, "and to go on our walk. I think the palace gardens will be lovely this time of day."

"The Oracle was wonderful, as you said she would be," replied Emily. "I thought we planned to meet this afternoon."

"Indeed, Governess, but something has come up and this morning would prove better," replied Hera. "I am hoping that you will not mind."

"I am a little tired be honest," said Emily. "Possibly we could meet tomorrow."

"Oh, nonsense," replied Hera loudly. "This will not take long, I assure you." Hera stood and put her arm around Emily. "Shall we?"

Emily knew that she couldn't refuse without seeming suspicious. "Very well, then," she replied. "Daxteros, will you escort us?"

"We are in the palace," said Hera, "and we are both strong capable women. We will fare fine by ourselves and my husband would love to remain here and entertain your guard. He longs for news from the outer realm. Is that not right, husband?"

"Yes, my dear," said Helios. "Worry not, Governess, I shall keep them out of trouble."

Backed into a corner, Emily found herself wanting to fight her way out. Both Dax and Michael were looking to her for what to do. Emily fingered the horn around her neck and felt a sense of safety. As long as she had water from the lake, she wasn't completely vulnerable. "My guards would love his company," she replied. Michael went to object, but a sharp look from Emily silenced him. "As Hera said, we will be alright. After all, what could happen to us inside the palace?"

Before she could talk herself out of it, Emily left with Hera. She felt bad for leaving the men behind with Helios, knowing who he really was, but they would have to fend for themselves. Possibly they

141

could learn something of use from him.

"So you must tell me, Elise, how fared your visit with our Oracle?" asked Hera as they walked through the palace corridors. "I am so enticed by the things she says. Tell me everything." Hera almost sounded giddy.

"She was very pleasant, thank you," she replied. "I too am intrigued by her. We spoke about the contest and who she believes will win."

"And what did she say to that?" pushed Hera.

"She claims the Gods have not told her, but she believes that Athena will prove the victor," said Emily with a smile.

"Athena? Did she say why?"

"She didn't," replied Emily. "Her mind seemed occupied on other matters, so I did not push the subject and left her shortly after. Perhaps she and I will have another opportunity to speak."

"I am certain that you will," said Hera. "I know I asked you this yesterday, but how fares your isle? I have not been to Carmour since before your father died."

"It is as beautiful as it has ever been," replied Emily. "My father left it in a great state and I have thankfully been able to carry on his efforts and legacy with little hassle."

"I am glad to hear it," said Hera as they rounded another corner and climbed a staircase. Emily then realized that they were not heading toward any of the gardens, but higher into the palace.

Emily stopped. "Lady Hera," she said, "are you certain this the correct way to the gardens?"

"Oh you silly girl," laughed Hera. "We are not going to the gardens."

"Then where are we heading?" asked Emily. Hera's eyes flashed red as Emily reached for her horn of water at her chest. She saw a blinding flash of light as she lost consciousness.

"Sweet girl, please do fetch us some wine and some dice," said Helios to Daria. In all of their travels from Saïs, he wondered where this motley crew had picked up this sorry excuse for a maid. When they had asked her for tea, Hera had to tell her how to make it. Hopefully wine would not stretch her skills.

The Diluvian had done her best to maintain her disguise, but knew too little of this world to fit in. The pair that sat before Helios was as mismatched as any two "guards" could be. One was too much of a brute, probably a sailor by the smell of him, and the other was so soft he would not be able to save his own skin in a fight, let alone his mistress'. But in spite of their failed deception, they still maintained their appointed roles. He would play their game. After all, he liked games.

"Do you gamble?" he asked them as Daria brought back three glasses, a clay pitcher of wine, and the dice. Apparently she was not completely useless.

"No, your lordship," replied the sailor. Daxteros, he was called. The soft man shook his head.

"Forgive my disbelief," said Helios. "All men gamble, for that is certain, if not with money, then certainly with their lives."

"Have you ever gambled with your life, my lord?" asked Daxteros. "Or do you stick to counting gold?"

Helios gave him a knowing smile. "There is no point in having a life if you do not test its endurance every once in a while. Why, some say that rising each morning is a risk."

"Indeed it can be, my lord," replied the sailor, "but while a ship in harbor is safe, it was made for the sea. There is no life without risking it."

"Well said, and gambling with coin can only add to the fun," said Helios. "Men labor hard for coin, yet give it up in the hopes that fortune may favor them. One could argue that to do so is placing absolute trust in the divine."

"You are saying that gambling is a spiritual practice, my lord?"

"I only insinuate that it can be, if the stakes are high enough," said Helios.

The sailor clenched his teeth. "Have you ever gambled with your soul, my lord?"

"My soul?" asked Helios. He could not help but laugh. *Has not everyone?* He thought. The smile that the sailor gave him was all too telling. The Oracle had clearly failed them. Smoothly, Helios took a long drink from his wine glass. "I do not call it a gamble, when I am certain of the outcome." Daria came over to refill his glass. "But to come back to my original point, you do gamble, if not with your lives, then with the lives of others." Daxteros looked at him questioningly. In one quick movement, Helios stood and grabbed the girl by her arm, drew his dagger, and slit her throat. Her eyes stared widely as she grabbed at her bleeding neck and fell to the floor.

In the rush of the moment, Daxteros stood and tackled him to the floor. The sailor managed to wrench the dagger from him and stabbed Helios in his side. Helios was surprised when he did not feel anything. Instead, he just laughed. Stunned, the sailor stood and backed away.

Helios got to his feet and removed the dagger. Blood poured from the wound and he staunched it with his robes. There was still no pain.

"What in the name of Hades are you?" asked Daxteros, anger burning his face as he gazed from Helios to the girl. *He loved her,* he thought. That made the act all more worthwhile.

"You know exactly what I am," replied Helios. "The Oracle told you, but do know that Hades is not done with you yet." Helios raised a hand toward the two men and their eyes rolled back in their heads as they fell lifelessly to the ground.

Helios laughed again and used the dagger to cut a length of fabric from the girl's dress to wrap his wound. Hades would not let him die yet, he knew. Too much work remained. Too much was left uncertain. Looking at the three bodies on the floor, he felt sated and left to seek out Hera.

Delia finally stopped crying. In her heart she knew that she had done the right thing in telling the Diluvian Hades' plan, but she feared he would find out and exact his wrath up her. She also felt bad for keeping this secret from her brother Doros. The first he had heard about all of this was from the mouth of the Governess. Lovingly, he soothed anyway.

"You did not have a choice in your secrecy," he told her after her repeated apologies. "I only wish that I could spare you from his torment."

"No one can save me," she replied. "I am the Oracle. You cannot save me, only love me."

"Then love you, I shall."

"Persephone sent a Diluvian to save us," she said. "In the stories, the Diluvians faced the deluge, death, and damnation to save us all. Here I am worrying about Hades' wrath when Emily has already risked so much more."

"What are you saying?" asked Doros.

"Only that I hide behind this lie, when she is facing this on her own," replied Daria. "I should be standing beside her and helping her to stop this plot."

"But she told you to carry on as if nothing had happened," he said.

"I know what she said, Brother, but I cannot let her face Hera, Helios, and Hades on her own. They are too powerful."

"What are you going to do?" he asked.

"I am going to find her," she said. After washing her face of the tears, she set out toward the Governess' rooms with Doros by her side.

As they came toward the Lady Elise's chambers, she saw Hera leading the Governess around a corner.

"That cannot be good," she said softly to Doros. Luckily, Hera had not seen her.

"Sister, we really should go back," he said. "What will Hera and Helios do if they discover you helping Emily?"

"They have not banished me to my rooms," she replied. "I am allowed to go about the palace. Let us follow them." She heard Doros sigh, but he trailed along after her.

The two women walked slowly, just seeming to make polite conversation. Hera smiled and laughed often, which only made Delia hate her more. Where were they headed?

Without warning, the pair stopped. Delia and Doros hid behind a wall at the far end of the corridor. Suddenly there was some quick movement and a bright flash of light. When Delia's eyes focused, both women lay unconscious on the floor. Fearful for Emily, Delia made to run to them, but Doros caught her arm.

"No, we need to leave them," he told her.

"Let me go, Brother," she scolded. "I need to find out what happened."

Delia ran the length of the corridor to the bodies. Emily clutched the strange horn around her neck, its cork now missing, while Hera lay several feet away and face down.

"We cannot help them," said Doros.

"They are not dead," she told him, seeing their bodies move softly with their breath. "We could help end this." Moving over to Hera, Delia rolled her onto her back. "We could kill her." For once, Doros did not question her. Straddling Hera's body, she slipped her hands around the woman's neck and tightened. To her surprise, she felt immense joy in the task. Hera's body began to convulse, but Delia did not care.

Behind her, Doros made a loud grunt and she turned her head. Her grip loosened as she saw blood trickle from the dagger that pierced her brother's heart. Their eyes met for a moment before life left him.

"Doros!" she screamed running to him as he fell to the ground. Helios stepped forward as she hovered over his body.

"Did you really think betraying Hades would be that easy?" he asked. Before she could reply, his fist flashed across her face and all became dark.

CHAPTER IV
THE SUMMONING

As Ubaid made his way back to the Temple of Neith from the docks, he thought about the Crystal Bearer and her mission to speak with Poseidon. It felt strange that she would return to Saïs only to leave it just as quickly. Certainly it was not his duty to question the will of Gods, but he could not shake the feeling. The sun peaked above the tree line as he entered the Temple and went to his office. The shattered bowl was still in pieces on the floor and the water had already evaporated in the early heat. Soon Queen Nefruneith and all of Saïs would be up in arms over the absence of the prisoners and he knew that they would come to him. The jailer would make certain of that.

The priest decided to leave the bowl on the floor and left his office. Passing the shallow pool, he made his way to the far end of the Temple, passing lesser priests going about their duties, and finally to a small room where he closed the door behind him. A small glowing orb hung from a chain in the center of the room and he removed it from its hook.

On the floor in one corner he lifted a small latch in the stone and opened a hidden door in the floor. Dust swirled into the dim light and he made his way down the shallow steps that led to the chamber beneath. Only the he and the queen knew of its existence. *Down here is our most sacred treasure*, he thought.

The length of the Temple sprawled above him as he approached a door. Taking a horn-vial from his robes the priest uncorked it and splashed its contents on the door. The water shone bright for a moment and then absorbed into the door as it opened. Ubaid was still amazed that there was power in the water of the sacred lake. So very little of that power was seen anymore.

Pulling the door the rest of the way open, he entered the stuffy chamber. Descending three steps, the room stretched out in front of him. The priest found it odd that such a large room held only a single statue, but then again there was no greater treasure in the entire realm.

Holding the orb before him, he approached the likeness of the Goddess Neith. She was completely unadorned, save for a single necklace with a glowing crystal hanging from her neck. *The Saitian Crystal.*

"Gracious Neith," he began to pray, prostrating before her. "I do not know what darkness has emerged for the Crystal Bearer to return to our land, but I beseech your reason, for I will surely die this day for having set her free. If it is your will that my time upon this earth is at an end, my life is yours to take, but I pray for your wisdom and counsel."

The priest had prayed here many times before, never truly receiving an answer from Neith, though in the silence and darkness, knowledge and wisdom would sometimes be imparted. He stood from his prayer and looked upon the statue and to the crystal. Legend said that the Crystal Bearer left it behind when she parted from this land as a token of good faith. If she returned, why did she not ask for it? Certainly she knew more than he. Some even believed that the Crystal Bearer was Neith taken human form. *How else can she perform such miracles?*

Curious, he touched the crystal and to his surprise, it began to glow brighter. He frowned. It had never done that before. He touched it again and it grew brighter still. Suddenly the air grew cold and he shivered. The crystal lifted and hovered in front of the statue. He was frightened, but could not look away. Then with a flash, it disappeared.

Ubaid scarcely believed what he had seen. When his eyes adjusted to the dim light of the orb, he saw that the crystal had indeed vanished. "Gracious Neith protect us." If the queen were to discover the crystal was missing, death would be a welcomed punishment. With the Crystal Bearer gone, Nefruneith would assume that he had indeed given it to her.

As he backed away, the statue began to shudder and its surface began to ripple. The stone appeared to take a breath and suddenly Neith stood before him in the flesh. Beautiful, she glowed from within, her blue eyes piercing into everything she saw.

She stepped off of the statue's platform as he fell to his knees at her feet. "Grand Priest, rest your heart for I have come." He dared not speak or rise. His will was hers. "The time has come to summon the Crystal Bearer to this land."

That gave him pause. He did not know what he had expected her to say, but that was not it. When he finally found his voice, he said, "But she has already come and gone, your graciousness."

"*A* Crystal Bearer has come and gone, yes," she replied, "but there is new bearer. One more powerful. One more desperate."

"Another?" he asked.

"Yes," she replied. "Summon the queen, for her blood is key and perform the rites immediately. There is no time to lose. I fear that we may already be too late to halt what is coming."

"What is coming, gracious one?" he asked.

"A dark power threatens to cover the world," she replied. "Summon the Crystal Bearer, for she and only she can set the world to right. Do not delay, dear priest."

"I shall do as you command, your graciousness," he said. "But…" Before he could inquire further, Neith stepped back onto the platform and she was once again stone.

Ubaid's hands were still trembling as he emerged from the secret tunnel. As he walked past his fellow priests, they gave him odd looks. He brushed off their concern and went straight to his office and shut the door. *The shattered bowl is still here*, he thought. He could use this as proof of the Crystal Bearer's power and the need to let her go. Too bad she took the slave boy with her. His life would prove her power. But then how would he explain the need for *another* Crystal Bearer? The young queen already felt threatened by the mere idea of there being a Crystal Bearer during her reign. Such a person could undermine her authority. He knew that he should call for the monarch, but she would arrive soon enough without his summons. So he waited.

He did not know how long he waited. Sitting at his desk, he nodded off for several moments at a time. Having not slept the night before weighed on him. Finally, the door opened.

"Her grace, Nefruneith," called one of the temple guards, "and captain of her royal guard, Musa."

Ubaid did not move or speak as the queen glided confidently into his office followed by her protector. Though he did not meet her gaze, he knew that she glared at him.

"What shall be done with you?" she asked him. He did not respond.

"Your queen addresses you, Priest," said Musa from behind her. Ubaid met his gaze, but still did not reply. "Did the terrorists take your tongue when you set them free?" He looked down at his folded hands and took a deep breath.

"I do not presume to defend my actions," he said finally. "You ask why they are gone. That is why." He pointed to the shattered bowl. "She did that. The one who called herself the Crystal Bearer. She harnessed the power of Neith, broke the bowl, and then brought a slave boy back to life."

"Did she now?" asked Nefruneith. "Why was she here to do so without my leave, Ubaid? Do you forget who it is you serve?"

"I serve her graciousness, Neith," he replied.

"You serve me!" she said. "I am the Daughter of the Flood! I was placed before the crown to rule Neith's people and that includes you."

"I humbly serve you, my queen, but there is still one whose authority is more supreme," he said softly. "The girl who broke that bowl was sent to us from Neith on a divine quest. I shall accept all consequences for my actions, even death if you would have it be so, but know that I acted only as I was governed to do. You failed to see, my queen, that the girl and the one that you still hold are Diluvians."

"Diluvians?" asked Musa. "What Diluvians?"

"The people of the flood," replied Ubaid. "You are familiar with the flood lore? The strangers that came to God-king Aha during the deluge to ensure the survival of Saïs were called the Diluvians. Now Neith has returned them to our world to once again save us from peril. If the lore is to be believed, we owe our very existence to them."

"Those are just fables," said Musa.

"They are not, Captain," he replied, "and she was the Crystal Bearer, she who I helped to leave."

"*Was* the Crystal Bearer?" asked Nefruneith. "Has she lost the privilege?"

"She still wields Neith's great power, but she is not the only one who can," he said. He told them about his visit to the hidden chamber and Neith's commands. "There is another who we must summon. Do what you will with me, my queen, but by the command of she who gave you that crown, we must call forth the new Crystal Bearer."

"The crystal vanished, you say?" asked Musa. "Are you certain you did not give it to this *Emily* before you set her free?"

"I would not give away such a treasure," he said standing. "Call me liar if you will, but there is work to be done. My queen, your blood is needed for the ritual. Walk with me to the sacred pool and I will tell you what must be done." Ubaid was surprised when she acquiesced. Musa followed behind, scowling the whole way.

Ubaid called for his priests to bring the sacred elements: a bowl of water from the sacred lake, a bowl of burning oil, a bowl of soil with a flower, and burning incense. Each was placed at one corner of the rectangular shallow pool. For the ritual, Ubaid had Nefruneith don one of the plain white linen dresses of the priestesses. As she stepped into the shin-deep water, he handed her a knife. She looked from the knife to Musa and back to the priest again.

"Am I to maim myself in your scheme, priest?" she asked. Musa puffed his chest as if to intimidate.

"Hardly, my queen," he assured her. "We only need a few drops of your blood. Now stay there and chant as I do. When the time comes, you need only reach into the water and pull up what you find there." She looked back at him anxiously. It wasn't often that the young queen showed fear.

"If this does not work, Ubaid…" she said.

"I assure you, it will," he said. *Neith, I pray, let this work.*

At Ubaid's instruction, she knelt in the pool and other priests formed around to support the rite. Musa stood off to the side, ready to jump in the moment the queen was in danger.

"Sacred alchemy of the universe," he called out, "and the forces of earth, fire, water, and air; gracious Neith we call upon the Crystal Bearer, for our world has need of her salvation. Bring forth she who shall do your will." The sacred water shone bright and the smoke from the incense came to settle around Ubaid's and Nefruneith's heads. "Chant with me, my queen." She nodded. "SA-HA, SA-HA,

SA-HA, SA-HA…"

As they continued the other priests joined in and they began to convulse as the sound overtook them. The scent of the incense grew heavy. The flower withered. The fire flared.

"SA-HA, SA-HA, SA-HA…"

Their senses and the elements melded as the air became heavy. The time was near.

"Goddess Neith," he cried out as they continued, "combine the elements with the sacred blood and bring forth your Crystal Bearer." He looked to the queen. "Now, Nefruneith!"

She hesitated for only a moment then sliced her palm. The blood steamed and trickled down into the pool. The moment it touched the water, the clay bowls shattered and the water boiled. A figure appeared beneath the surface. "Reach for her, my queen!" Nefruneith lunged into the water and pulled up not one, but two screaming bodies.

"Ahh!" one cried out. The chanting settled and Ubaid saw a woman holding a child, both now held by the queen. The woman had been the one to cry out.

"Lord, what in the hell was that?" she yelled, pushing the queen away and holding the child close to her. She seemed to take stock of her surroundings. "Get away from me! Get away!" The child squirmed, but the woman only held her closer. "What happened? Who are you? WHO are you!"

The queen, surprised the ritual had worked, regained her composure. "I am Nefruneith, Queen of Saïs. Welcome, Crystal Bearer."

They sat in a small dusty room with a single window that appeared to be the old man's office. They called this building the Temple of Neith. Kimberly held Allie on her lap, not letting her out of arm's reach for a single moment until she knew who these crazy people were. "The queen," as she called herself, lounged on a cushion, while her muscly bodyguard stood sentinel by the door. *Where would I even run to?* she thought. Kimberly hardly knew where she was outside of this temple, and judging by this god-awful heat it was in a desert. Even with her years in Egypt, this was still too hot. As if sensing her discomfort, a servant brought her a clay cup with cool water. She remembered the Temple of Neith at the Sa-el Hagar site. Was this the same one?

"I told you, I don't know what a 'Crystal Bearer' is," Kimberly told them. "We were just told to find the crystal and wait, then this morning the thing came to life and went crazy and here we are." She held Allie closer, causing her to squirm.

"Ubaid, you said there was only one other Crystal Bearer," said the girl queen. "Surely, they both cannot be it. What would the world do with three Crystal Bearers?"

"My queen, Neith was hardly specific," said the man called Ubaid. "She only said that this one would be more powerful and desperate."

"Desperate?" asked the queen. "Desperate for what?"

"I do not know, your grace," he replied.

The queen turned to Kimberly. "Are you desperate?"

Desperate to kick you in the face. "Not that I am aware of," she answered. "But I am wondering what we are doing here."

"I had a similar query," said the queen.

"What do you mean…?" asked Ubaid.

"Kimberly," she replied. "My name is Kimberly, and this is Allie. We were told by Alexia, or I guess you call her Neith, that our friends were in trouble and this crystal would help us save them. But I'm not sure why we are here in this stuffy room in the middle of the desert. Our friends were supposed to go to the Underworld. I figured whatever this crystal did that it would lead us there, not here."

"Are you so certain you are not in the Underworld?" mocked the queen.

"Look, I don't know you and I already don't like you," said Kimberly. "From what I can tell, we were just pulled from another world into this one. Not to mention we were stark naked and screaming." Kimberly took a moment to be grateful they'd given her and Allie the white linen dresses to cover up.

"Not so different than birth, one might say," said Ubaid. "You are *not* in the Underworld, Kimberly. Of that I can assure you."

"I knew that already," she replied. "I've seen Hades and none of you look like him, though it is hot as hell in here." That made the queen laugh. *Oh good, I thought she was frozen.* "And to set the record straight, I'm not this Crystal Bearer you keep going on about. If it's either of us, it's Allie."

"She said I was the key," said Allie. Kimberly smoothed her hair.

"You say you've spoken with Neith," asked Ubaid.

"Yes," Kimberly replied. "She came to both of us in dreams and told us both to find the crystal to save our friends." The queen laughed again, but Kimberly repressed her frustration. "Don't believe me if you want. I won't lose sleep over it, but if you say this is the Temple of Neith, then I'll tell you there's a secret chamber underneath us where you keep the crystal. That is if there's only one. I guess we have it now." She held out the crystal hanging around Allie's neck.

Ubaid looked startled and the queen frowned.

"No one knows of that chamber, aside from us three here," said Ubaid.

"She knows too much for a foreigner," said the queen.

"Do I?" asked Kimberly. "Then help me figure out what I'm supposed to do here and I'll be out of your hair as fast as I can. Trust me, I have no desire to be stuck in here with you."

"You will show more respect to the queen," said the bodyguard.

"She's not my queen, and I was raised to respect those who respect me," said Kimberly. "And I'm not going to even mention she's half my age. What are you, sweetie, 16?"

"That's enough," said the queen. "Musa, do not begrudge our guests. They do not know what they say and as our priest will attest, they are sent by Neith. We can forgive them their trespasses and insolences. But, Kimberly, I agree that you need to begin whatever it is Neith sent you here to do. So let us continue to riddle that out, shall we? Dear priest, please continue."

"Yes, my queen. From your attestations, the child is the Crystal Bearer," said Ubaid. "But then who are you, my dear?"

"Neith called me the 'guardian'," replied Kimberly, "and she charged me with looking out for Allie."

"I see," he said. "I do not know any lore of a 'guardian' but surely your presence is necessary. Tell me more of your friends that you have been sent to save."

Where do I even begin? "Well, there are five of them," began Kimberly. "Two of them left first. Sean and Erin Henry are Allie's parents and they sacrificed themselves to Hades to save her life." *I can't believe I'm saying this. This sounds so crazy.* "Sean's brother didn't like that, so he and his wife, along with one of my friends, went after them to steal them back. That's when all of this crystal stuff started happening."

"Ubaid, why do those names sound familiar?" asked the queen.

"I think I know, my queen," said the priest. "Kimberly, what are the names of the three who followed?"

"Sean's brother is Pete and his wife is Emily," she replied. "And my friend who went with them is Michael Turner. Why?"

"Oh dear," said the priest. The queen looked shocked as well, switching her stare between her bodyguard and the priest.

"What's going on?" asked Kimberly. "Do you know where they are? Are they here?"

"Not exactly," said the queen. She rose from her cushion and knelt before Kimberly and Allie. She looked about to cry. "I fear that Emily and Michael have already left. You see, they arrived just yesterday needing to leave for Attica at once. Our dear priest Ubaid hurried them along on their quest."

"They're alive?" asked Kimberly. "Oh, thank god!" She sighed in relief.

"The other…" began Ubaid.

"The other never showed," the queen said quickly. "They mourned for him when they arrived, but he never made it out of the Underworld, I fear."

"What happened to Uncle Pete?" asked Allie.

"I do not know, little one," replied the queen. "They did not say." Allie began to cry.

Kimberly held her close, not knowing how to feel. At least the child had one family member left. "We need to follow them," she said.

"Follow them?" asked the queen wide-eyed.

"Yes, follow them," she said. "You might not like me, I can tell, but this little girl needs her family. If she's this Crystal Bearer you keep talking about, then you have to help her."

"But…"

"Nope," said Kimberly interrupting. "She'll call Neith down on you and you don't want that. I didn't want that, but she put her hand on my head and knocked me out."

"My queen, surely it would be best to send these pilgrims on their way," said the bodyguard.

"Well then," said the queen, now standing. "Captain, we have a voyage to plan. Ubaid, I trust you can keep our guests comfortable until we are able to leave. We should have the royal ships ready for sail by first light."

"As you say, your grace," replied the priest.

Nefruneith and Musa returned to the palace with their tails

between their legs. The Queen of Saïs felt too ashamed to admit to the Heralds that she had their kin beaten and imprisoned. Even now, one was hanging by his wrists in the palace courtyard.

"What are we to do with him?" she asked Musa.

"He is kin to the Crystal Bearer," he replied, "and one of the Diluvians."

"I know!" she yelled as they walked through the palace. "The little girl will bring down the wrath of Neith upon us if she discovers our actions."

"We could just dispose of him," said Musa. "We will hide his body in a tomb and continue our story that he never arrived with the others. Ubaid knows better than to mention him. Not after you cut him off."

Nefruneith stopped, to think. Could they keep Pete a secret? They had to get the crystal bearer out of Saïs as quickly as possible. "As you say, Captain," she replied. "I will make all arrangements for the ships to be ready by morning. Make certain his body is gone."

"Yes, my queen," he said, taking his leave.

"I beg you to forgive Nefruneith's temperament," said the priest once the queen and her bodyguard had left. "You were correct in naming her young, and with youth come certain scruples. With any luck, age will sort her out."

"I'm afraid I lost my temper too," admitted Kimberly.

"Have no fear," he replied. "The day has been long and night comes on swift wings. Follow me, if you will, to your sleeping chambers for tonight. Our accommodations are modest at best, for we are humble priests."

"Thank you for your help," said Kimberly, standing and leading Allie with her. They walked down a corridor; the sun was about to set outside. "Did Emily and Michael really not say what happened to Pete? Pete and Emily were married. She'd be devastated if anything happened to him."

"I fear they did not," he replied. "But then again, they were here for less than a day."

Kimberly didn't know whether to believe the man or not, but he had been amiable enough so far. They entered a small chamber with two beds and she laid Allie down to sleep.

"Before I leave you to rest, Kimberly, might I have a word?" asked Ubaid.

"Not here," she replied looking back at Allie. "She needs to rest." Kimberly stepped out into the hall and closed the door.

"Did her holiness happen to mention from what you must save your friends?" he asked.

"No, she didn't," replied Kimberly. "She only said that they are in danger and will be lost without us."

"Gods often speak in riddles," said the priest. He made to speak, but then hesitated for a moment. "We shall depart as quickly as we can and help save your companions."

"Thank you, Ubaid."

The priest gave a weak smile and walked away.

Ubaid crossed to the center of the lake as quickly as his arms could take him. There had been no time to summon a slave to do the rowing, and he could not afford anyone to know of his leaving. The glow of the lake, which usually filled him with a sense of wonder, now shone ominously. The power of Neith bubbling to the surface to soon cast her wrath upon them.

He didn't bother pulling the boat onto shore and ran into the palace, making his way toward the courtyard. As he approached, he heard screaming and ran faster. Entering the clearing, he had just enough time to yell "STOP!" as Musa drew his dagger across Pete's throat.

"Gracious Neith, protect us all," said the priest as Pete's body fell to the floor. "What have you done? You have doomed us all!"

"Only if you tell the girl what has happened, priest," said the captain.

Ubaid knelt and held his hand over the gash in Pete's throat, blood pooling around him. "The Crystal Bearer, she can save him! I've seen it before with the slave boy. You must send for the child at once. This can still be undone!"

"This had to be done, Ubaid," said the captain. "She would unleash Neith upon us if she knew how we tortured him!"

"Do not argue, there is little time," said the priest. "He is slipping away." Pete looked at him, his body convulsing, causing blood to pour faster from his wound. "No, no, no!" Pete's body stopped moving and his eyes became void. "Gracious Neith, forgive us sinners. We know not what we have done."

The world seemed surreal to Kimberly as three ships sailed up the river. Less than a day ago, she had been within reach of a good cup of coffee and now she was on a boat in a long lost world heading to save Michael and the others from god knows what. In such chaos, the gentle breeze and rising sun was almost comical. Almost.

The priest had woken them before dawn, looking distressed as ever and hurried them down to the docks where the queen and her head goon waited. Nefruneith greeted them hastily and boarded her ship. Kimberly and Allie, the priest told her, were to sail in an adjoining ship, and the priest sailed in the third. The sun began to peek above tree line as they set sail.

Kimberly still held the child close to her. Pete had not made it out of the Underworld and who knew the fate of Sean and Erin. All Allie had left was Emily. *If we fail to save her,* she thought, *I will have to be the child's guardian.* The thought struck a chord as she remembered Neith's words. *I am her guardian.*

Book V:
The Contest

GERALD M. GIVENS

CHAPTER I
LOOSE ENDS

Taking a deep breath, she opened her eyes. Her head felt like it was split open and the light coming through the windows cut at her brain like a razor. Closing her eyes for solace, she tried to recall her dream. As the first few fragments pieced themselves together, she remembered it being as lucid as it was crazy.

She had been back in Athens, or Attica as they had called it. Though she had clearly been herself, she also hadn't been herself. Her name had been Hera and she was an advisor to the Attican king, but also a spy for Hades. The mere thought was completely ridiculous, but it had felt so real. She had a husband too, a relatively handsome man named Helios, who was a fellow spy. Part of their plan had been to use the Oracle of Delphi to convince the king to name Hades patron God of Attica, but that of course was just silly. No king would ever let a monster like that claim patronage of his people.

Again, it felt so real. The last part came back to her slowly. There had been something about a governess, from the island of Carmour. She had never heard of the island, but in the dream she knew it well. The governess had been a fake, she knew from the start, but she was playing her as well. She called herself Lady Elise, but Hera knew her as someone else. Someone important. In the dream, Hera led Elise down a corridor in the royal palace when something went wrong. Hera leapt for Elise, but a flash of light erupted from her necklace.

The last image she recalled was... Emily.

Erin quickly sat up. As she opened her eyes, the world in front of her came into view. She was in a lavish bedchamber, surrounded by golden silk curtains, ornate rugs, and the scent of incense in the air. This was not New York. This was not even her world.

"Where's my daughter?" she said aloud to no one. "Where's my husband?"

Standing, she crossed the room and went to the window. In the distance, there were mountains and hills, all lush and green. Beneath her window sprawled a giant city full of people, noise, and clamor. This was Attica, she knew.

"But if this is Attica, then..." she said as the events of the past month solidified in her mind. What was she doing? What had she done? Panic filled her. And Emily... Emily was here in Attica, but why? "And if she's here, where's Allie?" She prayed her child was at home in New York with her aunt and uncle, but something deep within her told her that was not the case. She had to find Emily.

Erin hoped against hope that whatever that light was hadn't killed her sister. Searching through Hera's memory, she remembered where the Governess of Carmour was staying in the palace, in one of the western towers. It was a longshot, but she might be there. She turned away from the window and made to leave the bedchamber and walked past a mirror and stopped dead. *Who the hell is that?* Erin was a proud brunette with dark eyes, but this woman in the mirror had curly blond hair and deep green eyes. She was also taller and paler. *This isn't right.* She touched her face, or that of the woman whose body she now occupied. "Damn you, Hades."

Erin opened the doors the bedchamber to a large sitting room, and in the center were three men. The man called Helios, surprisingly Michael Turner, and a sailor who Hera's memory named Daxteros. They were in the King's tower for some reason.

"Ah, Hera dear," said Helios rising from his seat and making his way over to her. "It is time that you were awake. We have work to do. I had feared that little bitch had knocked you out for good. Tell me what happened?"

Erin's stomach clenched. She knew that he was actually Sean, but she couldn't tell him that. He wasn't himself and he might kill her. She had to save Emily. He couldn't tell that she was somehow not under Hades' spell. She'd have to act. "Um... We had a little scuffle, and she struck me, but not before I could land a blow on her," she said, surprised how convincing she was. "Tell me, what became of our dear Governess?"

"You need not worry about her," said Helios with a smile. "Michael and Daxteros locked her and the Oracle in Thebos' Chambers. With their joined strength, the Great Lord will have use for them. He has not yet given us leave to dispose of them." Erin remembered that Thebos' Chambers was actually the jail tower, the name being a final jab at the former steward of Athens who had turned his people against Olympus.

She understood that Michael and Daxteros too must be under Hades' influence. Why had Michael come?

"The Oracle?" she asked. "Why was she detained?"

"I came upon our dear little Delia attempting to strangle you," he replied. "And had I been moments later, she would have succeeded. I killed her brother for her trespasses."

"Killed him?" she asked, in spite of herself. *No Sean, please God, not again.*

"A means to an end, my dear," he replied. "And speaking of ends, we need to move. The Oracle's disappearance will soon be noted and we have one more stop to make before heading to the games. The contest will begin quite soon."

"Of course, Husband," she replied, trying not to cry. "To where must we go next? I would like to visit Emily... I mean the Governess?" Erin scolded herself for her slip.

"Time is against us, my dear wife," he replied. "What do you want with her now?"

"To repay her in kind for my splitting headache," she replied. "I do not see why I should suffer alone."

"Alas, that is not the Lord's will," replied Helios. "You are not yourself, dear. This is Hades' vengeance, not ours."

"Indeed, Husband," she said, regaining some of her composure. "My headache clouds my judgment, it seems. Shall we go?"

Walking beside Helios, Erin's mind ran fast. She had to find Emily. She had to save the Oracle. Worst of all, she felt compelled to stop whatever events Hades was planning in his takeover. If she was lucky, she'd be able to save her husband as well. Seeing him as Helios made her stomach turn. *This isn't Sean,* she thought. *This is a monster.* She'd even save Michael Turner. No one deserved that fate.

Helios' course told her they were heading to the Oracle's chambers, but why? The Oracle was imprisoned in the jail tower.

Michael and Daxteros stalked close behind them. There would be nowhere to run, even if she could.

"Husband, what business do we have in the Oracle's chambers?" she asked.

"Loose ends, my dear," he replied. "Loose ends."

Moments later, they arrived at the chamber doors and knocked. An old man wearing robes of the priests of Apollo opened the door, looking oddly relieved at their arrival.

"Helios and Hera," he said. "Thank Apollo, you are here. The Oracle and her shadow have gone missing. Helena and I were just on our way to find you. The entire palace must help in our search, as she truly is our realm's most sacred jewel."

They entered and the old man continued talking about the Oracle's importance. Within, an elder woman, a priestess of Apollo, stood by the window looking concerned. Erin knew that Helena was taking the Oracle's disappearance very personally, as one of her guardians. She felt bad for the woman.

"Strange, it is, that she would stray, dear Delphinios," said Helios. "The contest approaches and her presence here is as important as ever. Tell me, priest, when was the last time you saw our sweet Delia?"

"She had a meeting with some Governess, and then went for a walk," he replied. "But that was early this morning. She was supposed to meet with the king today."

"Indeed, and his highness does not like to be kept waiting," replied Helios. "But I am afraid he will have to."

"I do not quite understand your meaning, Counselor?" asked the old man. Flustered as he was, he didn't notice Michael and Daxteros spreading out in the room.

"I am afraid I have some news, dear priest," he replied. "Please, both of you have a seat." He motioned to the couches in the center of the room. Nervously, Delphinios and Helena sat down, while Erin and Helios came to stand in front of them. Erin was just as nervous, her breath becoming shallow. What was his plan?

"What news do you have, Counselor?" asked the priest in a demanding tone. "Do not waste our time. The Gods do not suffer the weary." Michael and Daxteros came to stand behind the couch. Erin's breath stopped.

"Time will not be an issue for either of you any longer," he replied. "Give our regards to Doros." Simultaneously, Michael and

Daxteros pulled daggers and drew their blades across Delphinios' and Helena's throats.

"NO, SEAN DON'T!" screamed Erin, lunging toward the dying pair. Their eyes were big as they gasped, drowning in their own blood. Unable to save them, Erin felt helpless. Seconds or eternity had passed when they ceased moving. Erin sobbed, becoming covered in their blood. "Why is he doing this?" she whispered. "What have we done?"

"You are a clever woman, Erin Henry," said Helios, standing nonchalantly behind her. He didn't even blink when she called him Sean. "What better punishment for those who have sinned against him, then to aid him in his vengeance. Tartarus is not just a place, no. Tartarus is suffering. We will always know what we have done, and we will always regret it." Helios spoke as if this truth didn't bother him.

"God damn it, do you even know who you are?" she asked him. "Not this body that Hades has given you to wear as a mask, but who you *really* are underneath. You are a good man that wanted nothing more than to love me. You never wanted to hurt anyone." She stood to look him in the eye. "And yes, we have suffered for it. A kiss sent us to Atlantis and we suffered. Our survival there and our love for one another sent us back to the flood and we suffered. And to save our only child, we sacrificed ourselves to the selfish whims of a dark god and we still suffer." Helios' stood stoic, giving her chills. "Worst of all, we are causing the suffering of others. What is this all for? How much more must we endure before fate is satisfied?"

"This is who we are now, Erin," he replied. "I am whatever I am needed to be. My soul is property of Hades and who I was before our sacrifice means nothing. We have no identity. We live only to serve, and we die only to serve."

Erin slapped him hard across his face. "But I came back," she said, tears returning to her eyes. "I don't know how, but I came back. Let me help save you, Sean." She placed a hand on his cheek and he swiped it away.

"Yes, that bothers me," he replied, growing angry. "Hades will not be pleased by this."

"We can stop him, Sean," she said. "Together."

"We cannot," he replied, "and we will not. Vengeance is his." Before she could stop him, Helios took her head between his hands and chill ran through her. When she opened her eyes, she felt a wave of calmness and pleasure. She smiled.

"What are we standing around for?" asked Hera, looking at the blood pooling around her. "I must change out of this bloody dress and we must summon the king. The Great Lord approaches and the games are about to begin."

CHAPTER II
THE BOY FROM SAÏS

The trip from Saïs to Attica was uneventful and took barely a week, much to Kimberly's surprise. From an age where one could cross oceans in mere hours, the thought of sailing a ship across a sea seemed like it would take decades. When asked, Ubaid said that the winds were in their favor, a good omen. She didn't know anything about omens, but she was happy to get off the ship and feel solid ground beneath her feet once again.

Kimberly was glad to have been rid of the snotty girl-queen during the voyage. Their first encounter had left a bad taste in her mouth and she didn't wish to repeat it. As young and foolish as the queen was, Kimberly knew that Nefruneith had the power to imprison and kill her, and she wasn't sure she had the capacity to hold her tongue through another interview.

She also thought it nice to be away from the priest, Ubaid. Nice as he was, he would have only asked her more questions she didn't know the answers to, or worse yet questions she didn't want to answer. Kimberly had learned years ago to not confide information until you knew who your friends were and who were your enemies. Especially in this world, everyone would have an end game. She refused to play the pawn.

She and Allie had been treated like royalty on their ship. The captain and crew looked to them with both reverence and apprehension. Reverence that Allie was the Crystal Bearer and she her guardian. Their every need had been met. Apprehension because they truly feared the girl. The child was strange, Kimberly agreed, but there was no need to be afraid.

Landing in a bustling port town that priest called Piraeus, there were so many ships in the harbor and anchored off shore that Kimberly couldn't even try to count them all. Allie was excited when she saw all of the ships and did try to count them, but she ran out of numbers long before she reached the sum. Kimberly helped her along, but her attention was soon taken away as they reached the docks.

The dock masters at Piraeus had not expected the Queen of Saïs to arrive, so they received many odd glances and sometimes glares as they came ashore. Nefruneith had brought many of her house slaves, most of which were now loading their shoulders with food, supplies, and the queen's belongings. Others were preparing a giant litter that would take them to the capital.

The priest now stood beside her and Allie as they waited.

"How far is it to the capital?" asked Kimberly.

"Hardly a day's march, Guardian," he replied. "If we leave within the hour, we will arrive near sunset."

Hardly a day's march to the capital and hardly a day's march to Michael and Emily. Kimberly felt a wave of relief that they were so close. Allie, too, seemed excited.

"Your auntie Emily will be there," Kimberly assured her. Allie beamed with excitement.

Kimberly then had a thought, recalling what Alexia had said. Michael and Emily were in danger, but danger from what? Though she loathed the girl-queen, she suddenly felt safe that she had the Saitians' protection. Who could tell what would await them at the king's palace.

A short time later, they were called over to Nefruneith and her guard. The litter was the size of a small bedroom and a dozen strong slaves surrounded, ready to carry them away. She tried to ignore the blatant disrespect for her fellow humans, as she just wanted to get this all over as soon as possible. It was with slight trepidation that she climbed into the litter with Nefruneith and Ubaid.

To her relief, the girl queen didn't talk much. In fact she tried not to make eye contact and sulked. She didn't want to be there either. The priest, on the other hand, became extremely long winded.

"…I find it interesting that Neith would prescribe a guardian to one who has the ability to wield her power…" he droned. Kimberly tried to appear disinterested, but the priest ignored her social cues and carried on. "…one would believe that Neith herself would play guardian to her heralds. Would she truly allow any harm to come to her?"

The short voyage from Piraeus to the capital somehow seemed more tedious than the trip from Saïs, now being in the company of the priest. At least the queen had sense enough to not talk to her.

Lying in the nook of her arm, Allie fell asleep shortly after they left. The swaying of the litter did have a lulling effect, and she too began to feel tired. But the droning priest insisted on impeding the silence. Kimberly was relieved when the city finally came into view, across a large valley, built atop a large hill and its surround area.

"…it is sometimes spoken of in our histories that the Crystal Bearer is actually an incarnation of Neith taken flesh. With recent events, I will disagree, but the idea does bear reflection, especially if you see the happenstance of their names. The child is named Alexia, as is Neith by the Atticans. I do not believe in such coincidences."

"Their names are just a coincidence," said Kimberly, finally giving into his banter. "Emily was the first Crystal Bearer, and her name has no relationship to Neith's."

"I see your point, but…"

A loud horn sounded from the city, cutting off the priest.

"What is happening?" she asked, leaning out of the litter to better see the city.

"The contest is about to begin," he replied, looking a little uncertain.

"What does that mean for us?"

"Only that we shall have a sparse welcoming," he replied. "Most everyone will surely be at the contest site."

Soon the large city loomed before them as Musa talked to the gatekeeper and they entered the city. The capital seemed deserted, the population all amassed at the acropolis. Ubaid had resumed his diatribe when a second horn sounded.

"And so it starts," he said, finally falling into a welcomed silence.

The king's palace, referred to as Attella's Crown by the priest, was a magnificent structure of towers and bridges. *If Michael and Emily are still alive, they'll be in there,* she thought.

As Ubaid foretold, the palace was almost deserted when they

arrived. Despite the clear reason why, Nefruneith still seemed insulted by the improper welcome. After waiting several long minutes for entry, Musa came up to the litter.

"What news, Captain?" asked the queen.

"They are opening the gates for us now, but everyone is at the contest," he replied. "But there's something else that the guard was hesitant to mention."

"And what is that?"

"The Oracle of Delphi went missing this morning," he replied. "Apparently the whole kingdom is in an uproar over her disappearance. Some citizens want the games postponed until she's found."

"The silly little thing probably got lost in this oversized monstrosity of a palace," she replied. "Why could not the Atticans maintain the humble statures of the Saitian architects?"

"She is not the only one to go missing," continued Musa. "A Governess from one of the outer islands went missing at the same time. Guards who are not at the games are searching the palace and city for them both."

"Well that has little to do with us," she replied. "The guards know we are here to pay homage to today's victor. We have no time to idle on missing prophets. The gates are open, Captain. Bring us in."

Once inside, the palace gates closed behind them.

"An emissary of his grace will be with you momentarily," said a guard.

"I do not wish to speak with an emissary," replied Nefruneith. "I am a queen and I shall speak with your king."

"Apologies, your grace," said a man walking toward the entourage. His voice made Kimberly jump. "King Cecrops is detained as the Gods will wait for no man, but he wishes your company hastily at the contest. It has only just begun. I am to first show you to your rooms, so that you may refresh from your journey."

"As you say…" replied the queen, stopping in mid sentence. Kimberly too was in shock as she saw the man they called emissary. "You!"

Kimberly made her way to the front of the procession, dragging Allie with her. "Michael?" she said. "Michael, thank god!" She pushed past Nefruneith and embraced her former partner. "I was afraid you were dead. This place is dangerous." She was taken aback when he forced her away from him.

"Apologies, madam, but I do not believe we have met," he said. "Good fortune you find the man you seek."

"What are you talking about, Michael, it's me, Kimberly," she said. He only gazed back at her blankly and then she saw it. Nothing. There was no light in his eyes, as if he were completely hollow. A zombie carrying out orders. "What have they done to you?"

"Your majesty, please follow me," he said, turning away from her.

The queen only hesitated for a moment before following him, Musa at her side.

Kimberly was dumbfounded and unable to move. Michael's disregard hurt more than she could say. *What was I expecting?* she thought as the Saitians moved past her. She rode in on three golden ships to save him and be hero, but now she felt foolish. "What have they done to you?" she asked to no one.

Kimberly snapped out of her trance when Allie pulled her arm. Looking around, all of the Saitians had departed and only a couple of guards were left.

"We have to find Aunt Emily, Miss Kimberly," said Allie.

"I'm not sure who she'll be when we do, sweetie," she replied. "But you're right."

They headed in the direction Michael had led the group, catching sight of the tail end of the procession. Trying to rush to keep up, Kimberly suddenly noticed that Allie wasn't with her. Panic filled her as she spun around to find the girl running in the opposite direction.

"Allie!" she called and headed back the way they came. Rounding a corner, she almost ran the girl over. Allie had stopped in front of a small alcove that held a fire bowl, which lit the corridor. "Allie, what in god's name are you doing?"

"Come out," she said to someone else. "We won't hurt you, I promise."

Kimberly looked closer and saw a small boy cowering behind the stone platform. "Oh my," she said. "Are you hurt?" she asked him. He didn't move.

"Allie, we don't want to get lost," she said. "Let's go find the group. This boy will have to find his own way."

"But he's from Saïs," replied Allie. "Look at his clothes."

"I don't remember him being with us," she said.

"He wasn't, Miss Kimberly. He was here already." Allie squeezed herself between the stone platform and wall to where the boy hid.

"Are you from Saïs?"

"I was… I mean I am," he replied timidly. "The priest of Neith, Ubaid, he was with you?"

"Yes, he's our friend," she replied. Kimberly had thought the man friendly, but never her friend.

"Please do not tell him I am here," he replied. "He will take me back to the Temple and I will be a slave again. The Crystal Bearer freed me, but now she may be dead. I cannot go back."

"But I'm the Crystal Bearer," said Allie. "See!" She showed him the crystal.

"That cannot be. The Crystal Bearer is older, with hay-colored hair."

"That's Aunt Emily," replied Allie excited. "You've seen her? Do you know where she is?"

"They locked her away in the jail tower, but I do not know if she lives," he said. "She was not awake when they put her in there."

Kimberly had a bad feeling about this. She called to the boy. "Who are *they*?"

"The king's advisors," he said. Allie took him by the hand and led him out of the alcove.

Kimberly knelt down in front of him. "Did the king do this to her?"

"No, just his advisors," he replied. "They were sent by Hades. The king does not know of their actions."

"I see," she said. They would have to move quickly. "What's your name?"

"I am Xho, a free man," he replied, adding pride to his freedom.

"Xho, I'm Kimberly and this is Allie. We were sent here by Neith to find Emily, the Crystal Bearer. If you take her to us, we promise that Ubaid will never take you back to the Temple. I promise you."

"Do you come from the same place as her?" he asked, referring to Emily.

"Yes," she said. "The priest summoned us from our world to yours."

"You are heralds?"

"That is one way of putting it," she replied. "Please, Xho, take us to this tower."

"I will," he said. "Follow me." The boy ran off.

CHAPTER III
ARRIVAL

Hera and Helios joined the king in the large amphitheater next to the palace that had been built into the side of the acropolis hill just for this occasion. Resembling a theater, there was special seating near the center dais for royalty, nobles, and other persons of importance. Dignitaries from far beyond the realm were present and honor demanded that they have a decent view of the deities. Front and center, King Cecrops sat on an ornate gold-plated throne with a sunburst carved into its back behind his head.

Smiling as she approached the king, Hera took her seat on a bench to his left, Helios taking his seat on Cecrops' right. The cronies that Helios had picked up from the Crystal Bearer, Daxteros and Michael, stood close. Hades would have use for them when he arrived. For the first time in her memory, Hera felt anxious. The moment was near. The Dark Lord drew close. If she closed her eyes, she could feel his presence approaching and she breathed in his might.

"It is almost time," she said excitedly to the king.

"Indeed, it is, Hera," he said. "Might I say that you and your husband have done a magnificent job organizing this sacred event. I only worry what has become of our dear Oracle. Has there really been no sight of her?"

"I fear not, your highness," she replied. "Sacred as she may be, the Oracle is still a child. I cannot imagine the pressure for her to

173

have to be present for this contest. So many citizens look to her for wisdom and counsel. Indeed, some say that her view of the events here today would sway your judgment, your highness."

"Yes, that is terribly unfortunate for her," he replied. "Too much responsibility for one so young. Her counselors are missing as well, then?"

"Not at all, your highness," replied Hera. "As her keepers, Delphinios and Helena are searching high and low for our lost prophet."

"I shall see them when they return," replied the king.

"As you say, your highness," she said. Hera found it empowering that she could influence the king so easily. Her intention upon arriving in this land had been to place the king under Hades' great influence, but that proved to be unnecessary. Cecrops was weak of mind and a simple suggestion would steer him where she needed him to go. Hades had been pleased thus far.

"Your grace," announced a page boy, who seemed to have appeared out of nowhere.

"You may speak," said Helios, answering for the king.

"Your grace, her majesty, Queen Nefruneith of Saïs approaches from Piraeus with a household contingent," he replied, eyes trained on the ground.

"Could the girl-queen have worse timing?" replied Helios. He always was quick to anger. Hera just smiled.

"Do not bother with her majesty, your highness," said Hera. "I will send an emissary in your stead. Gods do take precedence over us mortals."

"Indeed, as you say, Hera," replied the king.

"Michael, see that the Saitian Queen is shown our hospitality and bring her here once she has settled into her rooms," she said, summoning him over. He was the weaker of the two and, should a riot ensue upon the lord's arrival, he would only get himself killed. Better that he serve as an ambassador. "And do press the urgency of her presence. The Gods do not suffer the weary."

Michael bowed and then walked away. She felt a twinge of concern at the queen's sudden arrival, but she quelled any uneasiness. The show, as it were, was about to begin.

The feeling of Hades' arrival became overwhelming and something deep within her knew that Hermes would appear in moments. She signaled to the trumpeter and he let out a long blow.

The crowd quieted as they brought their attention forward.

A small ball of light appeared, floating in the center of the dais. The light turned from gold to silver to red and back to gold again several times, growing in size and intensity. Soon it was too bright to bear. She would not look away. The messenger's theatrics would not faze her. Suddenly the light folded within itself and turned into the Hermes himself.

"Darkness has turned to light," he sang, *"and Olympus with all her might, will now bow to the world below, and to your will your fate bestowed. We shall not wail for the ending of this tale. We shall not weep for the fruits that you will reap. And should the darkness envelope the light, day shall always succeed the night. Darkness has turned to light, and Olympus with all her might, will now bow to the world below, and to your will your fate bestowed."*

When it became clear that his song had ended, the crowd roared shouting praise to the messenger. Scribes scribbled furiously, taking down every word he sang. After several long minutes, the clamor died down.

"Today the age of Attica comes to an end," said Hermes. "For once the sun sets beneath this day's horizon, a new patron will have been bestowed upon her beauty. From darkness to light and from death to rebirth, Attica will rise. Let us not weep for the ashes.

"Your king sits before you. With his blessing, this land will be immortalized by the grace of the divine. Each God will present you a gift. Think well on the value of such things, for whoever's gift is greatest shall be your new sovereign in the realm beyond this world. Choose with wisdom, your highness."

Cecrops sat surprisingly stoic. An immortal had just addressed him and he did not even offer the courtesy of bowing. Hades would make short work of him. Hera made sure to not let her distaste show.

"Your highness," said Hermes, "I present to you the goddess of wisdom, courage, and strength, Athena."

Hermes disappeared as the clouds above the acropolis broke open, revealing a light brighter than the sun, and a large hawk descended on the rays. The crowd gasped as the hawk landed lightly on the dais and immediately transformed into Athena. She was beautiful, yet terrifying to look upon. Standing taller than any man, she wore a white dress with bright golden armor and elaborate golden belt of live snakes. A gold cape fell from her shoulders and her long red hair flailed beneath her helmet. On her left arm she held a large round shield, and her right hand was closed into a fist.

"My children from an age passed," she called, her voice surprisingly melodic. "I come to you not as an Olympian, but as a mother. In the time of creation, I bore this land from my womb and gave your ancestors life. We are kin and I have once again come to give you life." She stepped from the dais to stand in front of Cecrops. She could not help but look down upon him, and her bright green eyes showed her excitement, and behind that, her potential fury.

Hera hoped against hope that Hades had a plan for subduing her and Poseidon. Trust, she thought. She must trust her lord.

"King of my kin," said Athena. "I give you a humble offering." She unclenched her right fist to reveal a single seed. Hera worked to compose herself as she stifled a laugh.

"Gracious Athena," said Cecrops. "We thank you for this gift. We are your blessed servants. What fruit will this seed bear?"

Athena took the seed back into her hand and broke the ground beneath her with her fist, revealing soil. Planting the seed, light poured from her hands to make it grow. Within moments, a small tree stood bearing small grape-like fruit. With all of her might, she ripped it from its roots and presented it to the king.

"The fruit of this tree is called 'olive'," said Athena. "Its offspring will provide this land food, oil, and wood. People will call to you from the far reaches of this world to trade with you for olives. Let this feed and sustain you, my children." Several men came over and took the tree from her and Athena went to stand to the side, allowing the contest to continue.

Without his former theatrics, Hermes popped back into the middle of the dais.

"One has come and bared her soul for a child she had lost," he sang, *"but another comes, who also had sons and lost them all with a heavy cost."* This time no one cheered. His words were somber and sobering. He seemed to have been hoping for that effect. After an uncomfortable silence, he continued his announcement.

"Your highness, I give you Poseidon, the Lord of Seas." He disappeared again.

The clouds darkened as if a storm approached and the wind picked up. Thunder roared above and the sound of crashing waves could be heard, though the sea was far away. A cyclone of wind mixed with rain appeared above the dais, swirling violently to the soundtrack of thunder. Suddenly the wind stopped and the water splashed to the ground, revealing Poseidon.

He, too, was terrifying to look upon. Taller than Athena, he wore billowing white robes, tied at the waist with a gold cord. He wore no helmet or crown, only carried his famous and mighty trident. Behind his long white beard and piercing blue eyes, the Lord of Seas was stoic. The storm above ceased.

"Brothers and sisters," his voice boomed, even echoing off of the clouds. Anyone within several leagues would be able to hear him. "I do not stand on ceremony or claim former ties to you. Men will ever need to join with the near and far reaches of this world. What I have to give is increased ability to do so. May your coffers ever grow from my generosity."

Poseidon lifted the trident above his head and began to twirl it in his hand. As it blurred, it began to glow. Thunder sounded again and lightning struck the trident as Poseidon buried it, forks down, into the ground with a swift motion. The earth began to rumble beneath their feet and within moments, water bubbled to the surface where the trident stuck in the ground.

Poseidon removed it, allowing a geyser to shoot up in front of him, and then settle back down. The water began to pool and eventually flowed to the edge of the hill and over its side.

"This will soon become a glorious river that will reach the sea," he said softly. "With it, you will have better means for trade and water. May it ever serve you."

"Your grace knows no bounds, great Poseidon," said Cecrops. "Your generosity overwhelms my people. Both of your gifts overwhelm my people," he continued, standing to face the crowd. "I do not make this decision lightly. The Gods bless us with every breath we take, and today they ask me to choose just one. I must choose one drop out of the sea of their blessings." Cecrops turned back to the two deities, Athena having joined Poseidon on the dais next to his forming river. "And so I must choose, as they have asked me to do. Know that this land holds you both in great esteem and choosing one above the other is not in disrespect." Hera's heart started to race as she felt her power grow. "Citizens of Attica, for you I…"

The ground cracked open beneath Cecrops' feet, sending him sprawling to the earth. Helios helped him to his feet and back to his throne. Grey smoke began to pour from the fissure in the rock. The thickness of the fog cleared in an instant and a tall white figure in dark wispy robes stood menacingly. The crowd flew into a panic.

Hera smiled bright.

"Dear Cecrops," said Hades over the din, "this contest has not yet reached its end."

CHAPTER IV
MADNESS

Emily opened her eyes to darkness. Her head felt heavy against the cold stone floor and her whole body ached as she sat up. The only thing she could see was a thin line of light on the floor, marking a closed door. Feeling at her neck, the horn of water was gone. She'd barely had a second to react when Hera attacked her. As she reflected, her movement to activate the water seemed involuntary. But where was she now?

Faint whimpering from within the room caught her ear. "Hello?"

"Emily?" asked the voice. It was the Oracle. "They have captured you as well? Of course they would. All is lost."

"Delia, what happened?" asked Emily.

"They killed him," she replied sobbing, "my brother, Doros. Helios killed him right in front of me. He is here. They threw his body in here with us."

Emily reached out toward the girl's voice, but found it blocked by cold flesh. Doros' corpse lay between them. Emily's skin crawled.

"How did they capture you?" she asked the girl.

Delia regained some of her composure. "I tried to kill Hera," she said. "I followed you and her through the palace, when there was a bright flash of light and then you both were unconscious on the ground. I ran to you and you were breathing, but so was she. I wanted to end it all right then and rid us of one of Hades' pawns. As I began to choke the life from her, Helios sneaked up behind Doros

179

and drove a knife through his heart." She sobbed. "And then he struck me. I woke here lying next to his body and yours."

"I'm so sorry, Delia," replied Emily. "We'll get revenge, I promise. We'll take down Helios and Hera and put an end to Hades' plot."

"I fear that it is too late," said the Oracle. "The contest has already begun. Two horns have sounded within the last hour. There is no way out of this room and Hades comes whether we will it or not."

"We can't give up hope," said Emily. "The world may be at risk, but so is my family. I haven't come this far to be defeated. It's always darkest before the dawn."

"What do you plan to do?" asked Delia.

"Something will come to me," she replied. "Something always does."

As if on her cue, they heard some scuffling outside the door, and then sound of bodies hitting the floor. Moments later, there was a blast and large burst of light, blinding her eyes. The dust rose and swirled around the room as she went into a fit of coughing. Before her eyes could adjust, the arms of two children embraced her. Instinctively, she pulled away and saw her niece and the Saitian boy, Xho.

"Allie?" she said, as she pulled her close. "And Xho, how did you... where did you come from?"

"You wouldn't believe us if we told you, Mrs. Henry," said a familiar voice. Looking toward the sound, she saw Kimberly Reeves, of all people, helping Delia to her feet.

"Kimberly?" she said, dumbfounded. "What on earth are you doing here? You're supposed to be in Cairo. How did you?" Before Kimberly could reply, Emily noticed the crystal hanging from Allie's neck. She shook her head. "No. No. No!"

"Yes," said Kimberly. "That crystal pulled us into this mess, trust me on that."

"But... no!" repeated Emily. "It's not fair. This can't happen." Emily quickly removed the crystal from Allie's neck and put it around her own. It wasn't fair to put such a weight on a child.

"It's okay, Aunt Emily," said Allie. "The pretty lady sent us here to rescue you." She smiled.

"Pretty lady?" asked Emily.

"Alexia," replied Kimberly. "She set all of this in motion."

Emily looked at Allie and could only hug her again.

"Let's get you two out of this cell," said Kimberly, leading Delia into the light. Emily rose to her feet and followed. The bodies of two royal guards lay sprawled out on the floor outside the door. "They're just unconscious," said Kimberly, reading the look on Emily's face.

Delia began to sob again, trying to go back inside the room. "We cannot leave him here," she cried.

Emily took her hand. "Delia, I promise you that once this is over, we will honor your brother with proper funeral rites," said Emily, "but now we have to go. Hades will be here soon." She turned away from the door. "Kimberly, how did you get here?"

"As I said, Alexia sent us," she replied. "You had no sooner gone into that tunnel when Allie knocked me into some dream. Alexia told us to find the crystal and wait. A week later the thing came to life and pulled us to Saïs, kicking and screaming. I know it sounds crazy."

"No," replied Emily. "It doesn't sound crazy at all. I've experienced it myself. What happened when you arrived in Saïs?"

"The priest, Ubaid, questioned us with the queen and her goon. They told us that you had just left and the next morning we set sail for Attica. We've only just arrived."

"And what about Pete?" she asked. "Is he here with you?"

"Your husband?" said Kimberly. "The queen told us that he never made it out of the Underworld. We came here to save you and Michael."

"She said what?!" fumed Emily. "He was there! They chained him up and beat him! You never even saw him?" She began to shake.

Kimberly looked scared and confused. "Emily, I swear that I didn't know your husband was in Saïs. I'm so sorry. Had I known…"

"No," said Emily as she fingered the crystal. "This is not your fault." Emily felt power rise with her rage as she donned the necklace. "Xho, where is the Saitian queen?"

"The emissary is settling her into her rooms, and then escorting her to the contest," he replied.

"Take me to her," she said. The boy led the way and Emily stalked after him.

The others hurried up beside her as Kimberly asked, "What are you going to do?"

"I'm going to tear that little bitch apart."

Emily raged through the seemingly endless corridors from the jail tower. No one saw them, as most everyone was at the contest. At her side, Delia tried to argue with her to not attack the queen.

"There is more at stake here than vengeance for your husband," the girl argued. "We must focus our energy on Hades."

"You won't sway me, Delia," replied Emily. "Tell me, what do you want to do to Helios right now for murdering your brother?" The girl didn't reply. "That's what I thought. Just stay out of my way."

Xho led them around a corner, down the hall leading to Nefruneith's rooms as the queen and her entourage headed toward them.

"Nefruneith!" yelled Emily. "Where is my husband?" The queen stopped short at the sight of her. The young queen's fear fed Emily's rage. "What have you done with Pete? Did you kill my husband?"

Unexpectedly, Michael Turner stepped forward. "Governess, so good to see you again," he said cordially. Emily noticed his lifeless eyes and seized power from the crystal. With a swift motion, she lifted him by the neck and threw him against the wall where he collapsed. She didn't care, she only wanted Nefruneith suffering.

Musa stepped forward next, drawing a sword in defense. Emily sneered as the crystal glowed, and sent a flash of light at the blade, turning it and Musa's arms to dust. He began to scream at the loss of his limbs. "You will tell me!" With strength that was not her own, she grabbed the captain by his neck and lifted him in the air, stifling his cries. "Where is he?"

His throat being crushed, Musa barely choked out one word. "Dead."

In accordance to her will, the crystal grew brighter and Musa burst into flames. Around her, she could hear screaming. The captain burned quickly and fell as ashes from her hands.

Her rage not sated, Emily reached out and took Nefruneith by the throat. The crystal glowed bright and then suddenly dimmed. Emily called upon the fire, but it would not come. Her strength failed her and she dropped the queen to the floor, coughing.

"Stop, Aunt Emily!" screamed Allie from beneath her. Looking down, the child was wrapped around her leg sobbing. Emily's heart broke as she gazed down at her niece. The weight of what she'd just done her her and she collapsed to the floor weeping. Allie removed the crystal from around her neck and put it on before falling into Emily's embrace. She could feel the power leave her instantly. The world was cold.

No one moved. Bits of ash that was Musa still wafted in the air. Kimberly bore no love for the Captain of the Guard, but she wouldn't have wished that death upon anyone, even if it was deserved. Pete had apparently been killed sometime in the day between Emily leaving for Attica, and her and Allie arriving. Nefruneith had lied to her. She wondered if she could have saved Pete.

Emily cried in a heap on the floor, clutching Allie to her. The child had saved Nefruneith from Musa's fate. To her surprise, the Saitian guards hadn't even moved to save their queen. They feared the Crystal Bearer more than they did their monarch. Now, mere moments after her rage, Kimberly could tell that the danger within Emily was now extinguished. The woman now only grieved for her dead husband.

The hallway seemed to exhale, as Ubaid moved to console Nefruneith. He, too, seemed in shock from seeing Neith's power wielded so violently.

"Kimberly…" she heard her name whispered from nearby. Turning her attention, she saw Michael rising from the floor and went over to him. She looked into his eyes and they held life again.

"Michael," she said. "You're back!"

"Hades had control of me," he said. The power of the crystal had broken the dark lord's hold over him. "I didn't have a choice, you must believe me."

"I believe you," she said embracing him.

"I've killed people. Innocent people. I didn't want to, but he made me do it." He began to shake and cry as Kimberly soothed him. "There's something else," he said regaining some of his composure. "Helios and Hera… they're minions of Hades. We have to stop them."

"Yes," said Emily. She, too, was regaining her composure, though she still held Allie close. "This must be ended. We must stop this now, before any more innocents die. Michael, take us to them."

"Hades is too strong and he is coming now," said Delia. "I can feel it in my bones." Kimberly felt a chill.

"We have all the power we need to stop him," said Emily as she looked Allie in the eyes. "Sweetheart, you must use the crystal to wield the power of Neith. I will guide you, but you must use it yourself. I will not use the power anymore. Not after this."

"Okay, Aunt Emily," the girl hugged her again. Kimberly felt sad for the child, to have this responsibility placed on her shoulders. It was necessary, of course, but it wasn't fair. Emily would guide her, but it was still Kimberly's job to watch over the girl.

"And you, Nefruneith," said Emily, climbing to her feet. The girl-queen's tear-streaked face looked up from the pile of ashes. "I can't forgive you for what you've done, but you can help make amends by standing with us against Hades' forces. It's time you grew up."

Nefruneith nodded.

Michael led them to the large amphitheater. The voice of Poseidon boomed from the clouds as they entered. From the back of the audience, they watched as the God of the Sea, larger than life, twirled his trident overhead and struck the ground. Water began to bubble up from the crevasse and over the side of the cliff.

"This will soon become a glorious river that will reach the sea," Poseidon said softly. "With it, you will have better means for trade and water. May it ever serve you."

"Your grace knows no bounds, great Poseidon," said Cecrops, as he began to praise the God for his gift. The king sat in front of the dais, with Hera and Helios to either side of him. Emily suppressed her rage and the urge to attack them immediately. She had Michael stay back, so that Hera and Helios would not catch sight of him.

"This is not the time to confront them," said Michael from behind her. Their time would soon come, Emily knew.

Cecrops declared both gifts, from Athena and Poseidon, to be amenable. As he went to name the winner of the contest, he was cut off. The ground beneath him cracked and he fell to the ground. Dark smoke poured from the new fissure in the rock. A thick fog formed, clearing moments later to reveal Hades himself, tall and pale in his dark robes.

"Dear Cecrops," said Hades, "this contest has not yet reached its end."

"What is the meaning of this?" asked Cecrops, as the crowd turned into frenzy.

Hermes popped out of nowhere, making Emily angry all over again. Hermes had abandoned them when they fled the Underworld. "Everyone, be silent," his voice boomed. The crowd froze and listened. "Divine law dictates that any God may present you a gift, King Cecrops, in the contest of patronage. In turn, you must consider the gift. I present to you, the Defender of Mankind and the Holy Lord of the Underworld, Hades."

"You have my thanks, Hermes," said Hades. Emily couldn't believe Hades was acting so calm. Even Athena and Poseidon seemed surprised by his peace. "I have not come to bring you distress," he announced to the kind and crowd, "but only to present you my gift for consideration."

Cecrops rose from his seat. "By what right do you, Hades of the Underworld, have to be considered for such an honor."

"My right comes from being your defender and savior, of course," replied Hades, "though your histories would not name me so. I will provide you stability and shelter from the forces beyond this world, unlike my fellow contestants. Poseidon once held patronage over a land. In one day and night, he smote Atlantis from this earth, killing all but one of its citizens. When Zeus flooded the world, where was Athena, your former patron? She did not once speak up to save you. Poseidon is not free from this crime either. It was he who struck down your king of old, Aktaios, at the last battle of Atlantis, and it was he who raised the tides to blanket the earth in ocean. What say you, Poseidon and Athena, to these truths?"

"How dare you curse my actions!" said Poseidon.

"However true they may be," said Hades in reply. "And Athena?"

"I could not stand against, Zeus, my father, once his mind was set to the task," she replied somberly. "I sorely regret my reservations during his deluge, but I am only one God."

"As am I, dear Athena," said Hades. "In truth, it was *me* who saved mankind from the deluge of Zeus. I sent forth the Diluvians upon my own ship to ferry the survivors of your world. Without me, every last person in your world would not be alive. You would not exist, dear King Cecrops."

"I do not believe your lies, dark one," replied Cecrops. "Present your gift and be gone."

"But I have presented it, dear king," said Hades. "I gave you truth, never mind that I gave you life. I will have your allegiance."

Everyone froze as dark smoke shot out of the crack in the earth and into the sky, blocking out the setting sun and casting the world into darkness. Furies poured forth from the smog and quickly bound themselves around Poseidon and Athena, who in shock fell limp in their clutches.

Cecrops rose in protest, as Helios threw him back and pulled a dagger to his throat. Helios placed his hands around the king's head, and in moments Cecrops smiled calmly. Hera stood and moved herself beside Hades.

"I will have your allegiance," repeated Hades. "I will never forsake you, so long as you remain obedient. I am now your patron and I shall rule this land myself. Any who defy me will be taken by the furies."

Emily looked to her group, all horrified. "You're right, Delia," she said. "We can't win this right now."

"What do you suggest?" asked the Oracle.

"We will go back to the palace and form a plan," she replied. "Quickly, before anyone sees us."

CHAPTER V
THE CHASE

"Her majesty, Nefruneith, Queen of Saïs and Daughter of the Sacred Lake," announced the palace steward. The governing forces of Attica, King Cecrops, Hera, Helios, and now Hades, convened in the Great Hall after the contest abruptly ended. Cecrops still sat on his throne, and Hades stood behind him like a puppeteer. Behind Hades, the lifeless forms of Poseidon and Athena hung suspended in the air by furies, their bodies a blur behind the dark swirling shadows. The messenger god, Hermes stood in a far corner of the room, trying to blend in with the wall. On either side of the throne stood Hera and Helios, smiling in their accomplishment of assisting their lord into this world. Michael stood with Daxteros just off to the side of the throne dais, nearest Helios. The Queen of Saïs would be the first foreign dignitary to recognize Hades as Lord of Attica.

Michael remembered Nefruneith at full strength back in her homeland, damning Peter Henry to his death, but all traces of that royal confidence were now gone. She was now merely a frightened sixteen-year-old girl playing a game far too big for her as she shuffled toward the throne. He truly felt bad for her. Despite her slights against him, Michael wanted to reach out to her and tell her to run, but that did not follow Emily's plan.

When they returned to the palace from the contest, Emily told Nefruneith that she would have to present herself to the king and Hades since they already knew she was in Attica, and her absence would be noticed. Michael was unsure if the queen was more scared of Emily or of Hades, as she agreed to the plan without argument. Michael was also told to return to his post alongside Hera and Helios. If he did not return, Helios would certainly seek him out. Michael had argued with her, saying that Hades would know that he was no longer under his influence, but in the end Emily's argument had won out. They were all safer if it seemed like nothing was amiss. They needed time to figure out their next move, she had said, and Michael could help to buy them that time. So he returned and acted as if he were still entranced.

Nefruneith was not alone as she walked into the Great Hall. With the captain of her guard now dead, her only entourage was the Saitian priest, Ubaid, who followed closely behind her. He seemed more squeamish than she did. Musa would have been more outwardly stoic, but Emily had exacted her retribution. Only the child, Allie, had saved the queen from that same fate. Ubaid now paid his own debt to the Crystal Bearer by accompanying the queen to face the dark one.

Stopping in front of the dais, eyes cast down, Nefruneith bowed deep before the king and Hades. Cecrops' voice was as hollow as his eyes, containing no emotion. "You are welcome to the Kingdom of Hades, sister Nefruneith. You come moments too late for the game of gods. It is a pity. Did you come for the contest?"

"Thank you, your highness," she replied, her voice shaking. "Indeed, I did come for the contest… though only moments too late, as you said. That and to pay homage to the glorious victor. I beg you to forgive my tardiness."

"Your tardiness is forgiven and the victor is present," replied Cecrops, motioning to Hades.

"Of course," she said. Michael watched as the queen struggled to look up at Hades. Keeping her eyes on the dark lord, she bowed again. "Congratulations on your triumph, great lord. I am honored to be in your presence." Hades only smiled coldly with his white, seemingly sightless eyes. An awkward silence settled as sweat formed above Nefruneith's brow. "M-may I present my counselor, Ubaid, the High Priest of Neith, who has accompanied me on this holy pilgrimage."

"You are welcome to my kingdom, Priest of Neith," replied Hades. Nefruneith's hands were now visibly shaking. Ubaid hardly seemed to breathe. "Dear queen, where is your guard. I have it that the captain never leaves your side."

"Indeed, great lord, Musa does not leave me, under normal circumstances," she replied, "but I have left him in Saïs to rule the realm in my stead and to keep my affairs in order until my return. This being an important religious affair, it seemed prudent that Ubaid should join me." Hades smiled coldly.

"Your grace, given your planned voyage, you still arrived late to the contest," said Hera, stepping forward from her post. "This seems odd given, as you say, the religious importance of this day."

"You are right," she replied. "The seas were not their best. We lost several days due to storms."

"Forgive me, your grace, I misspoke," said Hera. "You actually *did* arrive in time for the contest. I was given word of your arrival before the games ever began. I sent an emissary, Michael, to see to your quick arrival. Is that not correct, Michael?"

Michael had not expected to be called out and stalled, his heart began to race. He quickly stepped forward before the king. "I beg your forgiveness, my king, for not delivering Queen Nefruneith to you quickly. It was my fault…"

Nefruneith cut him off. "It was my error, your highness. I felt rushed from my voyage and demanded to be allowed to clean up before attending to you and the Gods. I was in no fit state for divine presence. Your emissary is not at fault in this matter."

"As you say," replied Hera, for the king.

Michael sighed relief and returned to his post, only to have Helios stop him.

"Wait, Michael," Helios called him forward again. Helios stood before him and looked him in the eyes. Michael was now sweating and visibly shaking. "You are not yourself, are you?" Michael flinched as Helios placed his hands on either side of his head. The world turned grey. His sweating and shaking ceased. The mere task of existing became easier. He only had one objective in his life: to serve Hades in all of his greatness. Helios smiled as he returned to his post.

Helios, the great counselor and right hand of Hades, turned and began questioning the foreign queen, her face now in shock. "Your grace, what exactly happened between the time you arrived in Attica and now? The king's emissary seems amiss."

"I do not know to what you are referring," she replied. "I have already told you, I was refreshing myself and settling into my rooms.

By the time I had finished, the contest was finished and the great lord, Hades, had been declared victorious."

Helios stared at the queen, as Hades spoke behind him. "She lies," he said, his voice deep and raspy.

"Your grace, who have you brought with you from Saïs?" asked Helios.

"Aside from my household staff, only Ubaid," she replied. "I do not see why you ask such questions; I am not on trial here."

"She has brought the Crystal Bearer of Saïs," said Hera matter-of-factly, "the one who wields the power of Neith."

"Alexia," hissed Hades.

"Yes, great one," replied Hera. "She hides here in this palace and must be found at once. The Crystal Bearer possesses the power to threaten the Dark Lord. Discover her!" Guards left the room in haste to search the palace as Hera stepped before Nefruneith once again. "Where do you keep her?"

"I do not have her," replied the queen frantically. "There has not been a Crystal Bearer in over five-hundred years. Not since the time of the del…"

"Then you are of no use to us," replied Hera as she pulled her dagger from its hilt and buried it into Nefruneith's side. The queen gasped. The foreign priest, Ubaid, screamed in terror as Hera smiled.

Life left the young queen as she collapsed to the ground. Her eyes became sightless and her body dissolved, turning into a black shadow mist, into a fury.

At the sight of his queen turning into shadow, the priest fainted. Laughing, Hera left him there and turned to Hades, a cold smile upon his face.

Their moment of reverie was broken by a guard rushing into the room, begging audience with the king. Helios talked to him quietly, his face becoming outraged. He stepped away from the guard and slit his throat.

"The Oracle and the Governess of Carmour have escaped the jail tower," he announced to Hades. "They must have fled during the contest. We do not know where they are."

"We do, dear husband," said Hera. "They have teamed up with the Crystal Bearer. I would swear my life upon it." She walked over to Michael and placed a hand on his shoulder. He felt eager to please. "Do you know where the Crystal Bearer is?" Michael nodded and smiled.

Emily stood in Nefruneith's chambers in one of the eastern towers of Attella's Crown. Around her sat Allie, the Oracle, Kimberly, and Xho, as the grown women discussed what they had just witnessed and their next move to fight Hades' uprising. Servants scurried around on their various tasks, continuing to settle the queen into her lodgings, seemingly oblivious to the results of the contest. Nefruneith and the priest had just left to join Michael in the Great Hall and to present themselves to the king and Hades.

"I just don't understand it," said Emily to everyone. "Why didn't the Olympians intervene when Hades took power? I mean, he just imprisoned two of them. Surely they care about their own."

"They were not able to," replied Delia. "I saw it. Hades unleashed his forces from the Underworld and immediately blackened the sky. I believe that he has created a barrier of sorts between this world and the other realms." She stood and walked over to the window. There was a swirling darkness in the sky, thicker than any cloud. It was night already, but the world had somehow become darker. "That is a legion of furies. No God will be able to penetrate it. Hades has ensured that, no doubt. The only Gods left on this plane of existence, aside from Hades, are Athena and Poseidon."

"But that isn't really true," said Kimberly. "The power of Neith can be harnessed by these two." She pointed to Emily and Allie. "That has to count for something."

Emily felt sick at the thought of using the crystal's power. She'd just killed a man. Yes, he'd killed Pete, but she never thought she had it in her. When Sean, Erin, and Pete had killed Thebos on the deck of the Persephone at the end of the flood, they had all been under Hades' influence. She had full control of her faculties when she burned Musa alive. Her hands started shaking. But he'd killed Pete, she thought over and over. Thinking of her late husband made her sad, and that sadness strengthened her resolve.

"We have to stop Hades," said Emily more to herself than the others. "This has to end."

"Emily," said Kimberly, "you and Allie together could overwhelm the furies holding Athena and Poseidon and release them."

"That is suicide!" replied Delia. "There are far too many furies, and how would you even get past Hades? He would never risk leaving his prisoners. There is no one he would trust to guard them aside from himself."

"Kimberly's right. We have to try," said Emily. "This cycle will never end if we don't. Hades will always have some grip on the world if we don't act. And I have a further idea. If we save Poseidon, he'll have no choice but to help us save Sean and Erin from Hades." With Allie's arrival and Pete dying, Emily had really been distracted from her original quest, to save Sean and Erin. She hoped they were alright.

"That is not our only option," said Delia. "There is another God here, though I cannot say if he will help us. After Hades sealed the world, Hermes was here. Since he cannot leave, that means he is *still* here."

More unsettled emotions welled up inside Emily at the mention of the messenger. "We cannot trust him," she said.

"I understand your hesitation," said Delia, "but Hermes has already proven himself to be just as powerful and manipulative as the superior Gods. I have read the histories and know his involvement in Zeus' deluge. He even helped you, if the accounts are to be believed."

"He abandoned us when we fled the Underworld," replied Emily. "If he had stayed with us... If he had just shown his face in Saïs, then my husband would still be alive. I will not put my faith in him. Not for this. Not for anything."

"Hermes did support Hades at the contest," said Kimberly.

"You are right," said Delia, "Hermes is on Hades' side, but he is not bewitched by Hades. Is it not beyond conceivable thought that he has his reasons? And if we can sway him to our cause, he could create a diversion to get Hades away from Athena and Poseidon long enough for us to free them."

"This is all hypothetical," said Emily, getting fed up. "We can't count on Hermes, and until we have a solid plan, we have to hide. Delia and I are still supposed to be locked away in the tower and it's only a matter of time before Hera and Helios realize that we've escaped."

"What about Nefruneith and Ubaid?" asked Kimberly. "What about Michael?"

"The Saitians will have to fend for themselves," she replied. "Hades knows they are here, so they have nothing to hide. Michael will have to continue his farce until it's safe to extract him. We, on the other hand, must hide and soon."

"But where do we hide?" asked Kimberly. "The hiding places in this palace are finite, and the only defense we have is in that crystal."

"That is not so," said Xho. His voice was kind and soft, and Emily had almost forgotten he was even there. Disappearing into the background was no doubt a skill he picked up as a slave in Saïs.

"What was that, Xho?" she asked.

"We have more power than just the crystal," he replied. "The orb lights we brought from Saïs contain water from Neith's sacred lake. The great priest used that water to test your abilities at the Temple, and that same water brought me back to life."

"Xho, you are a genius," said Emily as hope filled her. "Shattering the orbs will come in handy. We have to gather all of them quickly. We'll want to take them with us."

"They are here," said Kimberly. "I saw the servants bring them to the palace with Nefruneith's belongings." Kimberly asked the nearest servant where they were stored and in moments, they had a dozen grapefruit-sized glowing orbs.

"We'll save these for the right moment," said Emily. "We don't really know what we're up against." They placed the orbs into a large sack they found among the queen's belongings.

"Where to?" asked Kimberly.

"Let us go to my chambers," said Delia. "Delphinios and Helena will help hide us. We can trust them, and it is better than us being here when Nefruneith and Ubaid get back."

"Sounds like as good a plan as any," said Kimberly, looking to Emily.

"Let's go then."

Hera burst into Nefruneith's chambers with the full might of Hades followed by Helios, Michael, Daxteros, and a contingent of royal guards only to find the rooms empty, aside from the queen's servants.

"Where are they!" she screamed, rounding on Michael. "Where did they go?"

"I do not know," he replied.

"How dare you spread falsities!" she berated. She turned to the guards. "Tear the palace apart. Find them!"

"What about them?" asked Daxteros as he motioned toward Nefruneith's frightened and bewildered servants.

"Kill them all," she replied coldly. "Their queen is dead. Let them serve the Great Lord." Daxteros, Michael, and the remaining guards drew their blades and slaughtered the dozen or so Saitians, turning them instantly into furies.

The fugitives and the Crystal Bearer were still in the palace, Hera knew. She could almost feel them scurrying around like rats. If Michael had been correct that they had been in these chambers, then they couldn't have gone far.

Hera remembered first hand how terrible the Crystal Bearer's power could be. That power had overwhelmed her and made her forget the loyalty and love she bore for her master. That power had taken away her very purpose in life. That power, and she who wields it, must be destroyed.

"We will head to the Oracle's chambers," she announced, "and bring the new furies." They left. Knowing that the Oracle was with the Crystal Bearer, it made sense that they would flee there first. Delia surely believed her caretakers were still alive. It was also nearby, so they could, at the very least, check the rooms off their list.

Michael and Daxteros came to stand outside Delia's chambers as Hera and Helios approached, awaiting their command to enter. "I will enter first," she said.

Daxteros broke the door down. Hera entered and three figures stood by the far window, away from the corpses of Delphinios and Helena, near the door to the tower's bridge. The Governess... no, she was more than that. The Diluvian shouted for the other two to run out the door.

"Furies!" Hera yelled and the dark figures attacked. Before joining her fellow fugitives, the Diluvian held an orb before her and it glowed bright. She threw it to the ground and it shattered, causing the dark shadows to dissolve to nothing, screeching terribly as they died, creating a veil of glowing mist.

Through the mist, Erin saw Emily, Kimberly Reeves, and the Oracle running away. "Wait!" she cried out, desperate for them to come back, her heart breaking at knowing her true self once again. She ran to catch up to them, but in escaping the mist she became Hera and rage filled her.

"Daxteros! Michael! After them!" she yelled. Thankfully, there were still a few furies left.

The fugitives took the high bridge that connected the Oracle's chamber with one of the northern towers of Attella's Crown. That path would lead them to the King's tower, near the center of the palace, and would eventually take them right back to Thebos' Chambers. Hera smiled and followed.

As anticipated, when she caught up to the Michael and Daxteros, they had the fugitives cornered in front of the locked door to the jail tower, furies floating nearby awaiting her command. They argued with Michael, begging him to come back to their side. She just laughed at their feeble attempts. Whatever that orb had been, they clearly did not have more.

"You cannot defeat us," she called to them as she approached. "Furies!"

The dark shadows attacked like black wind and consumed the fugitives, who fell helplessly into their embrace. Hades would be pleased.

Having been a slave his whole life, Xho had a great talent for not being seen when he wished. He now hid behind the statue of a king in one of the palace corridors as Hades' henchmen and the palace guards stalked by, heading toward the queen's chambers. In his arms, he held the sack of Saitian orbs, eleven now, since Emily had taken one with her. Allie crouched quietly beside him.

Xho felt guilty for leaving Emily, even though it had been his idea to hide the orbs separate from the group. They knew that Hera and Helios would be looking for them and they could not risk the orbs being taken, or worse being shattered before they could be used.

Bringing Allie along had not been his idea. Kimberly, knowing that there could be no safety for the girl if they stayed together, begged Emily to let Allie accompany him. It was a short argument, but in the end Emily gave in. Allie had tried to give her aunt the Saitian Crystal, but Emily refused. As a consolation, Emily took one of the orbs, just in case.

So Xho led Allie in the opposite direction of the group. They would hide in the Governess' chambers until Emily, Kimberly, or Delia came for them. No one aside from their group even knew Xho or Allie was in the palace, so no one would be looking for them.

Ducking around corners, slinking through corridors, and in and out of towers, Xho and Allie finally made it to the Governess' chambers. He was startled when he entered and he had to stifle Allie's scream as Daria's lifeless body still lay on the floor, her neck sliced open and her eyes sightless. The blood that had spilled from her was now sticky and brown upon the floor. He could not stand the sight or the growing smell, and Allie's face was white as linen, but they could not leave these rooms, so he resolved to take Allie out onto the balcony.

Darkness swirled in the sky above. No stars or moon could shine upon the earth. He and Allie huddled in a corner with the bag of orbs settled in between them and waited.

Book VI:
Heroes & Victims

CHAPTER I
THE VIRTOUS SOULS

Persephone sighed as she lay across her chaise in her chambers high within Erebus. The bright colors and sweet fragrances of the flowers did little to lighten her mood. The Crystal Bearer had failed and now Hades wreaked havoc on earth. Her husband was intelligent to a fault, securing his dominion by cutting off the mortal world from both the Netherworld and Olympus. No one could break his hold.

Petals on the flowers around her began to flutter, as if moved by a light breeze, though there was no wind. Persephone steeled herself as Alexia appeared before her in a burst of light.

"I had wondered when you would come," said Persephone as she rose and embraced Alexia. "I beg your forgiveness; the Crystal Bearer has failed in her task. I should have done more to help her defeat Hades, but I feared his wrath. Now we are all cut off from him."

"Dear Persephone, you did what you could to help her," replied Alexia. "Your fear of Hades is not ungrounded, but do not fret yet, as all hope is not lost."

"Is that so?" asked Persephone.

"Indeed," she said, "I have a plan that just might save mankind."

"You are ever their savior," replied Persephone.

"It seems ages ago, but I was one of them for a short time," said Alexia. "Gods can be quite cruel. I will not allow their misdeeds to stand."

"We cannot cross into the mortal world," said Persephone.

"What is there that can we do?"

"Very little, I am afraid," replied Alexia, "but we can orchestrate the means for mankind to help save themselves. There are not one but two Crystal Bearers in Attica at the moment. With any amount of fortune, they will be able to use my crystal to free Poseidon and Athena from the furies."

"That is all well, but surely Hades is smart enough to not let them leave his sight," said Persephone.

"Indeed, which is why we need to create a diversion... a distraction to lure Hades away," said Alexia. "We may be able to buy the Crystal Bearers enough time to save the Olympians. Once freed, Poseidon and Athena will be more than capable of disarming Hades."

"What is the diversion of which you speak?" asked Persephone.

"We will send mortal souls back," she replied. "It has been done before, and I am certain that Hades will not see it coming. That should provide enough reason for him to leave his captives, but I will need your help in procuring these souls."

"What if he does not take the bait?" asked Persephone. "Will he not see it for what it is?"

"Maybe, but maybe not," replied Alexia. "With the hand that we will play, I am confident that he will have no choice but to face the mortals."

"I trust your plan has a few surprises for him," said Persephone. "What would you have me do?"

Thoughts came and went. Thoughts of New York. Thoughts of family. Thoughts of friends. Thoughts of hatred. And thoughts of love. But most of all, thoughts of Emily. Pete took a deep breath and he became overwhelmed with the scent of wildflowers. The smell brought him thoughts of his wedding day. The smell of flowers in the reception hall, the flowers of Emily's bouquet, the flower on his lapel. She looked so beautiful in her white dress, his diamond in the rough. Pete remembered when he first met her, and how he knew then that she was the one. He was so certain that he journeyed to the Underworld to save her from death.

Death. The thought stirred in his mind, hanging just out of reach of his understanding. He had passed over twice now, both times with his soul intact. The first time in search of Emily, and the second time in search of Sean and Erin. Why did that matter now? He had made it out of the Underworld both times, reborn beneath the sacred lake of Saïs. The first time he had outlasted Zeus' deluge and the second time he… was taken prisoner… tortured… and killed.

Pete's eyes shot open as he tried to comprehend his death. The scent of flowers remained and he sat up. "Hermes!" he screamed as he looked around. This was not Purgatory and he wasn't shrouded in darkness. Turning around, he met a familiar gaze. "Persephone? But… but I died. Why am I not in Purgatory?" He was in the Goddess' chambers, high in Erebus. It made no sense.

"I know no soothing words or songs, as the Psychopomps would recite, so forgive me for my boldness," replied the Goddess. "You are dead, Peter Henry. Fully, this time, I fear. Your soul no longer has an attachment to the mortal world."

"I was killed in Saïs," he said sadly. "I remember it all. The Saitian priest even came, wishing to save me in my last moments." His thoughts trailed off for a moment. "But why am I *here*? I should be in Purgatory, awaiting the ferry to bring me… well, here."

"These are desperate times, Peter," she replied. "I brought you here in secret. My curse to this realm has left me with a few advantages, one being able to cross the different planes of the Netherworld at will."

"But why?" he asked. "Hades will certainly find out. If not him, I'm sure Hermes will notice my absence."

"Neither will have a second thought about you," she replied nonchalantly, "because neither is here in the Underworld. Hades has taken Attica, and Hermes went with him. The contest for the patronage of Attica is over and Hades has forced the king to name him the victor. Upon claiming the land, he created a barrier between the mortal realm and the immortal realms. No Gods of Olympus or otherwise can stop him now. Which is why I stole you from Purgatory, Peter?"

"Surely, you don't think I can defeat Hades?" asked Pete. "I'm dead, remember. And now he's in the mortal realm."

"No, you cannot defeat him," replied Persephone. "Nor will you. But your wife can."

"Emily? What do you mean?"

"In taking Attica, Hades managed to capture Athena and Poseidon. Emily, with the power of the Saitian Crystal, which she now possesses, is the only hope of freeing the Olympians. Once freed, Athena and Poseidon can break Hades' hold on the world with ease."

"So where do I come in?" he asked. "Again, I'm dead."

"You of all people should know that death is not an end, just another transition between planes of existence. Like Ptollen of the Sea before you, you will lead a band of virtuous souls to the mortal world to wage war on Hades."

"But you said I have no chance in defeating him," replied Pete.

"You cannot defeat him," she stated, "and you will not defeat him. The mission I am sending you on is not one that I intend for you to survive, Peter Henry. But if you do not do it, you will leave the world you have left behind to crumble. Everyone you knew and loved will be destroyed, souls and all. They will not cross over. They will cease to exist."

"So what is the goal of my mission, if not to defeat Hades?" he asked.

"You are to be a diversion," said Persephone. "Hades will only leave Athena and Poseidon under the most dire of circumstances. You and your band will sail Ophion, the serpent demon, to Attica. Hades will take this as a slight, using his vassal against him, and will therefore have no choice but to face you head on. His pride is his weakness. You will face Hades and also his furies, which act as his army."

Pete looked at her uncertain. He knew from before that Persephone had no love for Hades, but his experience has made him leery of the guidance of any Gods. "How do you know that this plan will work? Hades is more devious than we could ever dream."

"This plan relies solely on you, Peter," she replied. "If you must know, this idea is Alexia's. I am not certain if that makes you feel better or not, but she has proven to be just as conniving as my husband. After all, she contrived the saving of your kind from Zeus' flood. For that, I would say you owe her this deed."

"Trust me, Persephone, I don't owe Alexia a damn thing," he replied. "But I'll do as you ask, as it seems there is no other choice. Who are the souls that I'll be leading?"

"I will show you," she replied and touched his arm.

Pete's mind went blank, and as it came back into focus, he stood in the light of the Elysian Fields. A soft breeze crossed a large open field lined with tall trees. A sense of peace surrounded him. He knew that if he crossed the field and into the forest, he would eventually come upon the Palace of Elysium, an inverted step-pyramid and the home of King Rhadamanthus.

"Peter," said Persephone. "I introduce your comrades."

Pete turned to see four souls lined up in front of him. Two he recognized, and two he did not.

"From your own time, here are Vincent Sanders, Allison Moore, Samuel Knight, and Julie Vane," announced Persephone. Pete ran forward and embraced Julie Vane, happy to see her holding hands with her love, Samuel Knight. Pete knew Sam from Sean's college days. The other two he knew only by name, as they had gone missing during Sean and Erin's first disappearance.

"From the realm that was Atlantis," continued Persephone as three more souls appeared, "King Hesperos of Poseidon, Ptollen of the Sea, and Pyrthens of Pythagoras." Pete had only ever heard tales about the king, but he acknowledged Ptollen and Pyrthens as old friends.

Six more souls appeared. "From the realm of Attica and formerly Athens, the Arch Priest Nikedemos of Zeus, the Queen Regent Attella of Athens, the Arch Priest of Apollo Delphinios, Priestess of Apollo Helena, Doros of Delphi, and Daria of Piraeus." Pete only knew Nikedemos and Attella, and wondered who the others were.

"And lastly, from the realm of Saïs, King Aha of Neith and…" she hesitated, "and Musa of Saïs." Beside Aha, the soul of the man who murdered him appeared.

"No," said Pete walking up to Musa, who looked surprised and what could be taken as afraid. "I will not take the man who tortured and killed me." To Musa, he said, "I'm glad you're dead, but I'm just sorry I wasn't the one to slit your throat."

"Your killer had a worse death than that, Peter Henry," said Persephone as she pulled him away from Nefruneith's former captain. "Your wife used the power of the crystal to incinerate him. Any vengeance you wish upon this man has been claimed by Emily Henry. The debt of life is paid in full."

Pete was taken aback. Emily killed Musa? Incinerate? He had so many questions, but before he could ask them, Persephone was gathering everyone together to explain their mission.

"You sixteen are the Virtuous Souls," she announced. "Ages ago, Poseidon created the Diluvians who have traveled through your worlds, sometimes damning and sometimes saving your people. At this time, Hades has taken what is left of your worlds for his own and threatens the entirety of mankind. Your connection to Hades' plot assures you the right to fight alongside the Diluvian, Peter Henry. Go to the realm of men, fight Hades and his furies with all of your might, and finally save your world from the hands of Gods."

They were all ghostly shells of their human selves, Pete noticed, but upon Persephone's call to arms, they began to glow brighter and cheered. This vengeance... this justice has been a long time coming for many of them. To his surprise, even Musa cheered loudly. Persephone said his life debt was paid, but his help in this fight would ensure his forgiveness.

"Ptollen of the Sea," Persephone shouted. "Will you sail Ophion to Attica and save your brethren?"

"Aye!" he shouted.

"Join hands!" When the last connection was made, Pete's mind went blank again and they reformed at the edge of a river of fire. Stepping toward the Phlegethon, Persephone made a high pitch screech to call forward the fire serpent, Ophion.

Like a sea monster of legends, Ophion bobbed and weaved through the lava, eventually arriving at the shore. Persephone whispered something to him and he threw his head, high into the air. She took several steps back as the serpent went up in flames and smoke. When the air cleared, a dark ship with a single red sail appeared.

"The Persephone," said Pete, more to himself than anyone else.

"Yes," replied the Goddess. "I cannot travel with you, but my namesake will bear you on your journey." Everyone boarded quickly, but before he made his way on the ship, Persephone pulled Pete aside.

"I hesitate to say anything, Peter, but you may face more than just Hades in the mortal world. Aside from your wife, both Sean and Erin are there, but do not hope to save them. They wear disguises and have become puppets of Hades. In some ways, they are more dangerous than him. Remember your goal: distract Hades so Emily can free Athena and Poseidon."

Pete felt conflicted. Knowing his brother and Erin were there as well, and possessed by Hades made him want to scream, but Persephone was right. He had to first help save the world, thus saving Emily. He could not save Sean and Erin.

Without another word, Pete boarded the dark ship and Ptollen sailed away from shore and into the darkness.

CHAPTER II
THE BELL'S TOLL

Emily woke up in darkness on a cold stone floor. Nearby, two women gasped.

"Hello?" she said quietly.

"Emily, is that you?" asked Kimberly.

"Yes, it's me," she replied. "Who else is there?"

"It is me, Delia," said the Oracle. "What happened?"

"We were captured by Hera," replied Emily. At that, Delia began to sob.

"Did you see them?" she asked. "Delphinios and Helena. They are dead. I have no one left." She cried.

Emily reached toward Delia's voice to soothe her, but she was blocked by something that made her cringe. "Where are we?"

"You are in Thebos' Chambers," replied the voice of Ubaid. Emily cringed as she realized the obstruction was Doros' body.

"Ubaid? What are you doing here?" asked Kimberly. "How long have you been here?"

"Not much longer than you, Guardian," he replied. "I was brought in less than an hour before the furies brought you in."

"If you're here, then what happened to Nefruneith?" asked Kimberly.

"The queen is dead," he replied somberly. "Or something worse than death."

"What? What happened to her?" asked Emily.

"Hera killed her," he replied, "because of you, Crystal Bearer. Know that I do not hold you responsible for my queen's death, but upon being questioned about your presence, Nefruneith denied that you are here. Hera was not pleased and that is when she placed the dagger in her side. Her death is a tragedy, yes… but her afterlife will be much more tormenting."

"Why do you say that?" asked Delia.

"When Hera killed her, Nefruneith's body dissolved and she became a fury," he said. "In her death, she has become nothing but a minion of the lord we now defy."

"It is the barrier that Hades has created," said Delia. "The furies block any coming and going between this realm and the realms of Gods. In death, our souls have nowhere to go. Hades will not care if any humans live or die in his new regime. Each death only makes his army stronger."

"How can we beat him?" asked Kimberly. "You were right, Delia, he's too strong."

"We can't give up," said Emily. "Allie and Xho are still out there. Who will keep them safe?"

"Emily, what can we do?" asked Kimberly. "We're locked in this dark cell, which I just saved you from less than a day ago."

The conversation paused as they all dwelled on what to do next. In her brainstorming, an unsettling thought came to Emily. "Wait," she said. "Ubaid, you said we were brought in by furies, right?"

"Yes, they held you until you woke a few moments ago," he replied.

"But why exactly did they let us go?" she asked. "It would have made more sense to keep us sedated."

"Because *I* told them to," said voice in a vacant corner of the cell. Emily recognized it well.

"Show yourself, Hermes!" she said, suppressing her welling rage. There was a slight buzzing and light erupted into the room. As her eyes adjusted, she saw Hermes holding his glowing caduceus. "In addition to backstabbing us, you're now spying on us, is that it?"

"Oh Emily, that is harsh," he replied, "even coming from you. You are imprisoned. Privacy is not a luxury afforded to those who are not free."

"You're a liar and a traitor," she accused. "You left us in Saïs with no plan or direction. You could have saved Pete from Musa!"

"You do not know the personal risk I took even leading you

through the Netherworld," said Hermes. "Nor do you know what transpired mere moments after you began your assent to this realm. I have fulfilled my debt to you. Every decision I have made since you left the Underworld has been for my own self preservation. There are great powers at play here, and the stakes are higher than the life of your husband. With Hades taking over Attica, the stakes are higher even than the lives of Sean and Erin."

"Then what did happen when we left the Underworld?" asked Emily. "At least tell me that much."

"I did not abandon you lightly," he replied. "Hades caught me as I was going to follow behind you. My choice was to serve him or be left to my fate in Tartarus. Forgive me, but I chose life. I do not ask for your forgiveness, but do try to see beyond your own goals and desires. I will not give up my life for you."

"I'm sorry," said Emily. "I didn't know, but you too must understand my frustration for seeing you paired with Hades in this takeover. I can't help but to see you as the enemy, since you are clearly helping him."

"I am helping only myself," replied Hermes. "Which is why you are awake right now and not under the spell of the furies."

"You released us," said Emily. "Why?"

"Despite what you might think, I do have a conscience," he replied. "I regret the situation you have ended up in."

"Then help us out of it," she said. In the dim light of the caduceus, pain crossed Hermes' face.

"There is no way," he said. "If there was even a glimmer of hope, I promise I would have helped you. I… I just wanted you to know that I am truly sorry. I have been ordered to take you to Hades. You can come with some civility, or I can call back the furies."

Emily felt broken, having come to this dead end. She sunk to her knees and cried. She had failed Sean and Erin, she had failed Pete, and worse Xho and Allie were stuck in the palace with no hope for survival. They'd be caught before too long. She had one last request of Hermes. If he truly cared about mankind as he said, he would help Allie and Xho find safety.

"Hermes," she began, "can you…" She was cut off by a loud cry, like the sound of thousands of screeching birds dying in unison. Hermes froze and the light of his caduceus went out. "Hermes?" He didn't answer.

"I think he is gone," said Delia.

"What was that sound?" asked Kimberly.

"I have a hunch," said Emily as a whisper of hope returned to her. "I think that was the sound of furies dying."

Hermes appeared on the balcony of one of the western towers of Attella's crown, overlooking the city and beyond its walls. Upon the new river that Poseidon had created, a charcoal black ship with blood red sails sailed into the city. At the ship's bow, a single bell tolled. "Ophion," he said to himself. Legions of furies rushed toward it, but with every toll of the bell, they scattered, some dissolving, only to regroup and rush the ship again. Nothing could deter the furies from upholding their mission.

From the balcony, he could not tell who sailed the Persephone, but he knew that no Gods could enter the mortal realm. Hades had made sure of that. He looked up to see the dark mass swirling in the sky, blocking out all but a subtle glow of the sun. No, whoever sailed the ship would be a mortal soul sent here by a God. The scheme reeked of Alexia. "When will she learn to cease her meddling?" Torn, he knew he had to tell Hades.

Suddenly glass shattered behind him, accompanied by a flash of light. Startled, he turned to see two children, a Saitian boy and a small girl with dark hair and big brown eyes, both silent in shock. The boy was holding a sack of Saitian orbs. The girl... he knew her, though he had never laid eyes on her. Like any good Crystal Bearer, around her neck she bore the Saitian Crystal of Neith.

As the glowing water puddled around the broken shards of glass, a plan came to him. Maybe it could even work. It was the only bit of hope to escape this nightmare Hades was crafting. He couldn't help but to feel uncertain. Could he risk everything? Hades had only just given him the caduceus back moments before the contest started. If this failed, the Dark Lord would truly break him. But he could not leave the humans to this fate. Not if there was hope.

"Do not be afraid," he said to the children. "I am Hermes. Your comrades have been captured. Did you know that?" The boy shook his head and tears formed in the young girl's eyes. "I did not think so." Hermes knew that his next step would be taking a big risk. If his quickly formed plan failed, Hades would end him. Furies screamed behind him. "We can save them, if you will help me." The boy recoiled, refusing to speak. "I will not hurt you, I promise. With your help, we can set this world right." The boy relaxed a little, but still held the sack close to him, shielding the girl with his body. She nervously clutched his shirt. "Would you like to save them?" Hermes extended his hand. The boy looked at it cautiously, and then curiosity got the best of him. Taking Hermes' hand, the three disappeared.

Pete Henry hardly noticed when the Persephone sailed from the void into the mortal realm. A haunting mass of furies swarmed the skies above, casting the earth in a sinister darkness. Try as it might, the sun failed to penetrate their darkness. Was that Apollo? He couldn't keep track of the pantheon. As they continued forward, the Persephone left the sea and sailed up river until the silhouette of the capital city of Attica appeared before them. Soft orange light glowed in windows of the temples and palaces upon the acropolis, signaling the burning of hearth fires and lit candles. No God-given warmth or light would come to Attica while Hades held patronage.

As he did during Zeus' deluge, Ptollen sailed the ship seemingly without effort. Nikedemos, who had been the Arch Priest of Zeus in his life, prayed to his sovereign for his justice. Pete wondered if his prayers could breach legion of furies above them. He was not so sure they could.

Aha, the former God-king of Saïs, approached him as he stared at the city.

"We can't win against Hades," Pete told him. "Persephone told me. We are to be a distraction and nothing more." Pete felt bitter he wasn't taking a more active role in overthrowing Hades, who had caused his family so much misery.

"Is that not enough for you, Pete?" he asked. Before Pete could answer, he continued. "I wondered, just before the flood, when you arrived from the tunnel beneath the sacred lake, what would make a man risk his life to save another? Was it honor, duty, loyalty, love? Your story became legend. Once you and your family returned to your normal lives, the story of how Peter fought through death to save his beloved, the Crystal Bearer, inspired lovers for generations. So what caused you to risk your life to save someone you hardly knew? The legends say it had been love at first sight that turned cause into action, but I think the root reason may be deeper than that. I saw it in your brother when he came to me from Atlantis, and I saw it in him again and in you during the flood. You of the Henry blood are determined to be heroes." Pete remained silent. "Do you know the ironic truth about heroes, Pete?"

"What?" he asked, knowing nothing he could say would be the correct answer.

"Heroes often become victims of their causes. I do not insinuate that the actions are not valiant or warranted, but each act of bravery ties the hero tighter to the idea that he must always be in protective pursuit. His identity as the savior will enslave him."

"What do you mean, Aha?" he asked.

"What I mean," continued Aha, "is that once you see yourself as a hero, it can be difficult to unsee yourself as a hero. You may always be searching for another way to save someone. It becomes your nature.

"You have now been given an opportunity to allow someone else to be the hero," said Aha. "You may give them the opportunity to overthrow Hades in your stead, but it seems that is not enough for you. This task is your lesson in humility, and you shall be as vigilant and brave as you ever were. It is an honorable thing that we do."

"I guess you're right, Aha," said Pete. "As always."

The city grew nearer and Pete began to notice a low hissing, first far away, but then growing closer. "Aha, do you hear that?"

"Yes," replied the God-king. "The furies are nearing."

Pete focused his eyes around the ship, along the narrow river and the shore, shadows wafted menacingly toward the ship. "Ptollen!" screamed Pete. The sailor didn't waste a moment and the bell at the bow of the ship began to toll. At the sound, the nearest furies scattered with an ear-piercing shriek, some of them disappearing entirely.

Though momentarily fazed, the surviving furies regrouped and attacked again. Aha had Musa man the bell, while Ptollen took the wheel and steered the Persephone toward the acropolis.

"This is really loud," said Pete to Aha. "Hades will hear us coming."

"It is our best way to deter the shadow," replied Aha. Even the furies swarming in the sky became agitated at the bell's tolling.

"We won't be able to stay on this ship forever," said Pete. "What do we do once we're overrun? Or worse, when Hades arrives?"

"We will wait to face Hades until he arrives," said Aha, speaking loudly over the din. The furies' shrieks were enough to almost drive Pete mad. "As for the furies, Persephone left us a failsafe below deck." As if summoned, Doros, Sam, Vincent, Allison, and Julie appeared with several long bundles. "Show him," said Aha.

They unwrapped the cloths on the deck to reveal sixteen long curved silver swords with bronze handles. One for each soul aboard the ship.

"What are these?" he asked .

"They are the fangs of Ophion," announced Nikedemos as he joined the group. "All serpents have their fangs."

"Where were these during the deluge?" asked Pete.

"They were here, though we were not fighting shadow demons then," said Nikedemos.

"And we're to fight the furies with these?" asked Pete. "Are we certain they'll destroy the shadows?"

"Yes," replied Nikedemos. "The fire serpent, Ophion, is a greater and more ancient demon than the furies. His power is poison to them." On instinct, everyone grabbed a curved sword and held it close; even Pyrthens, who would look odd holding any weapon.

"Together," began Aha for all to hear, "we are the heroes and the victims of the Gods. We are the survivors and the sacrificed of the flood. Together, we will help to end Hades' reign upon our former home. Do not be afraid, for your fear is of death, which you have already met. Today, we fight for the living... for our descendants. We will take this world back for our children!" Everyone roared.

The Persephone, bell tolling its arrival and the furies screaming in protest, passed the walls to the city and sailed unnaturally upriver toward the acropolis. Pete was on fire to fight and he glared toward what Doros told him was the crown palace, named for Attella.

Torn from focus, he heard Allison scream and the sound of metal striking metal. He turned to see Hermes standing with his caduceus held up in defense, and Allison knocked to the ground.

"Peace!" shouted Hermes. The air grew silent and still, yet thick with tension. "Musa, keep tolling that bell!" The rhythm of bell tolls and shrieking resumed.

"What are you doing here, Hermes?" asked Pete. "You can't stop us. Not if we all gang up on you."

"Peter Henry," said Hermes, "even you do not believe your words."

"Maybe not, but give me one reason why we shouldn't try."

"Peace," he said again. "I do not come here to fight, but to offer aid."

"Just like you helped us in the Underworld?" asked Pete. "You abandoned us in Saïs, and I ended up getting killed by that man over there!" He pointed to Musa. "Worse yet, Emily had to go on and try to save Sean and Erin on her own."

"She had help," said Hermes. "And it was not my choice to leave you, as I explained to your wife only moments ago."

"You've spoken to Emily?" asked Pete, his concern for her outweighing his hatred for Hermes.

"She lives, if that is your fear," replied Hermes. "But I did not come here to argue, or to banter about the welfare of your family. The mortal world is at stake here. I will help you and you will trust me or we have no chance at succeeding. Now, tell me who sent you."

Pete remained silent. He couldn't bring himself to trust the Psychopomps. To his relief, Nikedemos answered.

"The Goddess Persephone sent us forth on this holy crusade, great messenger," said the priest.

"To what end?"

"To our own end, I am afraid," replied Nikedemos. "We are to be merely a diversion. Fight Hades' army, is our mission, although futile. It is the hope of Persephone that we will draw the dark lord to us, providing an opportunity for someone to free Athena and Poseidon."

"That is good to hear, dear priest," said Hermes. "Your plan may succeed. I must leave, but I will return to you as quickly as I can. Know that I am truly on your side." Hermes turned, but Pete called to him.

"Wait," he said. "Emily?"

"She may survive if you do your part, Peter Henry," replied Hermes. "If not to save the world, fight to save her." Without another word, Hermes leapt into the air and vanished.

Hera cringed at the unmistakable sound of the furies fighting and dying outside. She and Helios remained in the Great Hall with Hades, the guards, and the zombie-like king, Cecrops. Of course, the lifeless forms of Athena and Poseidon still hung in the air, each in their own cyclone of furies. Somewhat hesitantly, she glanced at Hades to see his reaction to his army's apparent slaughter. Pride swelled within her when Hades gave no outward inclination of his anger. His wrath would soon become apparent, no doubt.

"Hermes, Psychopomps and Messenger, I summon thee," said Hades firmly. Hermes had just been sent to the tower cells to retrieve the Crystal Bearer and her entourage, but had yet to return. Moments passed and Hermes did not come. Hades calmly but firmly repeated his summons. After too long of a silence, Hermes popped into the room. The sight of him sickened Hera. How dare he make the lord summon him twice! Hades should destroy him now.

"I am here, Great Lord," said Hermes with a bow.

"I summoned thee twice," stated Hades.

"Indeed you did, Great Lord. I was gathering your prisoners when I heard the death cries of your vassals. I locked the prisoners back up, investigated the commotion, and then returned to you as quickly as I could. I humbly apologize for the delay."

"Tell me your report," said Hades.

"Ophion in the guise of the ship Persephone has arrived on the river Poseidon made," replied Hermes. "It is from the Underworld, sire, and sailed by mortal souls."

"Mortal souls?" asked Hades. "They cannot think to fight me. Who has sent them?"

"The scheme smells of Alexia, Great Lord," replied Hermes. "I am uncertain of this, but given her track record, it only makes sense."

"I will destroy Alexia soon enough for her continual interference," said Hades. "Go and send the ship back to the Underworld. Even with your meager talents, you should be able to manage that much."

"As you say, Great Lord," replied Hermes. He leapt foolishly into the air and disappeared. Hera only envied his divine power. Given the same strength, she could serve the Great Lord far better than Hermes could ever dream.

"Do not fear," said Hades. "Hermes will not fail me, for if he does, I will break his wings." Even Hera became uncomfortable as a smile formed on Hades' pale cold lips.

GERALD M. GIVENS

CHAPTER III
THE BATTLE OF DARK AND LIGHT

Hera knew better than to express any concern. Though Hades had never seemed outright anxious, she knew that he was moments from bursting. Hermes should have been back by now with word of Ophion's return to the Underworld. The thin smile that had crossed his face had sunk everso slightly. She found herself holding her breath, anticipating an impact.

As if ice around him melted, Hades moved from his post behind the king and over to Helios. He did not erupt, she was proud to see, and spoke calmly, if not quickly. "Go find him." Helios did not hesitate as he bowed and left the throne room.

The tension before was thin compared to when Helios was gone. If he did not return, Hades would surely send her next to face whatever fate waited outside those gilded doors. Her sigh was more audible than she intended when Helios returned in a huff.

"Great Lord, I bear ill news," he said as approached the throne.

"Speak," commanded Hades.

"Hermes has betrayed you," he said. "He did not send Ophion back to the darkness, but joined forces with the mortals against you. He now fights with them, slaying your furies."

Hades seemed indifferent, if not determined. "So be it," he replied. "Hermes has chosen his lot, and I cannot afford to be merciful to him as I once was. I shall destroy him myself and end this rebellion." A black iron pitchfork appeared in his hands, its two prongs sharp as razors. "I charge you Hera and Helios to guard our prisoners. Eternal damnation awaits you should you fail."

"We shall do as you command, Great Lord," said Hera bowing with Helios. When she looked up, Hades was gone. She shuddered.

Caduceus in hand, Hermes fought with all of his power. A lesser God in divine power, he knew that with enough time and numbers, the furies could overwhelm him and render him inert like Poseidon and Athena. Regardless of his impending doom, he pressed on, dissolving the shadows by the dozen. Hades would discover his betrayal soon enough and when that happened, the furies would be the lesser of evils.

After leaving Hades and his minions in the Great Hall, Hermes had returned to the Persephone and organized the virtuous souls for battle. Musa, Doros, Hesperos, and Ptollen were experienced fighters, but the others seemed just as determined to fight the furies, despite their lack of skill in combat.

They passed through the broken wall that allowed the river to flow out to the sea and upon reaching the acropolis, they left the ship and began hand-to-hand combat with the shadows. Their battle field was a modest strip of land between the palace and the newly-made river. Furies attacked them from three sides, the Persephone and the river to their back. Hermes kept an eye on the virtuous souls and was pleased to see that they all held their own with surprising skill.

Despite that skill, for every fury that turned to dust, a dozen more took its place. This really was a fool's errand, he thought as he cut down another. But that was, of course, the whole point.

Hades was sly and cunning, but he was also predictable. Too many odds had grown against him with Hermes switching loyalties mid-game and the uncertainty about who sent the virtuous souls. Of course Hades assumed it was Alexia, but truly any God could have done so.

As if Hermes had summoned him, Hades' voice boomed across the field of battle, cursing Hermes. "Foolish Psychopomps," said Hades, "now I shall break your wings!"

Hermes left them again in the jail tower. Frustrated, Emily still didn't know whether to trust him or not. Moments earlier, he had arrived with Allie and Xho in tow. Those two were supposed to stay hidden and out of sight, but apparently Hermes had found them on the balcony off of her rooms. The messenger god instructed them to remain in the cell until his signal. Apparently he had a diversion in the works that would allow them to free Poseidon and Athena.

"I just don't know if we can trust him," she told the others. Xho had taken several orbs out of the sack to provide dim light within the small cell. "He's left me to die before, so who's to say he won't do it again?"

"You're being too harsh on him, Emily," said Kimberly as she held Allie in her lap, braiding her dark hair. Ubaid and Delia sat quietly near the door, and Xho sat next to Emily, leaning against her. She put her arm around him.

"You weren't left to die, now were you," she snapped. Immediately, she regretted her rage. "I'm sorry for my anger, but I can't stand being a pawn anymore. I don't want to be a piece their game, to be discarded when my use has run out. I've lost everything in this quest to save my family." Tears streamed down her face. "My husband is dead. My friends are dead. Allie is the only thing I have left, and now I can barely look her in the eye after what I did to Musa. She saved me from killing the Queen, but even that was in vain. Hera killed her anyway."

"Giving up won't make this any better," replied Kimberly. "I regret your losses, but I know that your family would want you to press on. And at this point, honey, the only way out is through. We're in this together. Let's end this together."

"I still can't trust Hermes," said Emily.

"You don't have to trust him," said Kimberly. "He left us the orbs and he left us Allie's crystal, so surely he means for us to use them."

"Yes, but to what end?" asked Emily.

"*The* end," said Kimberly. "I've been around a lot of sad sorry people in my life, Emily, and I refuse to become one of them. No matter what happens from this point on, we have to try and save ourselves and this realm, even if we die trying."

"But death is not an end," said Emily. "I've seen death. I know it well."

"Then you have nothing fear, my dear," replied Kimberly. "Now hopefully Hermes will sound his signal soon. We have to be ready for it." She finished Allie's braid and stood up.

Emily stood, followed by everyone else. "As you say," she stated.

"You've broken down the door before," she said to Allie, "are you ready to do it again?" The girl nodded, fingering the crystal. She still wished that Allie had never been called to the crystal. Not for the first time, Emily damned Alexia in her mind.

From outside the tower, they could faintly hear the sounds of furies dying grow louder. Suddenly the palace shook and Hades' voice boomed from the sky. He called to Hermes and cursed him.

"That is our sign," said Ubaid. "Hades is not guarding Poseidon and Athena."

"Okay, do it Allie," said Kimberly, turning the girl toward the door. Xho held the bag of orbs, while Emily held one in each hand. She could trust herself with just a small and finite amount of the power.

The crystal floated in front of Allie as it grew brighter, and with a flash the door shattered open, spraying iron and wood into the hall. Emily moved past her niece quickly and shattered her orbs just outside the door, causing the two guards to burst into flames, incinerating them instantly. She clenched her fists and shouted for them to move.

In the darkness, they crossed the bridge that connected Thebos' Chambers to the King's Tower without being seen. Making their way down the spiral staircase, they stopped in front of a small door that led to the back of the throne room. On the opposite side of the wall, Poseidon and Athena hung lifelessly, she knew. She also knew that Hera and Helios would be likely guarding them now, along with Daxteros and Michael.

"We only have a few minutes," she whispered to the group. "Fight off any extra guards, and I'll take Hera and Helios." Before they could argue, she slowly opened the door. Hera and Helios were talking on the opposite side of the dais. Daxteros and Michael stood zombie-like next to the throne and the equally vacant king. The prisoner deities were hidden behind two dark cyclones of shadows behind the throne.

Inching out of the passage, she led Allie close behind her, and she again held an orb in each hand. They were almost to the Gods when Hera spoke.

"I see you have escaped," she said loudly, rounding the throne to see them clearly. "I always thought furies were lousy guards, but the Great Lord swears by them, so who am I to judge. Let us be on with this then. Seize them." Michael and Daxteros turned from the king, swords in hand, to attack.

Emily resisted calling upon fire and instead chose pure light to shine from the orbs before she hurled them at her attackers, spilling the glowing water on them. They stopped and dropped their swords, covering their heads with their hands and screaming. Emily saw that Helios was doing something to them. His hands were stretched out toward them as he muttered under his breath. The darkness was fighting the light. He had to be stopped.

Without thinking, Emily ran forward, picked up the sword Michael had dropped, and rushed Helios. He broke his concentration and deflected her attack with his dagger, clearly more skilled than she at hand-to-hand combat.

"Get Michael and Daxteros out of here!" she heard herself scream, as she attacked Helios again. As her blade met Helios', Emily felt a sharp pain in her side and screamed in agony. She released her grip on her sword and fell to the ground.

Confused, she looked up to see Hera standing over her, holding a bloody dagger. "It is time to end you." She raised her dagger to strike.

A piercing scream sounded as the remaining orbs shattered around Emily. Time slowed down as the spilled water floated together in the air to form one large bubble. As the scream ended, it split into two and slammed hard into both Hera and Helios, sending them sprawling to the ground.

Upon arriving on the field of battle, Hades summoned his golden chariot and raced through the legions of furies and toward Hermes. Furies rushed around incessantly, fighting the virtuous souls and dying by their blades. "Ophion!" Hades called to the serpent demon, still in the form of the ship Persephone. "Return to the Netherworld!" The ship was suddenly aflame. In the midst of the smoke, a great serpent roared. Ophion thrashed violently in the water and then vanished down river, smoke and steam trailing behind him.

Thankfully, they never intended to escape, but any sanctuary they might have had with Persephone's bell was now gone. This was it. All or nothing.

As Hades pursued, he lashed out at the souls fighting his army, slaying both Musa and Daria with his pitchfork, turning them into furies, and thus adding them to his already overwhelming force.

They couldn't defeat Hades. The Crystal Bearer had better hurry.

Kimberly screamed at the same time as Allie. The glowing crystal floated in front of the girl as she grabbed her head. Allie's rage had sent the remaining orbs soaring across the room to save her aunt in a flash of water and light, throwing Hera and Helios to the ground. The crystal dimmed, and Kimberly ran and caught the collapsing child, as Ubaid, Delia, and Xho attended to Emily.

"It's okay, sweetie," she said to Allie, who was still clutching her head between her hands.

Several feet away, Hera and Helios coughed and began to stir. Xho picked up the sword Emily had dropped and approached them cautiously. Kimberly wanted to call to the boy to stay away from them, but she couldn't bring herself to do it.

Hera moaned as she lifted herself onto her elbows. It was then that Kimberly noticed something was amiss. Her hair was now black instead of red. And Helios now had light brown hair. "Xho, stop!" she found her voice as their identities clicked in her head. The boy looked at her confused as she set Allie down and ran over.

"I'll be damned," she said as she helped them sit up. "Somehow this makes sense." Sean and Erin Henry looked haggard, but whole. "Xho, these are Allie's parents."

"Allie?" asked Erin. The girl looked up from where she lay and ran to her mom and dad. All three cried as they held each other close.

"But she stabbed Emily," said Xho, angered and pointing to his savior bleeding on the floor. Ubaid and Delia were trying to staunch the wound, with little success. Emily was growing pale.

Breaking from her husband and daughter, Erin rushed to Emily's side. "Emily, I'm so sorry," she cried. "I didn't... I..."

Emily hushed her, her breath growing ragged. "End this," she whispered, half pointing to Poseidon and Athena. Erin understood.

Kimberly watched as Sean and Erin took Allie by the hand and led their daughter over to the swirling dark cyclones. "Allie, use all the power you can," said Erin. "Free them and this will all end." Allie looked back at Emily, who smiled despite her condition.

The girl closed her eyes. The crystal began to glow again and the air became charged with electricity. Floating in front of her, Allie screamed again, sending a flash of light forward shattering the crystal as the mass of furies screamed their death cries and dissolved.

When the light dimmed, Poseidon and Athena fell to the floor and reawakened. Only a tangled cord of rope remained around Allie's neck. The crystal had destroyed itself.

"What has happened?" asked Athena to all present. Ubaid came forth and told them about Hades' takeover, the furies, and their being captured.

"So brave of you to release us," said Poseidon, climbing to his feet. The Gods towered over everyone menacingly. "We are in your debt."

"Can you save Emily?" asked Erin, moving back to her sister's side. "I'll do anything." She cried again.

"No," said Emily faintly. "Free my family from Hades forever. Stop his tormenting." Erin made to argue, but Emily stopped her. "This is why I came here," she said. "To save you. My death is nothing compared to your eternal suffering. Poseidon, please save them!"

"It will be as you say," said Poseidon. "Their souls will be their own, for now and eternity. This I swear."

"Thank you," replied Emily.

"Poseidon," called Athena as a golden sword and shield appeared in her hands, "the battle will not wait."

"Then neither shall we, Athena," he replied, calling his trident to him.

Hades struck hard, again and again, cursing Hermes as he went. All around them, the furies cried in anger and death. Finally, the strike Hermes had feared came and Hades' pitchfork shattered his caduceus, leaving him defenseless.

What was taking the Crystal Bearer so long? Hermes had to keep Hades' attention a little longer. More as a distraction than a strategy, Hermes began to fly, narrowly dodging Hades' blows. Back and forth he went, until the dark one caught his leg and threw him to the ground. Hades placed his foot on Hermes' chest. "I told you I will break your wings."

Hades raised his pitchfork to kill him, when a beam of light shot up from the palace and burst a hole through the dark clouds above them. Hermes laughed manically and disappeared.

Poseidon landed next to Hades, his mighty trident in hand, along with the Warrior God Athena bearing her sword and shield. Turning from where Hermes vanished, he struck out at them both, but they easily deflected his blows, knocking the pitchfork from his grasp and sending him sprawling to the ground.

The remaining darkness above dissolved, and lightning flashed from the sky, striking every last fury from the face of the earth, their final death cries ringing in Pete's ears. One by one, other Gods appeared beside Poseidon and Athena, the Olympians, he guessed.

"You were given dominion over the darkness, Brother," spoke the tallest and grandest of the Gods. Light seemed to emanate from him. "But that was not enough."

"Curse, you Zeus," spat Hades. "You and Poseidon tricked me into taking the Underworld!"

"Your actions are petty and cruel!" replied Zeus.

"No worse than when you drowned the earth," said Hades. "You and Poseidon both have committed far grander sins than me."

"Sins for which we have since atoned," said Zeus. "You have earned your place in the shadows."

The Olympians formed a circle and channeled their divine power to open a pit into the earth. Iron shackles formed around Hades' pale wrists, their chains trailing deep into the earth.

"None shall suffer at your leave again," said Zeus. "Dine with the Titans in Tartarus."

"You cannot do this," said Hades. "I am a God! I have those who will fight for me! I have those who are bound to me and will free me! Such sweet wrath I will bring down upon Olympus, this I swear to you!"

"The Diluvians are no longer yours to command," said Poseidon. Hades' eyes flashed hatred. "They are born from the flood, and they are all my children. You are now alone."

"Curse you all!" screamed Hades.

"Go back to your shadows, Brother," said Zeus as the chains pulled Hades away, deep into the pit. Even after the Gods sealed the earth again, Pete could still faintly hear Hades' curses echoing from below.

CHAPTER IV
THE VICTOR

In a column of light and fury, Athena and Poseidon blew a hole in the ceiling of the Great Hall and rose above the city to battle Hades. Their power burned away the perpetual darkness the furies had bestowed upon the world, and the sun shone in through the windows of the throne room.

Sean huddled with his family near Emily, as she clung to life. He remembered everything he'd done as Helios. Delia, the Oracle, wouldn't look him in the eye. That was for killing her brother Doros. She could only assume that he'd killed Delphinios and Helena too. Daxteros, the ship captain, stared at him blankly. That was for killing his love, Daria. Both knew that Sean and Erin had been under Hades' control, but now their individual quests for vengeance were extinguished. Sean pitied them.

Sean pitied himself. His family had tried to save him, and had succeeded, but his brother had died. Now it seemed that his brother's wife would soon join him.

Allie held the cord from the crystal in her hands and cried. With the power of the crystal, they might have been able to save Emily. The water from the orbs had been used up. The Saitian boy looked most distraught.

Emily's breathing became shallow and with a low hiss, life left her body. Erin and Allie sobbed. Xho threw the sword at the wall.

Lightning struck all around in a series of flashes and cries of furies dying, breaking their mourning.

"It's done," said Sean. "Hades is defeated." He didn't feel any better.

A hawk flew into the Great Hall from the hole in the ceiling and touched down, transforming into Alexia.

"I mourn with you," she said as she approached the group. Her face showed her remorse. "Truly, I do."

"Is it really over?" asked Erin, staring blankly at Emily.

"It is indeed," she replied. "Hades is banished to Tartarus. He cannot torment you anymore."

"He may not be able to," said Erin, "but his memory certainly will."

"We have all lost in this war," said Alexia. "I lost my home. You lost your brother and sister. Nobody wins at war. There is only the one who has lost the least. Hades has lost his hold on both life and death. Rhadamanthus will take his place in the Underworld. Though it came at great cost, all realms have gained from your sacrifices."

"Forgive me if I don't feel better," said Erin, still holding Emily's hand.

"Perhaps saying goodbye to those you have lost will help," said Alexia.

"What do you mean?" asked Sean.

"Follow me, and I will show you," she replied.

Xho refused to leave Emily's body, so they left her in his care. Hades' hold over Cecrops vanished with him, and the king stirred in his throne. Sean and Michael helped him up, and Alexia led them all outside to the battlefield.

Looking out across the trampled field, Sean saw a dozen or so figures standing with blades in their hands. "Who are they?" asked Sean.

"They are the Virtuous Souls," she replied, "those who have been affected by the wraths of Gods. Your brother, Peter, is among them."

Alexia led them across toward the river, and Sean was overwhelmed by who he saw. King Hesperos, God-king Aha, Ptollen, Pyrthens, Nikedemos, and so many others who had perished in their journeys. As she said, Pete was there too.

The brothers embraced and cried, both happy and sad to see one another. "It worked!" said Pete. He looked around anxiously. "Where's Emily?"

Erin told him what happened, and a look of sadness came to Pete's face. "Did she die before or after Hades' was beaten?"

"After, why?" said Erin.

He looked relieved. "If she had died before, she would have turned into a fury and I'd never see her again," he said. "Be sure to give her a coin before you burn her body. I'll be with her soon."

The group spoke with the virtuous souls a little longer, Delia being reunited with Doros, Delphinios, and Helena. Sean and Erin embraced Sam Knight and Julie Vane, along with Aha and Nikedemos. Pete told them that Vincent Sanders, Allison Moore, Musa, and Daria had all perished in the fight against the furies.

After a time, Alexia approached them and told them it was time to go. "The virtuous souls cannot remain in this plain any longer," she said. Sean held Erin and Allie close as the souls of their companions vanished. The sun was setting and she turned to the group. "I have spoken with the Gods of Olympus. I can return you to your own time, as a meager payment for your contributions in defeating Hades."

Sean looked to Erin and Allie, then back to Alexia. "We're staying," he said. Alexia didn't seem surprised. "We can't exist in our own time anymore. We've changed too much."

"You are welcome to remain here in Attica, should you choose," said Cecrops.

"Thank you, your highness," he replied.

"And you, Michael and Kimberly?" asked Alexia. "Will you remain?"

"You charged me with looking after this little girl," said Kimberly. "I take my assignments very seriously. If Allie stays, so do I."

"I came here because I had nothing," said Michael. "Here I can truly start over. I'm staying too."

"As you will it, so it shall be," said Alexia with a slight bow of her head.

After sunset, Emily's body was burned on a pyre near the river where her husband had fought the darkness. Erin honored Pete's wishes and placed a gold coin in Emily's mouth before setting her ablaze. She was surprised to see Xho so affected by her death. In her saving him from slavery and indeed his own death, he had come to worship Emily as a hero. He stayed at the pyre until all that was left were smoldering ashes.

The next morning, Erin watched as he collected the ashes on a large leaf and placed them in the river. When asked why he did so, the boy replied that she was a daughter of Poseidon. He will protect her now. Erin vowed to look after the boy in her sister's stead.

Even in her time spent as Hera, Erin had never seen the Great Hall of Attella's crownso full. The dignitaries and statesmen from around the world, who had fled or gone into hiding in the city during Hades' brief reign, were now present. The games were officially over and Cecrops still needed to choose a patron God for his kingdom. Both contestants, Poseidon and Athena, were present, along with Alexia and Hermes.

Standing in front of his throne, the king seemed more alive and vital than ever. Indeed, the experience of being controlled by Hades might make him a more just ruler, having experienced tyranny and manipulation firsthand.

"Citizens and friends of Attica, I welcome you," said the King. "We have been steadfast in the face of adversity, and praise the Gods of Olympus for delivering us from such evils. Hades, the great manipulator, had many of us spinning webs we would not have otherwise. I, myself, was victim to his poison, as were Sean and Erin Henry, Diluvians of Zeus' great flood. Together, they acted as Hera and Helios, inflicting irreparable damage. The realm forgives them of their slights, and begs Olympus to have mercy on their souls." Sean and Erin stepped forward to receive the king's blessing. "May you suffer not for the rest of your days." They bowed and backed away.

"Though we were without the light of just Gods, two people found their own light to dispel Hades' darkness. The Diluvian, Emily Henry perished in her fight against the shadow, but her niece survives her. Allie Henry, Crystal Bearer of Saïs, I commend you for your courage and for your aid. The realm of Attica is forever in your debt." Erin led Allie to the king, and she bowed at his gratitude.

"And lastly, our thanks go to Poseidon and Athena, who brought down the light of Olympus to forever cast away the shadow. For this and for your gifts, I find myself torn in choosing which of you will prove the victor."

Poseidon stepped forward. "Cecrops, King of Attica, I hereby remove myself from the contest for your patronage." The crowd gasped, and Cecrops' eyes went wide. "What Hades has done to this land is only comparable to the destruction I have waged upon this world with my own hands. I find myself unworthy of any dry earthly kingdom. I shall continue to rule the sea"

"As you say, great Lord of the Sea," replied the king as Poseidon stepped back. "Gracious warrior, Athena, I return to you the patronage of Attica. From henceforth, this realm will forever return to its given name, 'Athens.'"

Taller than life, Athena bowed to the king. "I hereby swear to protect your kingdom. I swear to never again allow the willfulness of Gods cause harm to you or mankind. Should my kin ever dare to lift a sword to your throats, I will sacrifice myself in effort to stop them. This I vow to you."

The king rose and bowed to her in return, followed by everyone else present.

"I am inspired," continued Athena, "by my sister in arms, Alexia of Poseidon. Time and again she has put the needs of mankind before her own, and has now twice aided in their salvation. Alexia, I grant you grace and honor you as a true Olympian."

Alexia bowed to her, as the crowd began to chant "Athena!" over and over again. Erin felt a glimmer of peace as Athena turned into a hawk and flew out of the hole in the ceiling and toward the sun.

EPILOGUE
CYPRUS

Sean sat on a shore, staring out at the sea. For all he knew, he could have been there for hours watching the waves crashing into one another. A storm brewed on the horizon. Erin sat to his left and they were alone on the beach. She smiled as he fixed a strand of hair behind her ear. Her hair used to be all black, but now it was streaked with grey and silver strands. "Another storm is coming," she said.

"Nothing we haven't weathered a hundred times over," he replied, and indeed they had weathered such storms so many times before. They had grown used to the summer storms over the decade since they had left Saïs and settled on the island that would one day become the country of Cyprus. It seemed fitting that they would end up here, back where everything began.

After Athena was named patron god of Athens nearly twenty years earlier, Sean and Erin, along with Allie, Kimberly, Michael, Xho, and Ubaid, returned to Saïs to help reestablish order in the wake of Nefruneith's death. The Saitian people mourned for their lost queen. Upon hearing about Allie's deeds in Athens, they proclaimed her their new sovereign. Sean and Erin didn't allow this at first. She was far too young and had been through so much already. It was far too much responsibility to place on one fragile girl.

In the end, Ubaid and Saitians forced their hand and Sean and Erin could no longer refuse. Their consolation in that time had been

Kimberly Reeves. To this day, Kimberly still looked over Allie, but in her first years as queen, Kimberly stayed by her side and protected her from those who might try to manipulate her. Truthfully, Allie had grown up to be a wonderful and just queen, and still reigned in Saïs. Relations between Athens and Saïs were now greatly improved, in the wake of Allie's actions in overthrowing Hades.

To their surprise, Michael trained under the Saitian guards and became a guard himself. Sean honestly didn't think he had it in him. The anger and spite that shaped his former personality had dissolved. Michael was well into his sixties at this point, but he served for nearly fifteen years before retiring. He still lived in Saïs.

Daxteros, despite Kimberly's pleas, returned to his trade ship and resumed his old life. Kimberly would have put him at the head of the Saitian navy, but the captain didn't want that life. Sean didn't blame him. Too many times, he had been forced into the schemes of others. They still saw him from time to time, as he made port at Cyprus, not so much to trade, but to take a break from the seas.

Delia had returned to Delphi to resume her role as the Oracle. Several times since the contest, Sean and Erin had visited her at the Temple of Apollo. Though she still grieved for her lost companions, she did forgive them for their deeds as Hera and Helios.

Now blind, Ubaid was still the high priest at the Temple of Neith. He counseled Queen Alexia of Neith, as he and the Saitians called her, on matters of state and creed.

"Queen Alexia", thought Sean. His baby girl had a destiny all of her own. When she was older, he and Erin told her their stories, about how they became the Diluvians. She could still wield the power of Neith, using water from the sacred lake.

Upon reaching manhood, the former slave boy, Xho, proposed to Allie. The pair was inseparable since their return from Athens and no one was surprised. Several years later, Sean finally agreed to let them wed. Ubaid oversaw the ceremony, and Xho was named king, though Allie still held the highest seat.

Sean and Erin spoke of Pete and Emily often. Several times in the past twenty years, they had been tempted to journey to the Underworld to visit them, but neither the Gods nor Ubaid would allow such a thing. "Death is not to be played with," the priest would say. "The dark pool is not a ship to ferry you hither and thither." After several failed attempts at convincing the priest, they gave up. Though sad for their own loss, Sean and Erin agreed that they were happy that Pete and Emily ended up together in the end.

"Let us go inside, my love" Erin said as she stood at the shore. "We need not weather this storm out here." Sean rose and let her lead him back to the modest house they had built near the beach. As Erin closed the door, a torrent of rain poured from the sky.

"We barely made it," he told her, smiling. She kissed him.

"We always do."

Acknowledgements

The Diluvians Series has been a trial by fire. I began writing the series in 2004 and now, in 2017, 13 years later, I'm finally releasing the conclusion to the adventure-fantasy series that proved to me that I can write fiction, create worlds, characters, and complex plots. From Eyes In Atlantis to The Deluge to Heroes & Victims, I can see my growth as writer. So, in this acknowledgment of Heroes & Victims, I'd like to first thank this series. I will write many more stories in my lifetime, but these three books and the process to their completion will always remind me of where I've been and how much further I have to go.

Over the six years that I spent writing, editing, and (for months at a time) ignoring, many people have come in and out of my life who have influenced this piece. I thank Karina Ayn Mirsky, my mentor, teacher, and friend, who has always been a resource and support system for this craft. Thank go to Kimberly Schewe (Kroemer), who was present and supportive in the earlier stages of this story (and hence has a character named for her).

Special thanks also go to Roseann Givens, Melanie Guidotti, Angelia (Dragon) Lane, Sandy Huynh, Kenny Givens, Julie Birman, Suzanne Roche, Lauren Thomas, Matt Giraud, David Nestor, Gerald Henry, and Alean Sims.

Thanks to my protagonists, Sean and Erin Henry. God knows I've put you through enough. Fingers crossed you'll now be able to rest.

Lastly, I'd like to thank my grandmother, Carole Henry, who passed away during the writing of this novel. From my earliest days, she encouraged my love for adventure, pushing me to travel the world and to write these stories. I miss you Grandma and hope you enjoy this new adventure.

ABOUT THE AUTHOR

Gerald grew up in Ann Arbor, Michigan where from an early age his interests in history and storytelling were built through frequenting museums with his mother. At age eight, he wrote his first story, a children's tale about a dog, a cat, and a mouse that became friends and lived together. In high school, his interest in writing grew through the study of poetry. Inspired by the poems of Edgar Allen Poe, Gerald began writing poetry, some bad and some good, and eventually self-published an anthology of his work. It was in college at Western Michigan University that he wrote his first novel, *Eyes in Atlantis* and has been writing ever since. In his spare time he likes to listen to music, spend time in nature, travel, and teach yoga. He now lives in Oakland, California.

For more information on Gerald M. Givens and his writing, please visit www.jerrygivens.net

www.ingramcontent.com/pod-product-compliance
Lightning Source LLC
Chambersburg PA
CBHW071301250626
47159CB00004B/1268